Sun
is
Sky

Jedah Mayberry

JACARANDA

This edition first published in Great Britain 2020
Jacaranda Books Art Music Ltd
27 Old Gloucester Street,
London WC1N 3AX
www.jacarandabooksartmusic.co.uk

'Would Be Twins,' 'Iron Bones,' 'Mouth, Eyes, Nose (Sun is
Sky),' and 'Sleep —Flashing for Kicks' have all been previously published by Snippet App
'Black Haired Momma' and 'Invisible Theory' have been
previously published by Linden Avenue Lit

A CIP catalogue record for this book is available from the
British Library

ISBN: 9781909762718
eISBN: 9781909762701

Cover Design: Christina Schweighardt
Typeset by: Kamillah Brandes
Printed and bound by CPI Group (UK) Ltd, Croydon, CR0 4YY

For JKLM—my wind, my wings, my softest landing.

Love is like the rain. It comes in a drizzle sometimes. Then it starts pouring and if you're not careful it will drown you.
– Edwidge Danticat

To describe my mother would be to write about a hurricane in its perfect power. Or the climbing, falling colors of a rainbow.
– Maya Angelou

Prologue

First Generation

Don't Cry Baby

The train is rolling again, carrying me back to Picayune. This child of mine is crying again. It's all she seems to do. Curls up that tiny lip of hers, opens her mouth to expose all her tonsils and tongue then wails like an ambulance siren. She looks harmless enough the few times I've managed to catch her sleeping. But, wake her for even a second and the water works begin again.

The night nurse confided in me that her firstborn child was a don't-cry baby. Never once shed a tear. She sat with me the first few nights at the hospital to keep me from throwing my baby out the window—a sho' nuff do-cry baby if ever there was one. She told me the bit about her don't-cry baby as a way I suppose of letting me know no two babies ever take to this world the same. Said her other three children did cry on occasion. She needed to care for each of them according to their individual dispositions as opposed to obeying her own wishes, as had been her tendency to do prior to any babies coming into her life. She assured me I would find my way in time. Time was never on my side.

These days, my used-to-cry baby has a baby of her own, grandbabies even. She just moved her eldest grandchild, Penny, down here to stay so neither of them would be alone. That one acts like she fell right outta the sky. Walks around with her head stuck in the clouds, worshipping the sun, calling on the moon, basing all her decisions on how the wind might choose to blow. Her grandma maintained that same head in the sky attitude when she was a girl, the two of them more alike than a couple of gumdrops, left alone in a jar, lookin' over at one another wondering what the other is going to do next.

That doesn't make her any less mine— granddaughter to the baby I didn't get to keep. But I've already said all I came to say. Besides, this is her story. It's best I let her tell it.

ONE

ONE

Women's Business

Anybody —

"Miss Penny."

"Yes. I mean—*Yes, sir.*"

"Your grandmomma sent me to fetch you."

"You know my grandmother?"

"There ain't a soul alive in this town who doesn't know your grandma."

He took the wheel with both hands and steered the car across an uneven span of railroad track. Another handful of lazy turns delivered us at Gram's front door. The man rattled the shift knob between gears, the purr of the engine idling ahead of us. This is as far as he intended to carry me.

"I appreciate you coming to get me," I stammered, pulling my suitcase from the backseat of his car.

"Just repaying a favour," he replied, already eyeing the series of turns he would make on his way back into town.

"Can I tell my grandma who dropped me?"

"She'll be looking for you, not for me," he insisted. "It could'a been anybody who dropped you."

He fiddled with the gearshift again then shooed me away with a tilt of his head. "Now go on inside and make yourself at home. Your grandma, she'll be along directly."

Tomorrow's Sun —

The year I was to turn fifteen I was sent to live with my maternal grandmother in Picayune, Mississippi—the kind of place that time moved slow on, drug a long finger across her skin, left a smudge. I had never known such a place.

They have something down here called a stink bug, claimed to possess as its special power the ability to put off a stifling odour, meant to warn other stink bugs of impending danger—but only after it's been squashed. I've come to think of myself as a sort of stink bug, cast from my home to serve warning for my two younger sisters who were left to endure whatever threat I am supposed to be fleeing. How the perils in Mississippi are meant to be any less than those in New York is beyond me.

My first full day in Picayune, two of the local boys got it in their heads to wet me with their water guns. Their eyes gleamed with the thrill of each squirt aimed in my direction, the air filled with the sound of their taunting: *"Enhhh, Enhhh, Enhhh!"* I stood staring, wondering what those boys meant to accomplish by wetting me until my dress was a tattered mass of jet stream tears, my hair lifted in several places, water dripping down either side of my face from make believe wounds.

The boys eventually grew tired of me—a moving

target that wouldn't seem to move—and continued on their way, shooting streams of water at the ground, at each other, into the wind. My grandmother, who witnessed the attack from her porch window, told me to warn those boys the next time they attempt to squirt me that I will lift my dress and make it rain on the whole world. She sent word by way of their mothers or grandmothers or whoever most held sway over the root of their devilment. She batted her eyes against a persistent sun, hung the message on the edge of a tilted sky listing from the weight of the burden it was sent to deliver.

By nightfall that evening, the sky was alive with the spectacle of events leading up to a storm: the low rumbling of thunder that escalates to a bone-rattling clap, the scent of rain as yet unseen transported on steam-drenched billows of wind. A hollow brightness filled the sky giving some hint as to the celestial whereabouts of the storm's inception. Together the storm's way of proclaiming, *'Ready or not, here I come.'*

A flash of light ruptured the soft underbelly of swollen cloud cover and the rains began to fall, in gargantuan droplets at first: *sphitt, splok, splook*—obviously from a common source yet strangely isolated in their onset. The rain eventually settled into a steady rhythm, the downpour having worn smooth the frayed edges of ruptured sky.

I screwed up my nerve to ask the question through

18

Gram's cracked bedroom door as she and I settled down for the night. "Was all this my doing?" I asked above the patter of raindrops keeping time on the rooftop.

"Silly girl," she replied, the titter in her voice showing the faintest hint of delight at the prospect that her words had carried, that her eldest granddaughter had grown to consider another person's way of seeing the world, an outlook that had eluded my mother under the same teaching.

"Magnificent forces exist out there," she explained. "Sunshine, lightning, drops of rain, the rainbows they conspire to produce. Vital forces, as undeniable as you and me. Yet none of them is small enough to fit between the tips of your fingers. The sky might on occasion heed your wishes, but it will never bow to your will. It's best you flush any such notion from inside your fertile mind."

She switched off the light resting on her bedside table before I could manage a response. The night air placed a hush over the space surrounding us, signalling it was time for sleep, not time for any further question asking about sunshine or rain or the sky's regard for my wishes one way or the other.

I lay nestled in the covers, contemplating my connection to those magnificent, outside forces. Had I been older, I would have recognised the coincidence between the timing of the threat Gram prescribed and the start of the rainy season in the Mississippi Bayou.

Any younger and I wouldn't have appreciated the kind of mojo a threat like this—mired in sexual innuendo—would have on the locals, the men especially.

"Evening, Miss." The man tipped his hat, resting a foot on the porch step, a lazy arm stretched along the length of the handrail. "Is the sun going to shine tomorrow?" he asked, his eyes as wet as any part of the sky, the brim of his hat, the tip of his boot.

"It didn't shine today," I replied. "Might not shine tomorrow either," I told him, reciting the words Gram had scripted for me.

Each night, somebody stopped by to ask about tomorrow's sun. Not always the same somebody, but every night without fail somebody came to ask.

Mosquito's Leg —

Midway through the summer, with the soybean crop in jeopardy not to mention the little league baseball season, a coalition of townsmen descended on Gram's tiny, three-room house, stamping mud from their boots as they made their approach. The racket echoed off a sky held low by days of endless cloud cover, beckoning Gram and me onto the porch before the men could get themselves fully organized.

The men seemed small standing down around Gram's front porch, heads bowed, hats twisting by their sides between nervous fingers like a gathering of school children assembled before an unyielding headmistress. Gram obliged them in this role, standing steady on her perch, peering at and beyond them with the same glance.

I stood silent by her side, studying the horizon for some cosmic event to intervene and calm the situation brewing between us. The sky seemed on the verge of another outburst, Mother Nature still unsettled by the water gun assault launched against me. Fast moving streaks in silver and gray circled the heavens twisting into one another, bullied by a common adversary. The treetops disappeared in a mysterious haze, giving the impression that an angry sky might at any moment open up and consume the earth, leaving Picayune to spend the rest of eternity locked in bitter turmoil.

Eventually one of the men mustered the nerve to speak, shaking me from my daydreaming. "Missus," he said with a tip of his hat. "We come to see if you would remove the curse."

After much conjecture and posturing, Gram instructed me to step to the edge of the porch, to hold my arms outstretched pointing skyward. She had me speak to the sky like a mother would a restless child.

"Be still," I said. "Be still."

Within days the rains stopped and the clouds began to part, leaving the townsfolk forever in my debt.

Never have I stood beneath a tree so big, enjoyed a shelter so complete as in the comfort afforded by the power of my grandmother's simple words. This was the start of a life I had never known. New York for me had been harsh, oppressive. Between Daddy leaving and Momma seeming to blame me for him electing to stay gone, it was inevitable that I leave too. One of the neighbourhood boys having been caught *showing* himself outside my bedroom window is the incident that sealed my fate. When I had done nothing, hadn't stood long, hadn't strayed near enough for him to take notice. Still, I was the one made to suffer.

Momma insisted that my luring him had endangered my sisters, had compromised their safety. What about my safety? When had I gone from fish to bait, the lamb separated from the herd to protect the other sheep? Now here I am in my new home making it be or not be—baseball or no baseball—as I see fit, the fate of an entire township hanging on my very word.

Had I not gone to school that year as I'd planned, I wouldn't have known Curtis Denby, wouldn't have let him touch me *there*. I wouldn't have gotten pregnant.

Curtis was a nice boy, even by Gram's standards. He smelled good most days, wore his shirt tucked neat inside the waist of his school pants. His most endearing quality, however, is that he appeared to like me. Not in the touch-and-grab-you way boys back in New York had liked me. Curtis liked me in a carry-your-books-home-from-school sort of way. He was in fact the first boy I liked who seemed to like me back.

I took to him like a bird to flight. The willow tree down by the river's edge was our secret place. It was on our way from school. After several weeks spent visiting on Gram's front porch, Curtis had earned her trust to the point she no longer insisted I come straight home— I suspect Gram liked Curtis, too.

Curtis knew a place where the river runs away from town, disappearing for good behind a thick fold of trees on its way to empty the full contents of its belly into the sea. My first visit there has forever altered how I choose to look at the world. I have since claimed that spot of trees as my own private sanctuary, nestling myself in their bosom whenever in need of a small refuge from the rest of existence. I find beyond those trees the promise of anything a person might want in the world held safe by a wall of tree cover on one side of me, the rush of the river moving past me on the other side.

Curtis and I soon found ourselves spending whole afternoons lying by the river bank, hunkered down in the tall grass. Curtis would flatten a square patch of grass with a piece of board, taking care to comb up the grass behind us to conceal the path we'd entered on. For hours we'd sit, watching the boats pass, tracing the birds' migratory patterns. Aside from the pigeons ever present on the rooftop of our tenement back in New York, I couldn't claim to know much about birds. Curtis seemed able to call every species on sight: Egrets, Ospreys, Belted Kingfishers.

The winds picked up midway into the fall semester. Curtis amused me by unbuttoning his shirt from the waist up, letting his shirttail fly in the wind. He strutted around our grass hideaway flapping his elbows in mock impersonation of the waterfowl we'd observed, tiny flocks of which kept a watchful eye on us from a safe distance down-river, suspecting like me that Curtis had lost hold of his senses. We fell to the ground in a fit, rolling around on top of one another like neither of us was wrapped too tightly. I wasn't sure how much I should like being pressed this close to a boy, my young girl parts just beginning to find their purpose. But I liked it a lot—a dull ache deep inside me longing to be touched. Before long, we were spending all our time down by the river, hidden away among shoots of tall grass.

The first-time Curtis kissed me, I thought I might melt on the spot. I didn't realize how much taller than me he was until I tipped my toes to match his height only to have my nose barely reach the sprinkling of fuzz sprouting inside the cleft beneath his bottom lip. He bent the full length of his body into mine, twisted his neck until our noses crossed swords. Then he kissed me, long and full, releasing a new kind of aching inside me. I didn't know where that aching might lead until I found myself pressed inside his arms again, my body tingling from the feel of his touch on my skin.

For my birthday Curtis brought me a bunch of black-eyed Susans from his mother's garden. The sky was especially blustery that day, fuelling Curtis's playfulness. He seemed to grow crazier with each new whip of the wind. After performing his ritual waterfowl dance, he let his arms fall slack, allowing the wind to carry his shirt to the edge of our hideaway where it hung itself in the tall grass.

He knelt before me, had me sit cross-legged across his lap, my legs hugging his waist. I wrapped my arms around his shoulders as fumbling hands worked to unhook my bra strap. I raised both arms and allowed Curtis to lift my blouse over my head, the tips of my fingers exposed momentarily above the crown of flowering grass surrounding our makeshift love nest. I silenced my breathing as he pressed his bare chest against mine. I felt his heart beating. Something deep inside me took hold, carrying me places I would never have thought to go with anyone other than Curtis Denby.

That night, I felt a needle pricking inside my belly against the calcified shell of a bird's egg—scraping, scratching, each touch of the needle testing the shell's surface for weakness. After several attempts to gain entry, the needle became a metal spike, its pricking ringing loud inside my eardrum like the sound you might hear on the train tracks as that spike is being driven to secure one end of a railroad tie. A few exaggerated blows and the metal spike transformed into a chisel hammering away against the glass skin of a light bulb, the bulb's shell transparent, its wire filament twisted around on itself, spindly as a mosquito's leg.

Eventually the bulb burst, spilling all its brightness deep inside my belly. I lay still in the darkness and let the soft glow from the light wash over me. Felt its tender warmth transform me, my womb taking the form of the light bulb it had swallowed, its mosquito leg glowing beneath my skin.

I awoke the next morning to find the glow still burning bright inside me, a new flicker glimmering behind timid eyes. By the end of the following week I consulted a calendar. I measured the time since my last period, began counting down the days until my cycle would begin again. I found instead that the month had run out on me before the cramps could get started, the energy draining from my body the way it ordinarily would come this time of month.

I rose from bed each day to discover a different part of me to have taken on an exceedingly unfamiliar shape while I slept. My fingers, my wrists, the paper-thin expanse of skin stretched tight across my ankles: all started to swell. It soon became difficult to fit my feet inside anything but the most comfortable of shoes. I ventured a glance in the bathroom mirror, examined with delicate fingertips what my eyes were registering, to find my nose stretched flat between vanishing cheekbones like my body was attempting to turn itself inside-out. With that, my suspicions were confirmed—I was pregnant, soft light and shattered glass having made their union permanent inside my belly, or so I had hoped.

Due —

At first I thought not to tell Gram, held a secret that my belly wouldn't keep silent for long. That's when I noticed the old woman across the street watching me from her porch window. On my way to school then home again, I'd find her peering through peach and green striped curtains parted just enough to reveal the shadow of a figure, the fingers of one hand the only things willing to be seen clearly.

I'd caught her on occasion making her way to retrieve the mail at the end of her walkway. Her mailbox, like the others on Gram's block, was made of corrugated steel, rolled over on top like the army barracks I'd seen in Biloxi on the bus ride to Picayune. Hers held her family's name painted so faintly against the contour of metal ridges that the name may as well not have been there in the first place: *Spinnaker*.

Gram never spoke of the folks who lived nearby. As a result, I couldn't say whether the lady across the street was widowed, divorced, or had ever married. I attempted to land a greeting as I left for school one morning, invoking a practice accepted throughout the south of addressing any grown woman as *Miss* whether or not she's married.

"How are you today, Miss Spinnaker?" I bellowed in the biggest voice I could muster. "Fine morning. Isn't it?" She never answered back. I continued on my way, fearing I'd mispronounced the woman's name. I ventured a look back as I reached the bus stop, by which time Miss Spinnaker's shifty figure had slithered from view. I decided not to speak again until she spoke first.

That was before my trouble, before I let Curtis touch me down by the river. Those days she just watched me, her face twisted in a way she seemed to believe might help cure whatever was going wrong with me.

I found her one afternoon posted next to her mailbox, smiling a simple grin trained in my direction. I didn't dare speak, still unsure how to correctly pronounce the woman's name. I didn't wave either, half convinced she had to be expecting somebody else. It eventually became clear that I was the one she'd been waiting on, had watched me the whole way from the STOP sign that leans lazily at the end of Gram's block, that simple grin plastered on her face. She craned her neck in my direction as I drew even with her mailbox, then whispered to make certain no one but I could hear, "When are you due?"

No other word carries such clear connotation, especially for someone in my predicament. She wasn't asking when I was supposed to arrive from someplace, how much money I was owed, when I expected payment. She was inquiring about the bundle growing inside my belly, that smile her way of indicating she knew, that she had twisted her face behind peach and green striped curtains long enough to have figured out. Now she wanted to know when my baby was due.

All I told Gram was that my period had stopped coming though I understood full well what that meant. I focused all my energy on suspending full realization of my ordeal, especially knowing we'd eventually have to call home and inform my parents of the trouble I'd gotten into. A lead weight lifted from me when Gram suggested we hold out a while longer. "Ain't no sense getting them all worked up over something that still might not be."

She took me to see a nurse lady she knew later that week. The woman gave me some pills and vitamins from the clinic where she worked. Asked me how long it had been since I'd seen the boy. I'd *seen* him the other day, but I knew what she meant. "Three months," I told her. "Maybe four."

Gram telephoned New York that night. From clear across the room, I felt the heat leap through the telephone wire connecting Gram to the sound of my mother's squawking. "What's that fool girl going to do with a baby? Can't hardly take care of herself."

Gram insisted we could handle this. "Everything's gonna be alright. Don't you fret over this none," she said, staring into a blank corner of the room, the phone cord twisting around an idle finger. Gram knew how to be cool under pressure. But all her cool words and calm reassurance couldn't keep them from coming—couldn't keep *her* from coming.

"Do whatever you think is best," Gram said into the telephone. "We'll see you in another couple days." She hung up the receiver looking defeated, a feeling I knew all too well. Even if my life was a mess, I wanted to be left to get out of whatever jam I'd gotten into the best I could on my own. Now they were coming, by way of a car Daddy had borrowed from one of his running buddies, intent on exercising as much influence over us as they could muster in a half-week's stay before heading back to New York.

Baby Girl —

A child in her mother's eyes is the most precious creature on earth, a gift sent to remind her mother of the wondrous possibilities the world has to bring. A mother to her daughter's eye is full of warmth and kindness and endless devotion. Sometimes between a mother and daughter, the eyes can't hold the lie.

Momma arrived with my father in the wee hours of the morning, smelling of road salt. "You're just determined to get yourself into trouble, ain't you?" she asked, nosing her way in between Gram and me with the angle of her pocketbook. No hug hello, no how you doin'. Their entire visit seemed like one long lecture. When she wasn't calling me simple minded, she was reminding Gram how irresponsible she had been to allow this mess to occur.

"What was I thinking?" she groaned. "You have no grasp on what it takes to raise a child, much less a grandchild. Wolves would have kept a better eye on her."

"Maybe you should have sent her to live with a pack of wolves instead of her own flesh and blood when your patience wore out."

"You're the one taxing my patience today," Momma responded, locking eyes for the longest while with Gram.

"One or the other of us is always taxing your

patience," Gram replied, holding steady on Momma's stare.

Gram turned and asked Daddy's thoughts on the situation but Momma interrupted again, claiming it was women's business. If the rate his opinion was sought in our household is any measure, everything must be women's business. Still, he had the makings of a terrific grandfather even if he no longer carried much weight as man of the house, father of the pregnant child with no say in how to handle the matter.

I couldn't take the way Momma was speaking to Gram, especially knowing it was my wrongdoing to blame. I headed for the river to get a break from the commotion. I hadn't set eyes on Curtis in days. Gram said it was best I not say anything to him until we had ironed out what we were planning to do. Little known to me, Momma was back at Gram's house laying out precisely what she intended to have happen as I sat alone by the river's edge, never stopping to think that I had any choice at this point outside of having my baby.

I touched my belly, thought about the life stirring inside me, all the goodness it might bring. "I will love you with all my might," I said out loud to the bulge in my gut, rubbing a loose finger across the soft indentation my bellybutton had begun making in the snug fit of any top I was still able to squeeze into. I wished for the stir of egrets to keep me company, longed for the whip of the wind that had lifted Curtis's shirttail.

I wandered back to Gram's house in time to see Daddy packing the car, this our only time alone their entire visit. He stared long at me saying nothing, his eyes a maze of discontent. I could see in his eyes as he continued to pack the car that he didn't agree with what Momma had been saying. But it had never been his way to go cross-grain where my mother was concerned.

He walked close by me on the way out, gripped my hand as he passed. "It's going to be alright, baby girl." I had always been his baby girl, despite how the rest of the world made me feel.

Momma stopped on the front porch, handed Gram a big wad of money, making sure I witnessed the exchange. "You let me know once things are taken care of. You hear?" Gram nodded a noncommittal response as a way to end the conversation. I felt nothing but breeze as Momma passed me, didn't expect any long good-bye at the end of a visit that started with no hello.

As they drove off, I asked Gram what kind of future me and my baby were going to have. She assured me the future would take care of itself, to concern myself instead with the kind of legacy I wanted to create. "We're sometimes better off breaking ranks with legacy to create a lineage all our own." She stood staring at the back window of Daddy's borrowed car like a BB gun trained on forgotten prey.

The next weekend Gram and I took the bus to

Hattiesburg. She bought me a bunch of new dresses with the wad of money Momma had left—ones that didn't make me look pregnant, but wouldn't make me look like I was ashamed of being pregnant either. Gram never told me what Momma had instructed her to do with that money. She wouldn't let me be a stink bug; wouldn't let me or my baby get squashed.

That night, I thought about my sisters back in New York. Edelyn, the closest to me in age, was named in true country fashion after two grandmothers put together—Edna and Evelyn. I suppose Evna would have been worse. The baby, Champayne, was named after another country tradition, anything you can't afford: an expensive wine, a fancy car, a faraway place you'll never live to see, only you change up the spelling a bit in an effort to disguise the origin of the child's name.

I felt sorry for them. For the first time realized that maybe I was the one who had escaped, that the stink bug had gotten away clean only they still risked the threat of stomping feet. I would have cried myself to sleep had I not slept in the front room so close to the sound of my grandmother's snoring. Instead, I lay still on the sofa bed to blank my mind and eventually I drifted off.

The next day I went to find Curtis. Gram had changed her tune once Momma left. She felt Curtis deserved to know.

"Me, a father," he said. His eyes showed an earnest

determination to give his all to the task.

"Ain't you scared?" I asked.

"Scared of what? To do what nature put us here to do?" Curtis replied, his chest puffed up like he had just planted a flag at the top of a new hill. He rested a reassuring smile on my face, rubbed a hand across the bulge that wasn't quite yet a bulge in my belly.

"Now, telling my momma. That's a whole separate matter." His eyes went wide with the prospect of sitting across from his precious momma, needing to deliver the news that she was going to be a grandma. I'd already been made to tell everyone in my world that I was pregnant, my mother especially. I needed him to stand just as tall for me.

Curtis began looking for work while we made plans to convert Gram's attic into its own apartment. Unfortunately, there were scores of grown men in Picayune far better equipped at not finding work than Curtis. His spirit sagged a bit further with each day spent pounding the pavement for work that seemed to prefer not being found, the playful energy that shone so brightly in him before now stamped down to the darkest corner of his soul.

Eventually, he found day-work building houses up in Purvis, expanding to absorb the sprawl touching off in and around Hattiesburg. This was no sprawl by New York City standards, but it was work for Curtis just the same. He set out each morning at daybreak, taking the hour's ride in the back of an open truck bed jostling alongside the other men strong enough to wield a shovel day in and day out, six days a week.

He used to come home some evenings so covered with dirt—*filthy-dirty*. "You building houses up there in Purvis," I asked, "or tunnelling to the centre of the earth?" Curtis didn't seem to take my teasing funny. He was struggling to earn a living for an unborn child. Meanwhile, his mother was pressing him more each day to return to school, advised against taking responsibility for any child he wasn't certain he should claim. But Curtis knew this was his baby as much as I knew it was mine.

Shhh —

Even the day work dried up once the last of the foundations had been dug. Framing and drywall were meant for skilled labourers. Curtis reverted to the one skill he knew with absolute certainty—obeying his momma. He returned to school the next week, explaining how it was an investment in our future: his, mine, and the baby's. I couldn't argue with fact. Still, I never felt more alone.

I was confined to Gram's house at this point, feeling too sick to go to school myself. I was becoming a bit self-conscious too, my belly beginning to poke out noticeably. Now alone in my predicament, I felt like every other girl to have lain down with a boy, not fully contemplating where it might leave her. I was no longer special, could no longer stop the rains from coming.

The nurse lady Gram took me to see warned that the pills might make me ill, having gone the first trimester without any supplements. I thought a pregnant woman was supposed to feel sick. So, I said nothing when I started spotting, took it as a sign the drugs were at work cleansing my womb for the baby to continue growing inside it. The morning I woke up doubled over in pain, I sensed things with my baby slipping to the wrong side of hope. Gram called over to the nurse lady who sent for an ambulance.

Everything inside the ambulance was loud and

bright except for Gram who sat by my side stoic as ever, all her attention focused on my face like she didn't want to know what was going on below my waist. I should have read the downturn in her disposition, the slump of her shoulders suddenly more pronounced. She touched my cheek, shaped her mouth to place a *shhh* on my suffering though no sound registered.

A pain ripped through my midsection as the ambulance rounded the curb leading away from Gram's block, like a portion of me tearing apart from the rest of my insides. I focused on the sound of my grandmother's breathing, the doughy softness of her hand against my skin, her swollen veins rolling beneath my fingertips. I squeezed Gram's palm into mine, and told myself this too shall pass.

One last firestorm inside my belly as we sped toward Crosby Memorial Hospital and the baby came out on the gurney. Half out of my mind with pain, I mistook the blaring ambulance siren for the sound of a baby crying. Rejoiced that the ordeal of my pregnancy was behind us, that my baby had at last seen fit to show herself, anxious to look out on the world.

But my baby never uttered a sound, never blinked an eye. She never took a breath.

Breath —

It may be good fortune that my baby was born three months early not breathing, with Curtis out of work, his momma not letting him see me. Gram corrected me to say no good can ever come from a baby stillborn. I failed to recognise a thing like this happens with sufficient regularity to merit a special term. God taking my own breath would have been less debilitating.

The next morning, Gram sent for a taxicab to retrieve us from the hospital. Neither of us should suffer the indignity of mass transportation after the night we'd endured. Only the swiftest, most private ride home was in order. I sat staring out the back window as the cab pulled into Gram's driveway, read the name on the mailbox across the street: *Spinnaker*. I strained to see the shadow of a figure in the front window, fingers peeping through peach and green striped curtains. I still didn't know whether she had ever married, how long she had been alone.

Gram set me up on the sofa-bed in the front room then put on some of that old-timey, sad music she sometimes played to help me know what it is that had its hold on me. She called it *The Blues*. If my mood ever had a colour, that day it was blue. Not a teary-eyed, hold-my-head-in-your-lap brand of blue. What consumed the whole of my being is a listless, don't-let-the-sunshine-in blues. Gram seemed to be feeling the same.

Curtis, on the other hand, was crazy with grief. Anytime I saw him he was sniffling and crying, or else not making any sound at all. He helped bury my baby on the side of a hill overlooking the river's edge. Carved a simple headstone marking that blustery October day where he had celebrated my birthday with flowers from his mother's garden, to the first day of spring. That's the time she had lived inside my belly.

Curtis joined the army at the end of the school year. He was sent straight from boot camp in Biloxi to the Middle East. I don't know what the army does to a man, but have witnessed firsthand how it can destroy a boy doing his best impersonation of what he believes a man to be. We spent our last day down by the river on his only visit home. He didn't love me the same, didn't touch me how he used to. Touched me like it was meant more for him than it was for me, like his touching wasn't meant for me at all.

I happened across Curtis's mother on occasion, working to replenish the Black-Eyed Susans that went missing from her garden in patches when her son first took up with me. She spoke one day from beneath the wide brim of a braided gardening hat, her hands never looking up from their busywork in the dirt. She felt obliged to relay that Curtis had been stationed for permanent duty someplace in Germany after his tour in Afghanistan had ended. Said he was doing fine.

"I'm doing fine, too," I told her, never breaking stride as I passed her front yard.

Inside Grace

The night my baby died, Gram and I mourned together, bent by communal regret. The next morning, I witnessed her sorrow transform into loathing, abject hatred for the ruinous effect she believed my mother's foreboding had inspired. Like Momma alone had ordained my baby's demise into being. Had squashed the life from her tiny body.

I didn't know to hate, but I eventually realized that's what was rooting itself inside me. I just as quickly rid myself of those feelings. But Gram's hatred was inconsolable. She consumed herself with guilt. Conjured ways not meant necessarily to bring my baby back, but to give me another one. It seemed in part to ease my pain but mostly to spite my mother, to goad her into another bout of wills so she could crush my mother's obstinacy with a force of her own. Gram's concern for my well-being, however genuine, became so intertwined with rage it was hard to discern her aim—to aid me or annihilate the person she believed had harmed me.

Patent Ignorance —

I had yet to determine my aim. Nearly making that baby with Curtis was the best thing I had ever done. When my pregnancy failed to produce a child, I all but lost the will to go on. It's all I could do to return to school at the start of the next term. Even then, it took summer school to fulfil my freshman requirements.

Miss Webster, my English teacher, spoke to me for the first time since having discovered I was pregnant. The skin along her cheekbones was oat brown, her eyes two shiny pebbles lost beneath a runaway bush of eyebrows. She held her lips pressed tight to keep her teeth from ever attempting a smile. Were she to smile, her lips would remain pursed, denying her teeth the chance to take part in the endeavour.

"It doesn't matter where you come from, but around here a girl has to make her own way," she said my first day back, her eyes peering out from beneath her heavy brow. "The sky has granted you the opportunity to do it over again, when you're ready. Until then, I want to see you fill your head with books. Not boys." Her lips swallowed up a woulda-been smile, her teeth making every attempt to shine through.

I listened as the words spilled over me, but wasn't ready to embrace the sentiment those words were meant to convey. The one thing I could say that I had truly done had slipped away, slid through my fingertips. When the love of my life up and blew away, I came away with the belief that finishing high school would require a will-power I could no longer muster. Gram convinced me otherwise.

"There are two kinds of heartache in the world, Penny," she offered into the darkness filling the front room. "The kind that endures and the kind that fades away. Eventually, one makes its way over to the other. If you allow it to."

She didn't stop to ask whether I was listening. She said what she had to say then pulled her bedroom door shut between us. The next evening, Gram met me at the kitchen table, another day having been frittered away, heavy window coverings keeping the sun at bay. She told me my mind is the one thing no one can ever take from me. Education was like religion with Gram. I could lay up in the front room with all the curtains drawn for the rest of my days if that had been my wish. But I was going to school. There was no questioning that.

She shared how at a time she had wanted to be a schoolteacher. "I was in desperate need of something to make my momma's spirit take notice. I am living proof that no child should be left to learn all she needs to learn from someone who herself hasn't learned half of what this child knows already. Not any child who looks like you or me.

"I prepared to take the state board exam, never telling a soul my ambitions to teach school. But the turmoil surrounding different kinds mixing in the same classroom made it impossible for a young black girl to get a teaching certificate in Mississippi.

"Moulding a fresh mind is like painting a picture whose colours won't dry for several years to come. Like helping shape the direction the world might take, one precious dot at a time." Her eyes flickered with light. I imagined the students' tender eyes trained on her with equal shine, like each dot mattered. To Gram they did.

She shook free from her daydreaming and got back to the lesson she meant for me to hear. "Kids aren't slow like grown folks to embrace new ideas. They hunger for knowledge. And so sweet, always quick to double back whenever they've caught someone beaming at them, never letting a smile directed their way go unrequited."

She then settled on the less rousing certainties of her everyday life. "I could have fought the system. At first, I did. That was before the boycott—the school board's response to a nationwide mandate to de-segregate the school system. Couldn't have made a bigger mess of things, their aim seeming set instead on no one getting an education." She sucked something between her teeth. "Like throwing out the Christmas goose to avoid sharing with your neighbour, never mind that both of you might starve to death. I recog-nised then I could never be part of a system so fouled up in its understanding of the value in education. I resigned from the idea of ever teaching school, the State of Mississippi in its patent ignorance be damned."

You'd think she was mourning a decision made just days prior. But this was a sorrow easily decades in the making, the passion behind which had only intensified with age. "Education isn't a privilege reserved for the chosen few. It's a God given right to be denied no one. That's what Martin Luther preached before they dusted him off. Medgar Evers had been around this way carrying the same message of *equal for everyone*. Oh, what they did to Medgar." She clapped the air with the open palms of her hands to release their anger. "Struck him down in his own driveway, for all his children to see."

She wrinkled the corners of her mouth like the taste of their murders was still foul in her memory. "I don't know when things are going to change. Not in my lifetime. Perhaps in yours. With any hope, your grand-babies will live to see the change we've been waiting on."

The memory of lost ambition washed her face in sadness. Her whole body folded in on itself. "It has taken a lifetime of helping people in other ways to even approximate the kind of joy being a schoolteacher would have brought me," she sighed. "Life can present an endless string of doubt and disappointment. What I'll tell you is to never give in to outside force. Let no one and nothing shake you from your dreams. After all, what are we without dreams to pull us along in the world?"

I believed at that point in the awesome power of Gram's presence. I felt the state of Mississippi had done itself a great disservice denying its children access to the likes of Evelyn Combs with her ability to shed light on things that should have been evident in the first place. Everyone should know Gram, should touch her circle if only for a moment.

She stayed on me about returning to school. "Take the worst situation you've known, consider how helpless you felt. Now imagine that feeling persisting the rest of your days. How helpless you'd be then. That's the existence you'll be left to endure without a proper education."

She was straightening my hair by the stove. The path of spent gas fumes plus the smell of hair burning had me light headed. Gram pressed on as lucid as I had ever known her to be. "There's nothing we can do to never feel helpless, but only a person who takes command of her own fate can avoid being rendered forever helpless."

"Some of us can't help but be helpless," I muttered, the side of my face hidden by an errant tangle of hair. "Some things are just meant to be that way."

Gram set the comb down on the stove, the teeth glowing bright orange at the edges and blue-green closer to the source of the flame. She leaned past my shoulder, looked me in the eye to measure the depth of comprehension for what I'd just said.

She took a seat next to mine, her body turned partway to face a distant window. "I didn't realize she had beaten you down this far." The words caught my full ear. It had been ages since anyone placed physical hands on me, but I was down as far as I felt I could go. That I had never really been up only served to conceal how far I had fallen.

Come What May —

We ate supper that night in silence, one side of my head still full of kinks and knots. After clearing the table, Gram and I stood at the kitchen sink doing the dishes: Gram washed, I dried.

As I set the last of the silverware out on a clean dish towel, I asked why she never says grace before a meal. "I say an inside grace," she replied, her hands never breaking rhythm beneath a mountain of soap suds.

I stood staring at my grandmother's shimmering reflection, just made visible against the sky growing dark outside the window. It was sometimes hard to tell whether Gram believed the things she said or simply said the things she believed I needed to hear. "God knows I'm grateful for all I've been given. *From my lips to God's ear.* Ain't that how folks in the church tell it? I just skip the part that passes my lips. No one else need hear my prayers."

Gram was slave to no religion yet at times seemed nearer to God than anyone I had encountered. I sought her counsel instinctively. "Does God love us equal?"

"What do you mean, *equal*?" She seemed more puzzled than perturbed which is sometimes how Gram appeared to me—perturbed that is.

"Does God love some people more than he does others?"

"God has more love to give than you or I can

comprehend," she explained. "You and me, we're small enough to love this person one way then not love somebody else the same. God's love doesn't know such bounds."

"Then why'd He do this—give me a baby only to take it away again?"

"To open up your eyes." She struck me with the intensity of her staring, her eyes locked onto mine. "That baby showed you're alive—able to sustain life. We may never comprehend why God took it before you got the chance to hold it good. But consider the blessing. Some women live their whole lives never knowing the joy of another life stirring inside them. Others still never warm to the task, even when fate places a baby right inside their feeble hands. It may not be evident today, but that warmth will visit you again once the right circumstance comes your way."

She let go with her staring, plunged her hands back into the sudsy water. "Now put away the chicken, Girlie." That's what she called me—*Girlie*. Mention of chores to do: food to put up, laundry to fold, a grocery list to fill, was usually meant to discourage my conversation, especially talk concerning God and boundless love. This time the warning didn't take. "Who do you love?"

"You're just full of questions tonight, ain't you?" Her eyes went shy, turned away momentarily from the stone determination they usually portrayed.

"Traipsing through memories of all the lives that have touched mine would be like chasing flocks of birds from the treetops—too numerous to count, too many complicated stories left behind for me to tell. Simply put, I love most people."

"Some more than others?"

She nodded her head rhythmically like she was trying to shake out a response. "Yes, I suppose... some more than others. Who loves you?" she asked.

"You do, I suspect?"

"And this you know for fact?"

"I believe I do."

"Okay then. Who else loves you?"

"My daddy loves me."

"Yes, your daddy loves you dearly. But I'm not talking about your daddy. I'm talking about folks in this room. Name someone else?"

"God?"

"Girlie, we aren't talking anymore about God tonight." Her eyes regained some of their toughness. "I'm talking about you. How do you expect someone to love you if you're not prepared to love yourself?

"You do love yourself. Don't you?" I took her question as rhetorical, an answer to which wasn't necessary.

"Well, don't you?" Evidently, I was wrong about not needing to answer.

"I'm not sure," I replied, reopening the floodgates on her lecture.

"What's inside you? You ever stopped to look?" Her disappointment seemed directed at me this time. "Just 'cause your Momma ain't sweet on you how you think she ought to be, you consider yourself damaged goods, a bruised peach that's determined to never heal?"

"Why doesn't she want me?"

"She hardly wants herself. Doesn't recognise the love she has to give. That's her burden. Don't let it be yours," she added as she rinsed the residue of soap suds from inside the sink. She wrung the dishrag between her hands, hung it across the faucet to drip dry then turned back in the direction of the kitchen table, her little question asker hot on her heels.

"Did you mean to have her?" I asked. "Momma, I mean."

Her eyes went shy again. She disappeared inside herself. "At that point, there was little I did on purpose. I took whatever life brought me—smooth or rough, come what may. Having a baby is the one thing I did with any clear intent. I only wish I had done it for better reasons."

She returned, a part of her still lost among distant memories locked deep inside her head. "It would seem I've been alone my entire lifetime. But it was harder to take back then. They say my momma died trying to push me into this world. I suspect that's how most people die—*pushing*. At least she was attempting something as noble as transporting a new soul to earth. But that's the circle of life, one taken for every one given, the rest of us biding time before we're called on to make way. If I'd only had more time with her—*any* time with her."

She rested her hands in her lap, stared into her palms like they held a picture of her momma that she alone could see. I longed for that kind of vision, wished I could crawl inside Gram's head to see a mother who loved me so much she would sacrifice all she had to give so I'd have a chance at a life of my own.

"My daddy worked himself to the bone trying to compensate for her absence. Told me bedtime stories about how smart, how sweet, how special my momma was. Had me wishing I could create someone just like her, renew her spirit in living form. Even named your mother Althea to help fit her grandmother's soul. But God takes souls. We learn that from our earliest bedtime prayers—*Should I die before I wake, I pray the Lord my soul to take.* What I got was your momma, for better or worse. And made the best I could of what I'd been given."

I considered my reasons for wanting a baby, what I would have done with her, how different my life would be, another being depending on me for every little thing. Feeling her stir inside me had altered my course already. Did Gram feel the same kind of love for my mother? Had Momma loved me that way at some point?

"What's wrong with her and my daddy?"

"Girlie, ties between two people made not of love is like a stomach that won't get full. You can stuff it with all sorts of things, but nothing will satisfy the hunger, a hunger for something one doesn't know how to give, the other doesn't know how to keep."

"How can you say he doesn't love her?" I asked. "He gives her anything she wants."

"Dear heart," she told me. "Love's nothing about possessions. Love is a bond formed between two people who find they want nothing more than each other. They work tirelessly to nurture love's bond, will give anything toward sustaining their connection to one another. It shouldn't matter that he gives her nice things." She searched my eyes for some show of light.

"Any gift given in the spirit of love is a token at best, a trinket meant to signify the depth of feeling you have for one another. But without trinkets there's still love. Without love, trinkets don't amount to a hill of beans. Love's absolute like that."

"Have you known a love that's absolute?"

"Oh, I had this Dominican man—his name was Ruben. He was something. Used to have to cross my toes when we kissed to keep my feet from lifting off the ground."

"Grandma Evelyn!"

"Don't get soft spirited on me now. I'm not saying anything you're not going to hear eventually," she assured me. "He had this little moustache that tickled my neck when we nuzzled. Tickled other places, too. And arms like two battleships, one with a strapping marlin tattooed across it." She squeezed her arm like she had big muscles hidden beneath her cotton shirt sleeve. Smiled like she was squeezing his arm for real in place of her own jiggly biceps. "Ruben was a good man, a good man with good lovin'. Now that's a hard combination to find."

"Did he treat you special?" I asked, imagining how things might have turned out with Curtis had our fairy-tale somehow managed to ring true.

"Oh, how that man worshipped me. Would wait on me hand and foot if I let him. But I didn't need all that. I could tell him to go to hell and he would turn up the next day with candy and flowers like the devil had invited us on a date."

I felt her foot tapping beneath the tablecloth. I tried to catch the rhythm of her tapping as she pressed her eyes closed, rubbed one hand over the other like she was trying to figure something. "I suspect he loved me, could have loved me had he stayed. But even a good man can't stay who isn't built for staying." She spread her hands across the table, letting her memory roam more freely.

"Ruben was born on the move. Met me on his way someplace. Now, I've been lots of places: Chicago, New York, DC. None of those places ever felt like home— too stark, the streets stripped bare, rock and steel replacing grass and trees. And cold. The kind of cold to pierce your soul, the wind rummaging beneath your skirt like y'all were intimate. Making love to an iceberg every time you step outdoors." She pulled her shoulders together in a mock attempt at generating some warmth inside her aching bones. "I like my wind outside my skirt. So, I made up my mind to stay right here and live out my days in Picayune. Didn't fret when he decided elsewise."

She held a one-sided conversation as though able to mind-read the questions tumbling inside my head. "Sure, I miss him, some days stronger than others. But you can't cage a bird who wants to fly. Your days will be filled with struggles if you try—some big, some not so big. Still, there'll be struggles. You don't want a man who's had his wings clipped either. Don't need that kind of weight on your hands."

I found myself staring. Tried not to blink for fear my shut eyelids might dull my sense of hearing. I felt a sudden rush of kinship for Gram. Held her tender in my eyes, for the first time weighed her vulnerabilities. I imagined her as a young woman, a girl even. How she could be me.

The boys back in New York used to joke me for my name—Penny Hill. Said you could take a hundred of me and just make change for a dollar. I hated those boys for what they did to my name. Handled it rough then rubbed it out in my brain like something no longer needed (a spent cigarette). Whatever a dollar's worth, they considered me a fraction of that weight, as easily lost as spent, given away freely at the corner store to avoid dispensing more of me into the world.

That night Gram told me that a worm lay down with a snake and produced a girl child, precious and small. They named her Penny to signify the value she brought to an otherwise empty existence together. "You gave them worth, Girlie, even of the smallest denomination."

We talked that night until darkness was well on its way back toward light, the window running bloodshot where its sill met the horizon. Gram wrapped my hair in a kerchief then kissed my forehead before heading to bed herself.

I thought about Gram's daddy as I waited for sleep to carry me away. How he must have felt upon learning she was pregnant. Delighted to learn his stories had stuck, had succeeded in preserving her mother's legacy.

I wished I had known her daddy. Wished I could see mine, could rest in his arms... And then I was asleep, my lids heavy, my heart light. Goodnight World. Goodnight Gram. Goodnight Baby Penny. I pray the Lord your souls to keep.

Wilt

I awoke the next day deep into the morning. I listened at the window for a familiar sound, but the songs of morning had been sung already, the birds of midday already at work chasing each other among the treetops. I rose to the must of stale air, felt summer's body heat rising all around me from the wood floor to the bead board ceiling, the front room of Gram's house catching the brunt of the noonday sun.

I retreated to Gram's bedroom. Her nightshirt folded neatly atop a tightly creased bedspread meant she was gone, had dressed and left for the day. Gram seldom spent time at home, especially during the summertime. She disappeared for hours on end then returned, simple as you please never saying a word about where she'd been.

I took advantage of these daily excursions to explore my new home, embrace my surroundings. When Gram was around, I ventured into her bedroom only out of necessity: to fetch her sewing kit from beneath the night table or bring her a cup of tea on a dreary afternoon. It housing the only bathroom, I also passed through her room on my way to the toilet. But when Gram was away, I could seldom be found anywhere outside of her bedroom.

I sat at the foot of the bed studying myself in the bureau mirror. I didn't look like the girls from Picayune. They had an easy way about them. Shared a bond of familiarity that only comes from having been reared in the same circle where their seeds were sown. They had known each other forever, saw in one another an extension of themselves—their own thoughts and views in another human form, separate yet similar. I was awkward by comparison. Knew no one like me. Even Gram was in many ways distant, was at least too large or too complex for me to recognise our similarities.

Put on Cute —

I'd begun to realize that I was cute—or could be cute is what one of the local boys told me. Eyed me from behind as I passed, his attention fixed like he needed to memorize something written across the back of my skirt. Curtis used to tell me I was beautiful. Would gaze at me, his eyes full of love's drunk. Gram says she loves me whether or not I'm cute. I love her the same.

After a while, having lost interest in my cuteness, I wandered over to Gram's closet in search of something better able to hold my fascination. Gram's closet housed things I had never seen outside her closet: hats and heels and form fitting dresses. Gram went nowhere to warrant that kind of wardrobe. It was like the things in her closet belonged to someone else, a silent stranger living in the room with her. Maybe it's Gram who was squatting in the stranger's bedroom, standing guard to keep anyone from disturbing the woman's things, the stranger's penchant for fur stoles and silk lingerie standing in stark contradiction to Gram's no nonsense demeanour.

Most had never been worn, still had tags attached. Like life had taken Gram on some endless shopping spree, leaving no time to ever try on the things she'd purchased. But Gram never shopped, couldn't stand the thought of some stuffy clerk deciding what looked best on her. Never seemed to consider how the way she looked might weigh on people's impression of her. I had yet to evolve that far. I worried incessantly how I set in other people's eyes, changing my look one week to the next—from braids to bangs to a pulled back ponytail—until I could at times scarcely recognise myself.

Gram on the other hand was the model of consistency. She had precisely two outfits defined by a pair of V-neck T-shirts, one red and the other blue, that she wore interchangeably paired with an equally sparse rotation of khaki skirts. During the winter months, she donned a sweater over-top the T-shirts and a pair of woolen socks inside the same sandals she wore barefoot the rest of the year. That's my Gram, simple and neat, down to the socks. Yet in her own way she had style. Carried herself with a quiet confidence that made her seem infinitely composed despite the frumpy getup.

I emerged from the closet dissatisfied with the understanding its contents had afforded me of the woman whose room it belonged to. I took a seat at the dressing table. Gram didn't have many things, but the few things she owned seemed the best money could buy. Off to one side sat a stained-glass vanity tray—coloured shards of glass surrounding violet dragonflies set in a lead frame. I bet if you held it up to the light you could see Paris, Milan, or Madrid through the images that tray would project—all the places I had been made to study during my stint in summer school.

Next to the tray was a candle holder topped by a

stained-glass lampshade matching the dragonflies on the vanity. At first glance the lampshade would have you believe it belonged to a regular lamp, but on further inspection I found resting beneath the shade a lavender candle nearly burned down to the end.

I searched the top drawer of the bureau for a box of matches, struck a match and touched the flame to the lamp. The light reflected around the glass shade brought to mind children frolicking in a mix of brightly coloured jumpers. Had it been dark outside, the flicker from the candlelight would have set the dragonflies dancing, Gram's bedroom a kaleidoscope of colour moving in rhythm to the flame's meandering. But daylight was too bright for that, the midday sun not likely to be upstaged by a couple lampshade dragonflies, bound to earth by reach of ordinary candlelight.

The contents of the vanity tray were equally impressive. A brush and matching comb, set in sterling silver, sat centre stage. The brush looked like its bristles had been cut fresh from the low, thick part of a horse's mane. I sometimes watched Gram brush her hair, a hundred strokes on each side, before retiring for the night.

Next to the brush and comb set rested a glass vial topped with a turquoise mesh atomizer. I studied the vial with my hand, giving the mesh atomizer a squeeze. The nozzle released a mist so fine it refused momentarily to fall to earth. I watched as the perfume laden mist swirled around with invisible air molecules, desperately clinging to one another before falling toward the vanity like a swarm of tiny fireflies suddenly stripped of their wings. I wiped the bureau top with the hem of my nightshirt. It smelled of lilac flowers.

An irresistible urge overtook me. I headed for the bathroom, turned the water on hot, dropped the rubber stopper into the chrome drainpipe, and prepared to give myself a makeover starting with a steam bath. I hung a towel over the window shade, lined the sink basin with candles, then eased into the tub, lifting my nightshirt over my head as I went, surrendering ever so slowly to the scalding water.

I stayed in the tub a full thirty minutes, felt wrinkles forming on the rubbery tips of my fingers and toes. I stepped onto the cool tile floor, dried myself then stood beneath a mist of falling lilacs.

I started to dress but recognised that my shabby clothes no longer suited my mood. I searched Gram's closet for something more befitting the path I'd started down with my steam bath. I slipped into a peach coloured camisole that fell just shy of mid-thigh, and put on a pair of Gram's patent leather pumps. I headed back to the bureau to check myself in the mirror. A failed pregnancy had done wonders for my breasts— now I had some, full and bulging at the sides of my slip. I almost hated to cover them, but recognised I couldn't go out like this. For the first time acknowledged that I had planned to go out—sneak out, dressed in the finest things Gram's wardrobe had to offer.

I lifted the lid of a heart shaped jewellery dish. A pair of pearl earrings caught my eye. I hurriedly swapped them for the gold studs that ordinarily graced my earlobes. I found a matching choker with an ivory cameo hanging from its centre, applied some lipstick, a hint of eye shadow. I brushed my hair up from around my neck and twisted a bun on top of my head before teasing down a few baby curls to frame my cheekbones.

From there, I went back to Gram's closet, trying on one dress after another. Most didn't fit well. Only one suited the steamy outside air. I emerged from the closet fully dressed: cream-coloured pumps and pearl accents offset by a floral print spaghetti dress. All dressed up and able to go nowhere—unless of course I could get back before Gram was to return.

A Bit of Shade —

I headed for the bus stop, Gram's heels still wobbly beneath unskilled legs. I eventually found my footing, planting a spiked heel firmly with each step before letting up on the last. By the time I reached town, I was the model of picture-perfect elegance—a refreshing breeze winding a path against the stifling summer heat.

The wind taunted me as I walked River Street, lifting the tails of my chiffon dress to expose a bare thigh every so often against the afternoon sun. I walked the streets of downtown Picayune uncharacteristically directed despite having no place to go, browsing store windows as if I had money to buy more clothes like the ones I had on. I felt thoroughly decadent, partly because of my breasts heaving gently as I made my way, unrestrained against my silk camisole, but mostly because the entire ensemble belonged to somebody else, the silent stranger whose life was packed away inside my grandmother's bedroom closet.

I eventually came upon a group of boys from school congregated outside the drugstore, talking undoubtedly about baseball or fishing or some other carefree matter. They had the same easy way about them I'd observed in their female counterparts, only their ways were less refined, primal even. The afternoon sky melted them into a sun soaked caricature of lazy smiles and dangling limbs.

They seemed as if nothing in the world mattered except what they were talking about right then, that plus finding refuge from the heat, the whole lot of them standing as still as they could manage beneath a bit of shade from the drugstore awning. And there I was in a hurry, no time to speak. I had things to do. Not important things, but things: clothes on the line outside Gram's backdoor that might not dry properly without me standing by to guide the wind on its path, a couple library books that would become overdue in another week's time, a refrigerator full of perishables that would reach their expiration before long.

Had I been paying better attention, I would have crossed to the other side of the street before reaching the corner where the boys had assembled. But my mind was lost in a window of endless bargains and markdowns. One of the mannequins reminded me of my middle sister, Edelyn, cast alongside a smiling family in a scene set against the river's edge. I hadn't spoken to them in ages. I let my mind drift home momentarily, trapped with my sisters back in New York.

The boys' chatter subsided as I approached. At least one of them looked like he used to know Curtis. Still, I couldn't call any of them by name—more reason not to speak. The sun's heat, plus the thought of boys from school catching me dressed this way, caused me to perspire. Not drip soaking wet. More a light glistening, starting at my temples before making its way around my hairline to the nape of my neck.

Beads of sweat formed between my shoulder blades. My slip began to stick to the front of my thighs. I reached to adjust my baby curls as they melted into thin sideburns plastered against the sides of my face, my flower beginning to wilt, put on cute threatening to come apart right before their eyes.

I gave the boys a pleasant nod once I recognised I could no longer avoid their path—part greeting, part thinly veiled masquerade to keep my heart from beating its way out of my chest. I focused extra attention on my stride as I approached the drugstore, hoping to avoid wobbling off the curbside in front of them.

The boys pushed away from the drugstore wall as I passed, straightening their shoulders one after the next, each aiming to greet me a bit taller than the last. My spirit took a leap that day, stood ahead of me, unabashed, imposing. I was melting on the outside, but my insides turned hard as steel, the uneasy waters that usually trembled inside my veins silenced by an icy self-assurance that seldom visited me.

"How are you-all?" I offered in their general direction. I'd been practicing my *you-all's* since arriving in Mississippi. Had waited nearly two years for the chance to use one out loud.

"We're doin' fine," they answered back, in perfect unison. "And you?"

"Just fine," I replied, giving the boys a farewell smile

while maintaining sufficient pace with my stride to put some needed distance between us. I hurried around the next corner hoping the river of sweat running down my back wasn't peeking at them through the thin fabric of my borrowed dress.

They didn't seem to recognise me, hadn't bothered to consider I may be someone whose acquaintance they had already made. Nobody knew me in that dress. I walked another block out of the way then headed for the bus stop. I'd had enough living the life of a stranger, longed to be back inside my own skin.

A Sliver of Brightness

Dress Down —

I arrived at the bus stop to find the bench completely empty. Even the most pitiful straggler might have offered some encouragement. But to find no one sitting there meant I had missed the last shuttle of the day to the outskirts, the evening bus running less frequently during the summertime.

I sat for a moment to adjust my feet in the pointy ends of Gram's high-heel shoes. I felt mounds of blisters forming on the outside edges of my toes, the bones twisting around one another like a deformed tree trunk separated at its base. The certainty of a punishing walk home loomed in my path, phantom-like, wavering with the rhythm of the beating sun reflected off the expanse of seething pavement.

A few minutes walking and I had to give up the high heels. As I bent to rub my feet, the bun in my hair gave way, sending a tangle of newly released locks tumbling around my ears like the loose head of a dry mop. I thought for a moment I could smell myself, my lilac flower scent lost deep in the musk of old sweat. I sat on the side of the road contemplating my choices: to walk the rest of the way barefoot or wait there for Gram to beat my cute behind. Either way, I was doomed.

That's when a car approached, a behemoth sedan in a shade of blue so dark it seemed to defy connection to any true colour—a car that's blue and green one instant then violet and black the next. The colours you might see at the vortex of a twister as all the hues in the rainbow swoosh away down the drainpipe.

I would swear on a stack of bibles that I had seen Gram's arm hanging from the passenger window as the car glided past me, her silver bracelets glistening in the sun as the car made its way toward the horizon, the smell of cigar smoke lingering long in its wake. But what business would Gram have in a no-coloured sedan, reeking of cigar smoke? Besides, I had to believe she would have stopped had she seen me walking, for nothing more than to dress me down for taking things from her closet without permission.

I got back to my feet, Gram's leather pumps dangling by my sides. I continued to walk, contemplating the trouble I was in. I tried to remember a time I'd seen Gram angry. Like anyone, she had her moods, but how cross she would be at me for borrowing from her closet, trying on her best jewellery, then parading myself downtown for the whole world to see? I could hardly imagine that.

I'd have been dead already had I been back in New

York, a lifetime of loosely related transgressions rolling against me like thunder in a cloud filled sky. Anger ruled our household like a drug. Momma would sift through the details of our lives, like a dope fiend in search of her next fix, some line one of us had crossed, to release the venom in her veins, deadly-sweet.

I was her favourite hit. She beat me once for sitting with my legs open too wide on the train. I was ten. Built like a boy, dressed like one too. I don't remember where we had gone that day. I sat with my feet tucked beneath me, my knees folded into my chest to keep my legs from sticking to the hard-plastic bench, the transference of moisture from bared arms and legs and thighs on nearly everything you touched.

I was awakened that night by an explosion of light at our bedroom door. I recognised my mother's house shoes moving across the carpet but could only make out faint traces of the person they were transporting— dark edges painted against hazy light filtering in from down the hallway. Her shadow cut a long path across my sisters' bed, holding a belt in one hand, the other hand reaching to push the door closed behind her. She waited for the door to click shut then stood silent to blend in with the night.

Ears replaced eyes. I tasted her anger, first with my tongue anticipating her heat then with my fingertips as I attempted to fend off the first few blows. Within minutes I was fully engulfed, her arms and mine the only things moving in the darkness, mother and child locked in battle against the blackest of nights. The belt on my soft flesh uttered the only sound. I'd learned early on to suppress my tears. Crying only made the beatings worse, my sobbing having a crescendo effect on her high, sending waves of fury crashing down ever harder on my puny backside.

The pummelling rained on me like two sets of fists, my mother and her shadow now one in the darkness. She eventually collapsed on the bed, breathing hard from the struggle, her full weight leaning against me. She pinched hard against the tender flesh along the inside of my left thigh.

"This what you want, somebody pokin' round down there?" she asked. "Make me a grandma before my time and I'll kill you first." Then she was gone, across the foot of my bed and out into the hallway, a sliver of brightness around the door frame the only physical evidence of our encounter. Before long, the sliver of brightness extinguished too.

I couldn't eat the next morning, a welt throbbing along the length of my thigh. Watched my mother play the happy homemaker, to good effect, as she served massive helpings of hot cereal from the stove. I held my tongue as my sisters smiled up at her, overjoyed by the apparent goodness of butter and brown sugar melting into creamy curds of cooked oats, ladled from the same hands that had assaulted me the night prior. Me, she let sit, an empty place mat set in front of me, content to let me starve if that was my aim. I don't know what I did to deserve such humiliation, but I never sat with my legs open on the train again. That much I assure you.

I listened as another car approached, the roll of its tires losing their urgency as the car rounded the bend I just exited along the roadway. Somebody lost no doubt, slowing to ask directions out of town on their way to Covington or Slidell. I'd have them on their way in no time.

I was greeted by a pair of grinning cheeks, the man hanging from the passenger window talking about me to the man seated beside him like I was a piece of produce left on the roadside, waiting to be squeezed. "Look at this fine, young thing. She fresh as a daisy." The driver leaned across to get a gander, the slow blink of his eyes conveying a need more depraved than anything my young spirit could hope to fulfil.

I took a long breath to contain the fright rising inside me when the blue-black sedan rolled up on me again, the windows rolled tight, Gram's dangling bracelets nowhere in sight. The sedan eased alongside the out-of-town strangers. The man behind the wheel drew down on them with a look transferring the fright from inside me fully to their slack faces. Their car made an abrupt U-turn, the undercarriage squealing with the steep angle of the manoeuvre as the rear tires scrambled against loose gravel accumulated along the roadside. The car scurried in the opposite direction, the blue-black sedan seeming intent on trailing the men to the county line.

By the time I reached Gram's block, my breasts had lost their sway, clinging tightly instead to the damp insides of my silk camisole. Gram's pearl necklace hung in an uneven circle around my neck, sticking in places to spots of evaporated sweat. I turned up the walkway thinking an ass whuppin' and a ride home would be a welcome substitute for a barefoot walk any day. As I climbed the front steps, I caught a glimpse of my aching feet, swollen and caked with dust.

A breeze shot past, licking the hem of my dress as it cut a path down the middle of Gram's tiny house. Gram was undoubtedly out back pitching wood chips into an old coffee can to while the time away, both doors open wide to let the day's heat escape for the night, the sun having successfully defended its turf against the kaleidoscope of lampshade dragonflies.

If I walked stiff legged and silent into the bedroom, slipped off her clothes, then hung them back in the closet, she'd never know they were missing. I could rinse and dry them the next time she was away.

I was astonished to find, when I pushed open her closet door, row upon row of empty wooden hangers, a jagged-tooth smile beaming in celebration of my pending demise. I hustled out to the front room, crept over to the trunk where I kept all my things—the wooden chest that doubled as a coffee table when the sofa-bed wasn't pulled out. If I was going to get my ass whipped, it wasn't going to be dressed in high heels and a strappy dress looking like somebody too grown for a beating.

I opened the trunk to find the other half of Gram's closet folded neatly in with the rest of my belongings. I changed into one of my regular cotton dresses then headed toward the kitchen, not knowing what fate might await me on the back porch.

I passed a pot simmering on the stove, the burner turned low to keep the water rolling slowly on itself. Gram caught me as I reached to push open the screen door. "Get the water for me, Girlie." She had me mix the water from the stove with a basin of cool water she had waiting on the back steps. She poured in some anti-septic smelling liquid.

"You shouldn't be out on your own like that." That's all she said to scold me, that I shouldn't venture out on my own. No mention of the dress I'd taken from her closet, the earrings I had lifted from her jewellery dish. Her lecture ran more in the direction of a gentle warning than a legitimate tongue lashing, finger wagging in my face.

"Lucky for you those boys were from your own school. Might not have been so well mannered other-wise." How did she know about the boys from school? I averted her stare to keep from giving away anything she might not have known already.

I'd had occasion to catch her downtown too—with a man, the one who drives the blue-black sedan in all likelihood. I recognised him as Mr. Graves, the funeral director. I found it an unfortunate coincidence for a man named Graves to take up the business of burying people. But the way I heard it, his daddy couldn't find any better occupation to pursue given the family name. Mr. Graves was simply following in his father's footsteps. Lots of things happened that way in Picayune, without the slightest question as to things going any direction other than how it appeared they ought to go.

The two of them were standing along the curbside in front of the post office. Mr. Graves was leaning against a lamppost, looking onto the street. Meanwhile Gram was turned, staring into the side of his neck or looking past him at seemingly nothing down the walkway whenever she wasn't looking directly at him. Every so often, one of them would say something in response to which the other would nod.

One such exchange eventually produced an extra-pleasant look on my grandmother's face like she wanted to smile if not laugh out loud, neither of which I could imagine she might do in broad daylight. Her face just as quickly swallowed up its pleasant look and Gram turned back to staring into the side of Mr. Graves' neck, waiting for her turn to nod again, depending who had last said something.

"Don't think I set out to follow you," she offered. "I was out minding my own business when I saw you pass in front of the drugstore all wobbly legged." Her teasing sounded almost playful.

"Put your feet in here," she said, pointing toward the lukewarm concoction resting at the foot of the steps. She removed the bracelets on both arms then began rubbing my feet. "Men are strange creatures. I'm not saying to never let your guard down, but approaching the wrong one in a frilly dress is like dangling fresh meat in front of a wild animal. Do whatever you like. Just make certain anything you do is of your choosing. Don't let your dress tell a false tale of things you're not truly intending." She gave my calf a rub. "You've got better sense than that." When she smiled at me, I couldn't help but smile back.

"If you want, I'll show you how to walk in those heels once the swelling in your feet goes down. And, if you're going to show that much thigh, make sure to shave first. No man wants to see a hairy leg, especially one as skinny as yours." She was most certainly teasing at this point.

"You watch yourself, Girlie." Her eyes turned serious again, waiting for me to acknowledge their shift in mood. "Not everyone's as nice as that Curtis of yours. And we don't need any more trouble around here. You hear me?" From there we let the night descend on us, sitting still on Gram's back porch and watching the day's events slip to the far end of the universe.

The sun hung in the sky as dusk approached like a red yo-yo dangling at the end of an invisible string. I know why the sun sets. That much I remember from science class. Still, I was aching to ask why the sun changes colours so frequently as it makes its way toward the horizon—from bright yellow, to blood orange, to yo-yo red. But I had used up all my questions to Gram the other night. Couldn't afford to disrupt the peace between us after the commotion I had already stirred.

I continued to ponder the question in silence. It was like the sun had turned its back on us, its bright yellow face gone to shine on a distant part of the galaxy. Meanwhile, mother earth had been left to accept this ruby red replica, never for a moment wondering why she'd been handed anything less than the sun's full attention.

For most people, the show's over once the sun has set. From Gram, I learned that the passing of the setting sun is more often than not the precursor of a spectacle yet to begin. The dwindling light spreads ever more broadly as the last memories of sunlight disappear over the horizon. Even the clouds get in on the mix transforming the sky into a spider's web arrangement of spiralling rays. It's as if God is at play with thunderbolts to carve snowflake patterns into the scattered cloud cover, a mix of brilliant colour bouncing in every direction at once.

The next morning Gram confirmed the clothes inside the trunk were for me. "Lord knows I've got no use for those things at this stage. You may as well get some wear out of them." Still no mention of where those things came from, why she needed them in the first place. More curious was that she wanted me to have them. She lectured me the whole night prior about the trouble I might get myself into then seemed intent the next day on showing me I could dress this way, so long as I didn't compromise myself in a way that produced a situation I couldn't manage.

I never wore those things again, not the full ensemble. No longer saw the point. Began to see the world through Gram's eyes, to comprehend that put on cute must on occasion fend for herself, even when that means walking the whole way home barefoot on a path paved in dust and hot tar.

Still

I'm haunted by the dream that my baby survived the ambulance siren, was born alive and breathing, just still. Initially I dreamed that, being so still, we hadn't noticed her breathing and buried her on the hill anyway. Lately I dreamt she's alive in the house with Gram and me. Yet she never makes a sound—not a sneeze, not a coo, not a teensy, little baby fart.

Being that she's quiet, I lose track of her for days on end—forget to feed her, forget to change her, never think to take her with me when I head out. I awake in a panic trying to remember where I've left her, when last I've seen her.

In the end, I recognise it's a dream, thoughts of my dead baby mixing with living details of the day's events—a long wait at the bus stop, a quiet walk along the riverside that in my dream appears will have no end. I find myself alone in Gram's front room, my bed covers tossed all around me. I sit up rail straight in the bed and wait for the sun to rescue me, for the events of another day to overtake memories of a baby stillborn. Eventually, they do.

TWO

Thunder and Lightning

Gabriel approached Saint Peter to inform him that someone had arrived seeking entrance to heaven. Peter recognised this immediately as one of Satan's tricks. No one arrives at the Pearly Gates uninvited, especially a form composed entirely in black smoke—no lips, no eyes, no swollen heart offered in exchange for God's forgiveness.

Peter alerted the Father who flashed the lights three times to put Satan on notice. He shook the sky to let the whole world know the devil was at work looking to take somebody's place in heaven. It's only when an angel enters heaven that the sky remains silent, the triumph and jubilation taking place beyond the clouds failing to reach those of us left to carry on without our angel.

Shine

Gram died before I could graduate high school, before I could get myself out of Picayune. Shut herself inside her bedroom one night complaining of a headache. I found her the next morning still as a bedpost, her hands and face ashen like the life had drained from her body in liquid form, starting with her skin tone. The medical examiner said it was an aneurysm in her brain, assured me that she hadn't suffered any. She didn't look like she had, tucked neat inside her bed like God Almighty had lain her there Himself.

I stood at her bedside, bid farewell to an empty form. Witnessed a lifetime of secrets, past lies evaporate into the sheets. A hollow shell rested in her place, the vessel that had carried her, or that she had carried. I couldn't decide which. In time, it too will dissolve into this earth, leaving only memories of Gram to live on inside my head.

Now here I am, daughter of a failed sharecropper turned New Yorker, next of kin to a dead grandmother whose own daughter seemed at best inconvenienced by the ordeal of her mother's death. My mother stayed at the graveside just long enough to witness the first shovelful of dirt fall onto the casket, her mouth seeming to wish to form the words *good riddance*.

Initially I thought not to notify them, remembering how she reacted last time we called with news to report. But I couldn't have that on my conscience, denying her the opportunity to pay proper respects to the only mother she was ever going to know. I would have obeyed my original instincts had I known she was planning to act out the way she did, would have weighed Gram's feelings over hers even if my conscience were to suffer. Still, I couldn't imagine standing by my lonesome at the funeral, the sole mourner appointed alongside the pastor to bid Gram her final farewell, leaving her as alone in death as she had been in life. My anxieties couldn't have been further from the truth.

People came from far and wide. Each claimed to have shared a special bond with Gram, yet none of them seemed willing to admit knowing one another. Women who looked all too sure of themselves as someone approached, then completely lost once the person passed them by.

The men, on the other hand, were all different, from hard-hat to business suit. You wouldn't have placed any two of them in a room together, yet somehow each of them had connected with Gram. Odder still, everyone seemed to know me, the women most especially. "You must be Evelyn's grandbaby," one of them proclaimed, her eyes taking in the full expanse of my skin. "You've got her shine."

Shine. I wouldn't have characterized Gram as having any shine. Then again, I hadn't known she had so many acquaintances, many of which had obvious shine.

After the funeral, the crowd congregated at Gram's house to consummate her home-going with food and drink and loud storytelling. I thought the floor might cave in from the weight of all those people, the corners of the room studded with pairs of sparkling eyes, each singing Gram's praises. Huge belly laughs echoed off the ceiling as one person after another recounted tales of unparalleled generosity, Gram's wit and humour and grace reflected in every smile.

It's funny how Gram dying managed to fill her house with life and the living in a way her being here with us wouldn't have permitted. The walls were still buzzing with the energy from their laughter long after the last person had departed, the light from their eyes still shining beyond lowered window shades—extra stars sent into the night to mark the day of my grandmother's passing.

I stayed alone in Gram's house for the first time that night, her snoring not there in the next room to dissuade my tears. I wondered what my being here had meant. Had I been help or hindrance, blessing or burden? Gram's mood altered so little it was hard to gauge how she felt about anyone or anything. I'd like to think she found comfort in my being here, took pride in knowing she could offer me refuge. That I needed refuge from her own flesh and blood is the only disappointment she seemed to register. It was my greatest disappointment, too.

Closest of Kin —

The next day, I was up to my elbows in a mountain of dirty dishes left piled along the kitchen counter when I heard a knocking at the door. I went out to the front room to find Miss Spinnaker standing on the porch holding a casserole of some sort. She seemed unsure what to say but felt she needed to say something.

"I've been meanin' to come by, see how you-all were doin'." Her eyes ran in the direction of her shoes, both of us recognizing I was the only bit of you-all left in Gram's tiny house.

Suddenly, the casserole she was holding reminded her of why she'd come. "I brung you something." She held up the dish in case I needed further evidence of its existence. "You'll be needin' something to eat."

All the home training I hadn't had kicked in. "Come in an' set a while," I offered. "Let me fix you a plate." I put her casserole in the fridge then set out some leftovers from the night before and poured a couple glasses of lemonade. We sat at Gram's kitchen table and nibbled and talked. Lord, did she talk. I've come to recognise how in the wake of death old people feel compelled to share their life story, in case they are next to go. To draw some dotted line to anchor them forever to this earth, at least for the remainder of your existence. Further still if you find their story compelling enough to carry forward, to pass along as part of your story.

I'd have thought this kind of talk was reserved for kinfolk. But with no kinfolk close at hand, I suppose most anyone will do. That day me and Miss Spinnaker became kinfolk, even if pseudo-so.

She was widowed though her husband had been stepping out on her long before he died. So, I guess she was sort of divorced, too. All that's certain is that she had been alone nearly as long as Gram, the two of them leading separate lives set on parallel paths of un-mitigated despair. She never mentioned children. I assumed she didn't have any. Perhaps that's why she worried so over my baby—keeper of all yet mother to none. That kind of energy has to eventually find some-place to go.

She was a seamstress back in her day. That explained the fancy curtains she had hung in her front window. Said she primarily took in work from across town. "Used to be there were mainly white folks over that way. Got a few uppity coloured folks livin' there nowa-days, mingling in their shops, learning alongside them in the same classroom together. Didn't think I'd live to see the day." Gram preferred simpler times, like us and other, whenever she felt a distinction was warranted. I could see why she and Miss Spinnaker hadn't been closer.

She faded in and out as the conversation wore on, a

lifetime of ancient struggles swimming behind tired eyes. I offered a thin-lipped smile in hopes of warming her up again. "How long have you lived here?"

"My whole life I suppose. Left for a little while when I was a girl. Couldn't have been much older than you are now." She scratched a place beneath her breast like she was alone in her own kitchen, not the least embarrassed to attend to such a private matter.

"Came back after not too long. Been here ever since, right in that same house." Then she went quiet on me. After talking my ear off the whole afternoon, my spirited little gossip went stone silent.

A heavy chill filled the air. Something I hadn't felt my entire stay in Picayune, that sick in the pit of your stomach feeling. The sound of my mother's voice passed over my head. "Look who has come a knockin'? Come to pay your respects after all this time. For what?"

Miss Spinnaker began muttering to herself, a frantic look taking hold of her expression. "I knew I should have stayed clear of this place. Ain't had no business coming over here, no how."

"Calm yourself, old woman. I'm not here to start any mess with you. Just came to say I'm leaving, headin' back to New York. Got no ties left to this place." She glanced at me, the look on her face almost apologetic—*almost*. Then she was back at Miss Spinnaker.

"I wouldn't exactly call this ending happy, but I'm glad it's over. Whatever we were to you doesn't apply any longer. What you should have been to me, I can't even say I missed." She gritted her teeth like she could grind Miss Spinnaker to dust had she come any closer.

"Take anything you want from the house. Can't say I need anything to remind me of this place. Anything else you find you need, don't call me for it. You know as well as I do how to get along on your own." She glanced around the room, breathed one last sigh inside Gram's house, liberated several lifetimes of regret, her lips held tight on the exhale like she might whistle had she only blown hard enough.

"Y'all play nice, now." Then she was gone. Into a taxicab she'd left waiting by the curb to carry her back to the railway station.

Miss Spinnaker stayed another minute to make sure the coast was clear, then scurried back across the street to retake her post behind green striped curtains. I sat bobbing in the wake of their exchange, treading water to make sense of their altercation. I cleared the dishes in silence, lifted shattered bits of conversation from the knotty pine table. I saw Miss Spinnaker's cracked face, Momma hurling insults at it as I rinsed our plates in the sink. I examined those bits inside my head, trying to figure why Momma had been so gruff. That was just her way I suppose—at odds with the world and everything in it. At least she was gone now.

Light Matters —

I gave Miss Spinnaker time to compose herself then went over to apologize. Not all us Combs women are mean spirited. She seemed embarrassed by the gesture, acted like nothing out of sort had occurred. "Come on in here, baby. I was just about to fix myself some tea."

She led me through the front room into the kitchen. The walls of both rooms were papered in a bright floral print meant to pick up on the peach and green she had in her window curtains. I only knew Miss Spinnaker's house from outside those curtains. The layout was identical to Gram's only reversed, like you were looking in a mirror.

She set right back to conversation once a bit of tea had settled in her. "Don't fret none over me and your momma. The cat in her has been at my dogs since the dawn of time. Your grandmother's passing isn't going to change that one iota. That's just how we get along."

"She's the same way with me," I replied, feeling we had struck a chord.

"Ain't nothing like the same thing. Her beef with me goes back way before you were even born. I don't blame her. She's got a right to expect certain things from me. But I'll tell you about that and more, in due time."

I'd been put off in a variety of ways, but none more aggravating than something promised in *due time*. It means I'll tell you when I feel like telling you, if ever I do. But you can't push old people to do things they haven't already made up their minds to do.

I searched the front room for the truth behind her lies. Everything matched like the walls had bred the couch then the couch gave birth to the armchair, each having had a hand in raising the curtains. And hospital ward clean—a speck of dust would find a lonely exist-ence inside Miss Spinnaker's antiseptic rooms. Yet it was far from inviting. The house seemed too still for anyone to have ever lived there. It was like Miss Spinnaker set aside a path between her bedroom and the kitchen that she seldom ventured from, the events of her daily routine confined to a series of runners laid down on the hardwood floor. The house stayed dark day and night like she was mourning the loss of some living thing, someone who would have brought light to her life had he or she been admitted inside Miss Spinnaker's household.

Maybe that's what I was to Gram—a source of light, a small flicker to remind her of the vast possibility of things. As self-sufficient as Gram appeared to be, I suspected she too had needs. Needs that went unful-filled before I arrived. She may have been missing me as much as I was missing her, our two souls yanked apart before we got the chance to fully connect. I hope to recognise her when I finally get to heaven.

I stayed at Miss Spinnaker's until well after the

sun had passed over Gram's house on its way to light the back side of the world. That night I added Miss Spinnaker to the long list of souls I said prayers over. I pitied my mother. Anger consumed her, a dense fog depriving her vision, the joyous reaches of her soul cordoned off like one of the finely furnished rooms inside Miss Spinnaker's dimly lit quarters.

I slept in uneasy fits that night. Left Gram's bedroom door open wide to escape the haunt of finding her the next morning lying in full repose beneath a stiffened bed sheet. Daybreak found me wide awake. I lay silent in bed, as guarded as the moon unwilling to yield its post until the sun is fully installed to take charge of the sky again.

I observed with patient eyes as the waning hours of darkness transformed the walls around me, watched the first glimpses of daybreak chase objects from the shadows. I sought comfort in the subtle movement of another shape in the room as layers of detail crept up from the floorboards. Took each shift in light as a sign that Gram was still knocking about, painting the walls with creeping shadows to assure me I'd never be alone.

Past Lies

I could tell from the sad shape of the windows across the street, the sag in the porch, gravel missing from the driveway, spots of grass showing through, that her baby had died. No right life's going to grow inside a house that's known no mother, Evelyn dropped there like the morning press bearing news of things I'd never grow to be.

I've watched three generations of my flesh and blood come and go in that house, years of lives, each broken in some way. Nearly saw me a fourth, my own livelihood stretched out a bit further with each birth. I touch my hand each day to the inside glass of my front window to heal whatever's going wrong out there only to realize the break starts where I sit. The original sin lies with me, a lie long past though not forgotten.

I fear at times I will rise to heaven to find that God hadn't minded my sins, recognises how poorly they reflect my true intent. What He had minded is that I failed to own up to the things I've done, spent an entire lifetime across from my only child never acknowledging her connection to me. I suspect she knew. She acted at times like she did though she never held over my head that she knew. Never let past her lips how I had denied her.

Alton Combs was good in that way. Accepted the role he'd played in our sin and settled into raising a daughter alone, his daughter, lost to me forever. Took the greatest responsibility when he was least to blame. He lay down with me to squelch my desires, to put an end to my relentless pursuit. Not that I could have resisted that man had he wanted me, but he never did. Asked if I'd gotten what I came for when it was over, his eyes vacant like he'd lost something in the exchange, an exchange we'd never have occasion to repeat.

Mother and Daddy sent me to live with my auntie in Jackson upon learning I was pregnant. They never once asked about the boy knowing full well it was the grown man across the street I had been drawn to. They will have with ease picked up on the spark smouldering between us from the way I lingered, waiting to catch him looking for me in the front yard. He had only been a handful of years ahead of me in school. But, having been left alone in his daddy's house for so long, he seemed older. I rushed in on the slightest provocation, the smallest sign that his feelings for me equalled the feelings I had for him. Spooked any chance the two of us might have had at forging a meaningful bond. Created a baby in the process. My parents couldn't have been more shamed. But Alton wouldn't allow the shadow of disrespect fall on the roof of my father's house. He met me at the railway station on my return to Picayune, that little bundle of stink wriggling next to me on the bench seat. He asked whether I would be able to manage then moved my baby across the street, raising her like she never had a momma. And I said nary a word.

That's what God's gonna strike me down for: letting the threat of how things might appear to the rest of the world dictate how I lived my life. Traded my momma and daddy's shame for whatever joy I might live to see. Spared the Spinnaker name one final smudge but lost my baby in the process. Ain't had a restful moment since.

I don't know how many turns I have left 'round this earth. I take each breath like it's my last, my life not nearly as precious as the one I gave away. Take what I can from the scenes I have chance to witness, content to play guardian from arm's length, protecting best I can all that I relinquished the right to claim as my own that fateful day at the railway station.

I stand each day on the edge of my determination to confess all I know, rid myself of sin. Yet I never do. I stay inside my daddy's house and pray to silent walls that God will have mercy on my piteous soul. That my only child died ahead of me underlines the fate that awaits my ascent to heaven. I see my daughter's finger shaking in denial, banishing me to hell. But I would gladly die just to see her again, tell her she's mine, even if she knows already.

Everyday Procession

Weeks after Gram's funeral, and the town was still in mourning. Not in empathy for my sorrow. The town's sentiment for our collective loss seemed heartfelt, down to the person. Folks didn't take on the face of remorse solely for my benefit. Feelings of regret filled a room long before I crossed the threshold.

Wherever I went, the reception was always the same. "How are you getting along, Miss Penny? Keepin' your chin up?" Then they moved on to tell how they were coping even before I had a chance to ask. I doubt Gram set out to accomplish it in this way, but her passing succeeded in connecting me irreversibly to the towns-folk of Picayune.

The woman who owns the hair salon approached me after paying her respects at Gram's home-going. She invited me to the shop for a wash and set. Said she could do something special with my hair. I explained that I didn't have money for anything extra. She told me to put concerns over money out of my head. Mr. Graves took the same stance when I asked about terms to repay him for the funeral ceremony. "Everything is taken care of," he told me. Has yet to ask for a red cent.

Another couple weeks of the whole town mourning together, and everything returned to its normal routine with one grand exception: I now had a part in it. I was no longer the centre of attention like I was immediately following Gram's departure, what with everybody's sorrows tucked away again, back inside private memories of Gram (or wherever sad emotions go once they've outlived their usefulness), but I now had a part to play.

Acting purely on instinct, I took up Gram's routine in the everyday procession that had been her life before my arrival in Picayune. I ventured into town most days, greeted people as they passed. Greeted them in the way Gram would have greeted them—cordial, sincere, but not overly engaging to invite too much conversation.

I made the stops Gram would have made: groceries on Tuesday mornings, never carrying the parcels home with me but indicating to the grocer the items I wished to have delivered later that afternoon; the post office on Friday if not Saturday mornings, depending on my time; and the hair salon on alternate weekends. And everything was taken care of. I couldn't spend a dime in this town despite my best efforts. My excursions were never outlandish, but I didn't want for a single thing. The end of the month had in fact come and gone before I thought to wonder about the rent, whether someone expected to receive payment. I'd been all through Gram's things but had yet to locate any of her business affairs. She didn't have any money stashed away.

Momma would have been back here to claim it had that been the case. But Gram always seemed to make ends meet.

I once asked Gram what she did to earn a living. She said she used to raise corn but, at the time I'd asked, claimed to be semi-retired. This I found suspect for a whole gang of reasons not least of which is that neither crop nor field stood in easy reach of Gram's front step. Plus, nothing moved in Picayune unless somebody moved it. Those same plants Gram claims raised themselves while she sat in semi-retirement would have stood stock-still awaiting her return. I pictured Gram standing over a freshly tilled expanse of earth instructing those plants on how to grow:

The sweat of a hundred struggling mules has fallen on this piece of dirt solely for your benefit. So, stand tall. Spread your broad leaves to catch every last drop of rain and bow your head to protect your fruit from the sun. Come harvest time, pluck those elongated ears from their stalks, rid them of husk and hair. I'll meet you at the cookin' pot. Got the water boiling just how you like it, fast and warm from the sun. Remind you of the ground you came up in.

I found myself raisin' korn the better part of a year before realizing that's what I'd been doing, before recognizing that to be the fate to which I'd been born.

Specters

My stillborn baby continued to visit me in my dreams, only those days I dreamt that Gram died the same night. Left with my baby inside an ambulance and never came back. Sometimes I dreamt that I'd never seen either of them in living flesh, Gram's life as much a fantasy to me as the one my baby might have known.

The dream usually ended at Gram's funeral. I couldn't see the body, couldn't bring myself to look inside the casket. I closed my eyes and focused all my energy on reversing the effects of the sun, on holding off the moon, to erase the day I lost her: my older, wiser, more determined self. Enough energy in the right direction and I'm no longer here. She's not me. Neither of us was lying, dirt and wood and soft velvet forever more separating us from life among the living.

Teacup Kisses

Miss Spinnaker said death resides inside each of us, lays dormant, suppressed by an abundance of living flesh. Life, death's vacuum fresh container, sealed tight by an overwhelming desire to remain among the living. It's only when the balance slides in the opposite direction that death begins to surface, emerges from its container in startling spurts.

Likely conversation from a woman whose own existence was living proof of the subtle distinction between dying and getting older—walking backward into the moon until the sun could no longer claim us, time on earth a penance we each must pay in exchange for eternal life after death.

I tapped her apparent expertise on coping with a lonesome existence. "Why is it that everybody leaves me?"

"It would be too simple of me to say life is fleeting. But life is just that, a train moving against all our will at times. Best if yours is a slow train, running along a smooth track. A train so slow you'll have chance to stroll alongside its easy locomotion, set up however you like, climb aboard a while then step down and let the train pass by if you decide that's best.

"But, take heed," she warned. "No two trains ever pass the same way twice. Even a train you know will be different if ever it comes your way again. You'll be different too. So pay special attention if ever you spot a slow train comin'."

I sensed Gram's voice inside the room with us, felt her gentle hand at my back. For the first time began to see in Miss Spinnaker compassion over curiosity, genuine concern over meddling interest. I channelled my questions through her to Gram, my ears longing again for the sound of my grandmother's reassuring tone. "How will I recognise which train is mine?"

"A slow train will make itself plain. Trust in that." I thought she might put me off again, watched as her teacup clanked against unsuspecting teeth, her lips taking a protective stance. She studied the rim of her cup, dabbed her tongue at a runaway drop of tea before setting the cup down again.

All I needed was *Girlie* at the end of her sermon to take me home again. I saw Gram's eyes in her head, felt Gram's spirit floating above me, her level-headed way of thinking guiding the movements of Miss Spinnaker's customarily spiteful tongue.

"And where's that train going to lead me?"

"Only time will tell. It might lead you back here, settled and staid, an old woman whiling away the years in the quiet confines of Picayune, Mississippi."

I thought about the prospect of staying. Weighed the possibility until another question popped inside my head. "How'd my grandmother wind up here?"

She seemed to mistrust the question. Trembling lips set off in search of the rim of her teacup, refusing to speak. "What I mean to ask is why she never left Picayune?"

"Where else is she gonna go? Most everyone she knew lives right here, all of 'em raised up from this here dirt."

"Everybody seemed to know her too."

"She inherited that from her daddy—surrogate Black mayor of Picayune. How he had a way with people." My eyes flashed for her to tell more. Fortunately, she obliged without her usual display of undue hesitation.

"Alton Combs was what's known as a bit of a sleeper. Wouldn't have stood out in a crowd of one. That was before his daddy died. Having no brothers or sisters to lean on, he assumed responsibility for their household and just as quickly grew into a man, the likes of which Picayune had never seen.

"The natural thing would have been to take his father's place, his feet planted in mud, and allow the sun and years and time to dissolve him into this earth, the same way they had done his daddy. But that's not what fate had in store for your great grandpa." Only sips of tea interrupted her conversation, each touch of the cup to her lips seeming a small eternity meant to detain me further from my family's history.

"It's a story anyone in Picayune is perfectly capable of telling. Alton's father didn't leave much, but life hadn't been entirely unkind to the Combs family. It was not unheard of for a landowner to extend certain kindnesses to one of his longtime field hands. Give him a little parcel of dirt to tend in reward for years of loyal service. The farmer's way of helping a man like the senior Mr. Combs, getting up in years, ease into retirement without his family starving to death. That plot of land also provided invaluable training ground for a new generation of field hands, a hidden motive for the farmer who would eventually benefit from their services too, the farmer's generosity fostering an inbred loyalty that couldn't help but regenerate itself a hundred times over.

"Trouble is, the soil was usually spent by the time the farmer came around to doling any of it out, even to his most trusted workers," Miss Spinnaker said, adding to the trail of breadcrumbs Gram had only just begun to lay out for me. "Those infertile bits of land amounted to little more than a hollow show of goodwill, providing little means for the worker to yield a crop beyond that needed to feed his own household." She freshened her tea with a bit of water resting just this side of boiling, then set right back to conversation.

"Your great granddad had different ideas about what to do with his inheritance. Why drop seed on a piece of ground that's already given as much crop as it has to give? He put a house on that piece of land instead. Rented the house out to itinerant workers who dust these parts at different times of year, depending on the growing season.

"Before long, he had two houses to rent, then three. Built this whole block one house at a time, renting at first then selling to GIs coming back from overseas. Only his kind heart got in the way of any real prosperity, never charging anyone more than that person could afford to pay. Rumours abound of folks leaving as deposit a pick axe or favourite hunting knife, anything they felt able to do without until arrangements could be made to finance their home purchase. He 'bout gave away as many houses as he sold what with so many widows left after the war. He turned a false show of good will into one with genuine intent."

"What about my momma's father, my granddaddy?"

"Oh, that one was a rolling stone. Come through Picayune one autumn. Rented a room from your great-grandpa. Boone was his name—more ghost than apparition. Had your grandma doing things she ought not be doing. Then couldn't catch hide nor hair of him once the gruntin' was over, your mother's seed planted inside your grandmomma's belly."

"He was a scoundrel then?"

"He was slick all right, but far from scoundrel. He could hardly help his ways, the women in Picayune drawn to him like flies to milk. Your gram simply had the upper hand livin' under a nearby roof.

"Not that your grandma needed proximity to gain advantage. She possessed gobs of charisma that she lifted from deep wells whenever the need compelled her. She could move people who didn't know they were about to be moved. Left them grateful for the change she'd brought about in their lives."

I felt a loftiness swell with the braggartly way she held her head cocked to one side whenever she spoke about Gram's movements around town, an excess of familiarity in the way she referred to Gram's father by his full name. I dismissed it as simple local pride, Gram being the sole offspring to a hometown legend.

"Your daddy was more of the same, had the look of pure sin. When he smiled, the sin only got deeper."

"How'd all that charisma miss my momma?"

"Your momma's a special case. A whole lot of good has escaped her grasp, but not for lack of trying. She latched onto your daddy figuring he had charisma enough for the both of them. Like a homely woman might choose a pretty man, hoping to balance her deficiencies. Plucked him right outta the dirt and took him with her to New York—that girl forever in a rush to go no place. And your father believing the world will bend his way by simply wishing it so, your mother filling him with the belief that nothing but good fortune lay ahead for them so she could hightail it out of here.

Could disappear among a sea of nameless faces and lose any ties to her past in the process."

Gram had long ago shared the story of how my daddy met my momma sharecropping his way across Mississippi. He rented a room at the far end of Ruby St., just beyond where it meets Stevens. He, like me, was a stranger to town, a wide-eyed curiosity intent on little more than getting himself out of Picayune, working his way north, hungry for a taste of life in the city.

The whole rest of the world was Chicago bound when they left Mississippi, following the river north. My Daddy had set his sights on New York, had had enough turning the land with his hands for somebody else to profit. Dreamed of taking part in the latest, come again resurgence sweeping through Harlem. He complained the clay underneath his fingernails was affecting his piano playing. Gram claimed having no piano to play was to blame for his decline in musical proficiency, not dirty fingernails.

I'd only ever heard my daddy play once in public. As far as I know, he's only performed the one time before a live audience. This slick lookin' fella came by the apartment complaining that their regular piano player was laid up with the flu, asked my daddy to stand in— Lyle Hill, always the replacement player. Momma was working then, cleaning office buildings late into the night. He had no choice but to take Edelyn and me with him, jackets over our robes, footie pyjamas stuffed inside our rain boots.

We watched the entire show from a little stairwell just off stage, Daddy labouring over every note, nothing from his corner of the bandstand sounding like he meant for it to sound. It's like the nightclub's piano was in fine working order, only the touch of my daddy's fingers on the keys was sadly out of tune. It got to sounding pretty good by the end of the second set. But that's the last time daddy would be invited to stand in with his buddy's band.

Miss Spinnaker eventually turned to questioning me. "Plannin' to carry yourself back home now that your grandmomma has passed?"

I heard the words escape my lips like someone else had spoken them: "Sometimes, home is the place you find yourself when no place else feels familiar."

Suddenly it occurred how much I wanted to stay, needed to stay. I had come to appreciate Picayune for more than its abbreviated winters, summers punctuated by fresh squeezed lemonade, sweet tea sweating in the palm of your hand. The easy way even the harshest words flew off the tongue in my direction, the sway of the wind that seemed to have a mind all its own.

Gram had started something with me that I needed to see through even though she'd never witness the finished product. It's like I was conceived the night my baby died, was born into a place where my grandmother had ceased to exist. That day I was an infant, left alone in a world that barely knew I existed.

"Maybe I'll teach school," I beamed, "like Gram." I was quite satisfied with my choice, not that I liked the idea of returning to the classroom. I instead liked the notion of fulfilling Gram's lost ambition.

"Your grandmother never taught in anybody's schoolhouse." Her face showed visible signs of fatigue, regret at needing to again explain who my grandmother had been, especially to somebody who she must have believed had squandered the opportunity to learn Gram's story firsthand.

"I mean, she wanted to be a school teacher," I stammered, shaken by her shift in attitude.

"Wanted lots of things. But nobody's gonna hire someone to educate their kids whose own life is so mixed up. Doesn't know her own momma, her daddy rentin' rooms and other things to any dirt picker to breeze through town—from moonshine to mud boots to midnight bed swappin'." Just as quickly, her tirade trailed off, her eyes running to the far corner of the room. She apologized beneath her breath for the outburst then began clearing the table in silence.

That's how most conversations ended with Miss Spinnaker. I'd touch some nerve or raise some wrong, the origins of which I had no clue. Then she'd either clam up or lash out at me, signalling it was time to leave. And leave I did, out of her backwards, left goes right, right goes left house. Back to the safe haven of Gram's empty rooms where nothing Miss Spinnaker had to say could rob me of the memories I had left of my grandmother.

night-right goes left house. Back to the safe haven of
Gram's empty rooms where nothing Miss Spinnaker
had to say could... the memories I had left of
my grandmother.

Carryin' On

With the tendency between me and Miss Spinnaker
trending toward the occasional falling-out, I turned
to the hair salon as my only social outlet. It became
a central part of my weekend ritual. I'd even begun
showing up on off Saturdays to keep a handle on the
conversation.

I was guaranteed to find nearly the same crowd
assembled regardless of what time I arrived, the shop
always alive with idle chatter. Even when the crowd
was too thin or too disconnected to hold a conversation
on its own, a handful of staff regulars were there to pick
up the slack. Miss Thula had two of her nieces working
in the shop part time, primarily on weekends, sham-
pooing so the stylists could spend more time behind the
chair, neither cousin having reached the point of doing
hair herself. One of them could be trusted to lead the
charge whenever any amount of pointless drivel was
needed.

Cecile was the younger of the two. If conversation were like driving, where you mash the gas to
talk then brake to listen, Cecile would be steady on
the gas cruising past me at a hundred miles an hour.

Meanwhile, I was creeping, crawling, barely able to squeeze a word in edgewise. Every so often, she'd pause to ask, "Huh, you said something?" Even if I had said something, I invariably shook my head, *No, I didn't say a thing,* letting her back into the fast lane of her one-sided conversation.

Sharaine was harder to figure. Being the slicker of the two, she didn't talk nearly as much. Eyed me like there was something she might want to say but couldn't put her finger on a line of conversation worth having with me. To hear her talk, you'd think she was from here. But, from the way she eyed me, a subtle distrust in any gesture thrown my way, it wouldn't have surprised me a bit to learn she'd spent a good amount of time in New York or Chicago. Chicago for certain. We might have found some common ground to connect on otherwise. She acted decent enough, but my New York instincts told me not to take any chances where that one was concerned.

Miss Bynum was the elder-stateswoman on staff. She only worked odd Saturdays, honouring the few long-standing appointments she still held. Even then, she never stayed the full day. There was inevitably someone whose path she'd rather not cross scheduled to come in at some point during the day to send her on her way.

Her conversation was usually confined to a series of hushed whispers with whomever she had in the chair.

She was a few quick hellos on her way in, then she was a hurried wave over her back on her way out. I don't think she much cared for me. Then again, I don't suspect she'd have noticed whether or not I was in the room.

Lamar, I especially liked. There was something familiar about the way he smiled at me, a soothing timbre to his voice. Though I don't believe necessarily in reincarnation, especially one that was premature, I do believe a person's spirit could outgrow the space afforded his body alone. When I looked at Lamar, I saw my daddy in part, his quiet wisdom leaking beyond the walls of his physical being, sent to keep his baby girl company all the way down in Mississippi. Like my daddy, Lamar knew how to listen. Listened like he cared about the problems I brought to him, unlike the salon gossips who instead listened to serve their own meddling interests.

Everyone suspected Lamar was gay. I fully believed the women in the shop needed for Lamar to be gay to keep any interest they had in him at bay (or to justify in their minds why he showed so little interest in any of them). I'd like to think it was a simple matter of being content with his life away from the shop, his mind set on keeping whatever business he had once he exited the shop door to himself, precisely as it should be. Still, the rumours persisted.

Possessing nothing worth gossiping about or being

jealous over, I invariably faded into the woodwork whenever I entered the hair salon. I took my usual position in the far corner of the room, crammed in next to Lamar's station, and waited patiently for something worth having shown up for to commence. Not being especially quick of tongue, my movements were confined to the back of the shop mostly for my own protection. I might have gotten trampled otherwise, standing too close to the main line of conversation.

It seemed no one in the shop was happy unless there was a scandal brewing, some negative outcome to celebrate. It would take a lifetime of calculation to sum the wage misfortune had exacted from folks who frequented the hair salon. It was only when you considered the gross similarities in their troubles that you shaved any time off the task. Even folks who'd suffered the same plight seemed to take pleasure in each other's misfortune, like they were unable to see the connection to one another's pain. Having little regard for each other, you could only imagine the feeding frenzy that ensued anytime a stranger entered the salon.

They once devoted an entire afternoon picking apart a newcomer to the shop—a woman of humble means from her dress, venturing into town to fix herself up for some special occasion. I reckon a loved one returning from war, needing to come in from the storm, hostilities continuing to rage half-a-world away. Maybe a lover whose eye she had yet to catch, somebody whose attention she was still working to secure. Either way, her demeanour showed telltale signs of budding romance carrying her higher than she might ordinarily choose to carry herself.

I thought she looked adorable once Lamar had finished curling her hair. The sparkle in her eyes, the smile she hid with both hands on first sight of herself in the mirror, said that she thought her hair looked adorable, too.

Cecile barely let the door swing shut before cutting loose on her. "Girrrl, did you see those turn't over shoes? Looks like she walked here all the way from Alabama."

"Yeah, by way of Detroit. Thula, you should have cut the girl a break. She ain't have but that much hair." Sharaine poked out her hip, snapping her fingers over her head to signify how long it would take to fix the woman's hair.

"Oh, you must not have seen her legs. That girl's part primate, you ask me." Lamar mouthed to me from behind his chair, *'Aren't we all primates?'* shrugging off their apparent ignorance. Never one to hold her tongue, Cecile continued, this little bit of truth lost on nearly everyone in earshot: "I bet she can climb the mess outta tree."

Ill regard hung in the shop like stale air on a steamy afternoon. Each day brought more of the same. *'Who gave her the nerve to wear that dress, paint her nails that colour, pluck her eyebrows bare comin' in here lookin' surprised all the time?'* Never once did talk in the shop aim to reach the middle of a person, examine a person's pain, her fears, her most outlandish hopes and dreams. Only Lamar seemed to care about maintaining a level of decorum. Never let the ignorance stoop but so low before stepping in, especially on behalf of one of the shop patrons. Even if Miss Thula didn't care about such things, Lamar most certainly did.

"That girl has never done anything to any of y'all," he said, drawing the focus of attention to his station— my daddy in spirit, standing in defence of the innocent.

Cecile was quick to respond. "Hurt my eyes is what she done."

"You're not doing anybody's eyes any favours," Sharaine replied, the cousins appearing to turn on one another. "When last did you pluck those eyebrows? Look like two tarantulas about to do battle across your forehead."

Daddy dismissed this pattern of deprecation as characteristic infighting among crabs in a barrel. Except these are the kind of crabs that don't give another crab a chance to reach for the top before pulling on 'em, curbing the tendency among crabs to reach in the first place. Sharaine and Cecile were forever on the lookout for a tattered dress or turn't over shoe to keep everybody at the bottom of the barrel, mashed on top of one another. I can only imagine what they had to say about me when I wasn't around. But, without their constant back biting and chatter about anyone unfortunate enough to be absent on any given day, I would have had no outside entertainment.

MmmHmm —

There were times when conversation in the shop ran as tame as the married women's crochet circle, moving from one member's front room to another in regularly scheduled rotation. Missus Graves entered the salon one Saturday looking for somebody to set her hair. I recognised her immediately as the undertaker's wife, the pecking order around town easy to discern: the mayor, the police chief, the fire marshal, the bank president followed by a prominent minister or two. Then the undertaker. On this side of town, the undertaker stood second only to the ministers—folks lookin' to catch that last bit of religion before they were called Home.

Missus Graves' hair looked perfectly fine to me, the obvious intent behind her visit to test the air inside the hair salon. A couple Saturdays later, she arrived with a few assistant air samplers in tow, their hair needing as little attention as hers had just a few weekends prior. She plopped down in Miss Thula's empty chair, her entourage standing close guard, pretending to wait for an available stylist. It took some time for their conversation to unfold, Thula resisting the bait with all her might.

"You do a fair business over this way."

"I do all right," Miss Thula replied, never lifting an eye from her curling iron.

Missus Graves continued, barely registering Thula's response. "I usually take my business across town to Rosie's, but might start comin' over this way instead." Rosie's was the first salon in Picayune to cater to an integrated clientele—by that I mean the few uppity folks Miss Spinnaker recalls to have only recently started living over that way. "Can bring a lot of business your way if the mood were to strike."

"I don't have any open appointments," Miss Thula replied. "But, we're happy to take walk-ins if you don't mind a few minutes' wait."

"MmmHmm."

There was something funny about her *MmmHmm*, a quiet tension in her exchange with Miss Thula, lost on no one inside the shop, save me. The women dragging by her side eventually came into clearer view. One I recognised as the grocer's wife. The other, Missus McCullough, was married to the man who owned the used car dealership in town. Whenever I saw her, her eyelids were plastered with a heavy covering of mint-green eyeshadow, leaving her brow in a permanent up-raised pose, like the world was too much, everything she saw catching her by surprise. Mr. McCullough had been in the hair salon the other day talking fast and low next to Miss Thula's station, the two of them looking like a couple bank robbers trying to get their stories straight before someone from the sheriff's department made it over to interrogate either of them. Mr.

McCullough's wife looked extra smug as the women prepared to make their exit.

Missus Graves issued a parting warning before leaving the shop. "There's a wind of change sweeping through Picayune. Mark my word on that." She waited for Miss Thula to return her stare. Not a bite. It's like whatever crime Miss Thula was party to obliged her to accept these women descending on her shop as part and parcel to her punishment, a sentence issued without judge or jury present.

The Saturday radio slow jam session was the only thing alive in the shop after the sister circle had vacated the premises. Phyllis Hyman was belting out her heartfelt rendition of *Betcha by Golly, Wow* from beyond the grave. Cecile and Sharaine were wailing alongside their departed songstress, showing little regard for Miss Thula's condition. At the very least, raining sunshine on her pity party when a little compassion for her predicament might have been more appreciated.

"I sure do wish you-all would go on and let her sing it. Sounds like somebody's standin' on your feet, mashin' all your toes." The cousins apologized to their aunt after turning down the volume on the radio, saying they didn't mean her any disrespect.

Miss Thula hurried through her last appointment then headed out early, leaving any walk-ins to one of the other stylists, something she was not in the habit of doing. After all, it was her name hanging outside the shop door. The room fell silent in her wake, everyone stunned by her uncharacteristic retreat.

The shop didn't stay silent for long. One cousin began to blame their aunt's early departure on the other's singing, likened it to the sound of a stuck mule. The other, in turn, accused the first cousin of sounding like a pig drowning in slop, whatever sound that makes. In time their bickering spilled over to the rest of the crowd, returning a sense of normalcy to the shop despite their spiritual leader having been chased from her post, the barrel of crabs left to carry on in her absence.

Draggin' Speak —

Ordinarily, I didn't find sufficient reason to call home. Eventually convinced myself that anything worth saying could just as easily go unsaid. I'd seen the seasons change in Picayune enough times to resist calling on the first warm day to hear they were still buried in snow. I didn't have any news to report—good or bad. It wasn't anyone's birthday back home. And I'd learned not to care any longer that they more often than not misplaced the anniversary of my birth. That day I called to reminisce momentarily in thoughts of home, my connection to which had grown increasingly faint.

Champayne was usually first to pick up the receiver, having reached the point like every child does where she believes all eyes are on her, the likelihood that somebody might be calling for anyone else in the apartment seeming highly remote. You could hear the enthusiasm drain from her voice once she realized it was me calling rather than one of her neighbourhood friends. Edelyn was tougher to read. Her voice never rose too high. She never seemed especially disappointed to hear my voice on the other end of the line, never seemed too disinterested in what I had to say.

That day I called simply to feel like something would have a familiar ending. Momma usually pretended she didn't have time to talk then relayed a hundred needless questions through one or the other of my sisters. This time she picked up the extension on the first mention of my name.

She asked straight away about the hair salon after shooing my sisters from the line. "How's Miss Thula managing?" How had word of the incident in the hair salon reached my mother so quickly? "You aren't giving her any trouble, are you?" she asked. "Forget what people around there tell you. Thula's good people. Don't let me hear about you giving her any mess."

That was my mother's way of showing concern for somebody she cared about—threatening to thump me if she caught wind of my having caused the person in question any grief. I knew she kept close contact with somebody around town. Even my own mother wasn't so callous as to leave her eldest daughter down here all this time without someone standing by to report back if I got into any more trouble. But I wouldn't have put her together with Miss Thula. I got the sense Thula and Gram had been friends. But she and momma were closer in age. Perhaps the two of them grew up together, Thula assuming the role of big sister, Momma's spirit gravitating toward hers to make up for any attention she found missing at home.

Whatever their connection, I felt duty bound to obey my mother's word. I hung up after assuring her I'd keep an eye out and report back if Miss Thula had another run-in with the sister circle.

When I entered the shop again, the conversation had resumed its familiar cadence. Even Miss Thula had regained her voice. I arrived in the middle of a light-hearted debate brewing between her and Lamar, no apparent mention of the sister circle in the air.

"Lula Mae's been wild her whole life. If you claim to know Lula then you've been pretty wild your own self." Miss Thula flung her opinion in the air, daring anyone to defy her authority on the subject.

Lamar had already adopted his characteristic stance, always prepared to defend anyone not present to stand up for him or herself. Hadn't been here in a long while from the sound of things.

"All I'm saying is she looks like decent enough folk to me." He seemed inclined to let go of the conversation, but recognised the necessity of this argument in Miss Thula regaining her footing around the hair salon. Letting go of his side of the argument would give the impression that he pitied her, a sentiment he clearly didn't wish to convey.

"You can't always judge a book by its cover. There's sometimes more to a person than meets the eye." Lamar took care to keep his tone in check, wanting to launch a strong enough defence to appear natural, but not so strong an attack as to let the discussion escalate beyond simple banter among friends, no battle lines drawn in the hair salon on that day.

Miss Thula kept hold. "I don't fault her for anywhere

she's been in life. Can't say I'm especially proud of every turn I've made. But there's no denying how far she's fallen no matter how sympathetic you want to be. Now that's all *I'm* saying."

Lula Mae was Mister and Missus Graves' only child, estranged from the family long before I showed up in town. That was the thing about Picayune—even when you were estranged from someone, the most you could afford to do was move across town from one another. Lula Mae made for a good bit of gossip once her drinking got out of control, less big once people got accustomed to the idea of the undertaker's daughter taking the place of the town drunk. Once the blush of having been labelled town drunk began to wear off, she became the town's ashtray, letting any and everybody snub out his tip in exchange for little more than a fresh bottle to snap open plus the promise of yet another night spent beyond reach of her mother's incessant glaring.

"She was nice lookin' back in the day," Thula proclaimed. "But she done dogged herself down to the point she doesn't look like anything anymore. Comin' around here, the smell of cheap wine spilling from her, the air of cigarette smoke lingering anyplace she's visited. Now she's supposed to be made over again. Next thing you're gonna tell me she's in the church. Wouldn't surprise me a bit to learn she's fallen in with that bunch 'a heathens."

I could see Missus Graves' face reflected in Thula's

remarks, her tendency to speak her mind working over-
time after having been made to hold her tongue the last
time the two crossed paths. "She and her momma can
kiss me in a place that's hard to find. Show up in my
shop draggin' on me, I'm gonna find something about
you to drag on twice as hard."

From that day forward, mention of Lula Mae grew
a thick lump in the middle of Lamar's throat. I left it
alone, figuring he'd eventually come around to telling
me what about Lula Mae made him go skittish.

Blue Cloud Cover

I brought the evening to a close the way Gram and I would have, resting on the back steps as the sun extinguished itself for the night. I sat pondering the apparent bond between Lamar and Lula Mae. He confided in me that the two of them had gotten close. He resisted my stare when I asked how close, though I knew already how close they had gotten without him having to spell it out.

I turned my attention toward the heavens. I never knew there was such a thing as blue clouds, able to blend in with the sky 'til you no longer recognised them as the clouds they were born to be. I never thought I'd live to see the sun skip a beat, jump ahead in time and disappear from view before ever reaching the horizon. Had I gone inside for even a second, I would have missed the whole affair. Would have sat wondering for the rest of eternity why the sun had set in such a hurry, who or what had rushed the sun along its march across the sky? How a thin line of clouds could turn itself inside out masquerading as not a cloud in the sky so blue?

I watched in dismay as the sun went flat on one side like a ruptured tire resting on its metal rim. Then the metal rim began to deflate leaving half a sun dangling shamelessly above the horizon despite having failed to complete its appointed rounds. The rim disappeared leaving behind a dazzling array of sunlight beaming from beyond the band of blue clouds, like an angel had cupped her hands over the sun, the clouds forming a shallow opening for the last remnants of setting sun to escape. It was only once the sun slid to its proper place beyond the horizon that I came to appreciate the illusion, could begin to accept the existence of a blue cloud cover capable of hurrying along the events surrounding the passing of the setting sun.

Would Be Twins

Gram oftentimes remarked how people were inclined to place all their trust in simple when simple was all they knew. Idle gossip, passed word of mouth around town, as simple as the wind rustling past, shall forever remain Picayune's most trusted vehicle of communication.

Booker—

The news caught up with me as I boarded the bus into town one morning. Even the bus driver took a hand in dispensing the gossip.

"You heard about Booker?" was the question put to me before I could assemble proper change to pay my fare. "He sure split his pants."

I had been down here long enough to recognise the bus driver meant that Booker had done something awful while the whole world looked on to see him do it. I stood staring at the top of the bus driver's smooth brown head, clueless about anyone named Booker much less what he might have done to shame himself.

The bus driver continued in his efforts to put an image of this man inside my head. "Tobias Booker, Thomas's baby brother. Folks used to go around calling him Bunk before he moved away to avoid confusing him with his brother who also sometimes goes by Booker." Still not a hint of comprehension. "You might have mistaken them for twins before Thomas, the older of the two, broke out with a case of vitiligo. You ain't heard the news?"

"Can't say as I know the man."

"Folks are saying Bunk shot his wife dead over in Natchez. Rolled up on Lorraine in front of the college where she works. Hit her with a single 20-gauge blast, barely letting up on the gas to steady his aim. Witnesses say the scattered buckshot left nary a scratch on the frame of his wife's lowered car window."

I detected a hint of boastfulness resting beneath the driver's otherwise sombre tone. The outside light lifted a twinkle of excitement inside his eye, one corner of his mouth resisting the first twist of a smile. "I tell you, a country boy and his shotgun are a force to be reckoned with."

I didn't know which way to feel. A man I hadn't known had done something I couldn't imagine someone having done, the news passed to me like the correct time or the day's weather forecast—should I expect sunshine or rain? I started in the direction of a seat adjacent to the driver's position, my legs quaking beneath me as I made my way along the aisle.

Each person to board the bus added a new bit of detail to the driver's account. It stood as common knowledge around town that Bunk had gotten wind of some untoward intermingling between his wife and Mr. Harrison, the men's basketball coach over at the high school. The turmoil surrounding their situation eventually prompted Bunk to move his wife to Natchez, about as far from Picayune as a body can carry himself and still reside in the state of Mississippi, looking to make a fresh start between them. His wife took a job in the administration building at Alcorn State. Meanwhile, Bunk found work delivering cleaning supplies to various institutions around town, the college cafeteria included.

Church folks were quick to remark how idle hands are the devil's workshop, the lax schedule of responsibility afforded anyone affiliated with the school system during summer break making way for some of the devil's most accomplished handiwork. It would appear over the course of the summer that Bunk's wife had begun slipping away again to meet up with Mr. Harrison in Brookhaven, Hammond, Monticello—any number of nondescript little towns lining the highway between Natchez and Picayune where their being seen together wouldn't draw undue suspicion.

The bus driver, still enthralled by Bunk's shooting prowess, put the finishing touches on the tale as the bus reached the centre of town. "The time his wife's sister drove up to surprise her in Natchez, while she was supposed to be down here visiting her family in Picayune, sent Bunk into a rage. He started dipping out of work early, showing up late in order to check on his wife's whereabouts. Pretty soon, riding along the highway in and out of town became Bunk's full-time occupation."

The driver eased off the accelerator as my stop approached, fit the final bit of detail overtop the waning engine note. "Word has it he was just let go the other day from his delivery job on account of the excess of unexcused absences. They say he headed straight for the sheriff's office, turned himself in ahead of the police knowing anything about a murder having taken place in their jurisdiction. The rest as they say is history, was bound to occur sooner if not later."

I stumbled off the bus dazed. Needed to take stock, to piece together with my own hand the commingling of events, the details of which the bus driver couldn't see fit to keep to himself. Picayune suddenly birthplace to a cold-blooded murderer, only one whose name was foreign to my ears until news of his crime had already shattered the tranquillity of meaningless discourse swirling around town, saddling me with the need to sort out the ups and downs of whatever had gone wrong between Bunk and his wife as best I could.

The Sound of Sweet Music —

I hurried through the few errands I had to run: returned a couple books at the library, picked up toilet tissue and hairpins from the drug store, some canned goods from the market. I headed straight for the bus stop, desperate to see what new detail of Bunk's crack up had been uncovered. Unfortunately, by the time I boarded the bus again, the story of Bunk shooting his wife was no longer news, at least none worthy of the bus driver poking his nose into the gossip.

He drove me the whole way back to Gram's block in near silence. Even the few passengers to board along the way offered little more than a passing greeting over the engine's drone as the driver manoeuvred the bus back onto the main thoroughfare, the wave of sensationalism surrounding the murder of Bunk's wife seemingly short-lived in people's minds. Though I did overhear Bunk's name spill from the driver's tongue again as I stepped down from the bus onto the curb, the driver apparently intent on dispensing only new news, to those who hadn't heard it yet.

I imagined Bunk's wife in the instant before she was shot, pictured her riding along, humming in rhythm to a tune on the car radio, her fingers drumming in time with the beat, a band of sunlight holding steady on the long arc of the steering wheel as she made her way through traffic. She must not have had a care in the world. Even the troubles in her marriage, the anxious moments stolen away with Mr. Harrison, the shadow of guilt dogging her every move were lost momentarily, might have been tucked away beneath the sound of sweet music inside her head.

She would find another time to fret over the lies she'd told, the string of excuses invented to conceal her indiscretions. Would set aside the time spent suffering before unyielding eyes, the sidelong glances from people who felt they had the right to judge her despite knowing things might have turned out the same for them had they found themselves standing inside her shoes, married to a man who had never learned to show his affection toward her, didn't possess the right assemblage of words capable of closing the distance growing ever larger between them.

Years of trying with isolated success had left Bunk at cross purposes where his wife was concerned: still wanting her despite recognizing the limits on his capacity to muster the attention she so desperately craved, weary with fatigue against seemingly impossible odds that life together with her might with the passage of time ease in the direction of happily ever after. That same man would never be persuaded to ever let her leave his side.

I saw Bunk riding along behind his wife's car, his shotgun resting beside him on the truck's bench seat, the action pumped, his finger never far from the trigger.

He took care to remain a few cars back, blending in with the flow of traffic so as not to draw his wife's attention, spook her and miss the chance at putting an end to their ordeal. The voice inside his head must have been choked down, knees bent in the dirt, wrestling against the pain inside his chest. He didn't want to lose her. But she had shown him with her actions, time over blessed time again, that she would never truly be his.

He had to put a stop to it, had to cut loud over the backdrop of sweet music pulsating inside his wife's head. Let go the bark of his shotgun blast in between strums of her fingers against the steering wheel to silence the voice inside his head, sentencing them both to die with a split-second decision.

The bus left me at the edge of the neighbourhood still burning for information. As I turned up the block, a man emerged from behind the row of towering cypress pines planted to block the sound of traffic emanating from the roadway. Irregular patches of pale skin marred the cocoa-brown complexion on either of the man's cheeks, his earlobes, the tips of his fingers. He wore gray pinstriped coveralls from the paper mill buttoned tight to the neck. Ordinarily during the summertime, you saw men coming from the mill with the sleeves of their uniforms tied down around their waists in an effort to survive the heat.

The man who stood before me didn't seem to care

about the heat. The tag embroidered above the pocket of the man's uniform matched the name that had been on the bus driver's tongue earlier that morning—*Booker*. I stopped in my tracks, causing him to pull up short too, the sudden lack of movement between us requiring extra time for him to process. It was evident from the slant of his eyes, the sway of his stance, that the man had been drinking. Less clear was what he wanted from me. What, given his brother's predicament, had him lurking outside Gram's block waiting for me to return.

"You-all were supposed to fix this." He spoke with enough spit on his tongue to send the words flying in my direction.

"Fix what?" I asked, baffled by the accusation.

"Fix it so that Tobias would understand." He tugged at the collar of his uniform, having just sobered enough to finally be cognizant of the heat, the drone of cicadas humming off in the distance before sounding again from a nearby tree line.

The slant of his eyes began to soften like he was on the verge of crying, only he was still too drunk to recognise his need for tears. "I put my trust in you-all to fix it. Now he's gone from me forever."

The man turned away a bit too sharply for the fog swirling inside his head to catch up. He stumbled back down the walkway, labouring the whole while to steady himself against a private breeze that seemed to have caught him alone, before pushing his way back through the row of towering cypress to wherever he had parked his truck.

Detective Daugherty —

Later that afternoon, a putty coloured four-door pulled into Gram's driveway, a stack of red and blue lights strapped to the rooftop. The sternest looking somebody I had ever laid eyes on stretched out of the car, donned a straight brimmed, Mounties' style hat before marching himself in the direction of the front porch.

He rapped twice alongside the door frame causing the screen door to tremble in place. The man stared like he knew me from someplace as I pushed the screen door past the brim of his hat.

"Althea Combs?" he asked, glancing down at his notepad, letting me know he was still reaching to know me.

"That's my momma," I replied. "But she moved away from here ages ago."

"Then you must be Evelyn Combs," he proclaimed, his voice showing only slightly less hesitation. He was most certainly reaching at this point.

"That was my gram," I responded. "But she no longer lives here either. Is there something I can help you with?"

He introduced himself as Detective Daugherty from the Mississippi State Bureau of Investigation. He asked if I'd heard about a crime committed the other day in Jefferson County. Naturally, by now the whole town had heard.

He wanted to know when last I'd seen Mr. Booker's wife. I told him that, until mention of the name this morning, I hadn't known Booker. Bunk is what he meant to say. He scratched this additional bit of detail into his notepad.

"How about Mr. Harrison? Have you made his acquaintance?"

Anyone made to complete physical education as part of the curriculum required to graduate Memorial High is assured to have made Mr. Harrison's acquaintance. That didn't mean I knew a thing about his supposed association with Bunk's dead wife.

We continued in the broken parlance of two strangers not sharing the same common language. Detective Daugherty spoke of allegations and perpetrators, co-conspirators around town. All I knew was that Bunk had shot his wife. Why he shot her, the circumstances surrounding the difficulties they'd been having with one another, prior to moving away from Picayune or since, I couldn't put my hand on. More curious was what had led the detective to Gram's front porch in the first place, her name and that of my mother loose on the detective's tongue. What had Bunk told him about Gram? What is it I was supposed to have known?

I started to mention my encounter earlier that day with Bunk's brother, Booker. But that was an added complication I had yet to get my head around. Booker hadn't done me any physical harm. From that perspective, there was no crime to report.

Detective Daugherty stepped away from the front porch as boggled by our conversation as his misplaced insinuations had left me. To my knowledge, I had done nothing wrong. At the same time, I couldn't offer him a single thread to draw the next line of his investigation on. I didn't know Bunk. I don't recall having ever laid eyes on his wife. Couldn't pick her out of a crowd even if I had seen her.

As for Mr. Harrison, he was little more to me than the men's head basketball coach—the Phys. Ed. instructor hanging onto fading youth through the prospect of budding athletes whose development had been left in his care. Perhaps he had known Bunk's wife, intimately for all any of us was concerned. Bunk may have been justified in his outrage, might have shot them both dead had he managed to catch them in the right compromising position, both their pants split open wide. But that was pure speculation, colourful embellishment set on top of idle gossip passed from one hand to the next on the bus ride into town. I was in no position to call it.

Between Here and Sleep —

That night, Tobias Booker joined ranks with Gram and the other lost souls haunting my dreams on a semi-regular basis, Bunk cast among the walking dead stuck on death row awaiting his eventual execution.

Later that week, I got caught in a dream where I couldn't wake up. I was lying stomach first, my face pressed into the pillow, a thin sheet pulled over me to protect my skin from the slight chill that had managed to work its way inside Gram's house, the sun on its way as dawn crept in to reverse the trend of cool air in the room.

Suddenly I felt a body lean into me. A man, I gathered, from the weight of the intruder climbing on top of me. I sensed his touch more than felt it, a light pestering on my skin like the bed sheet had gone double or triple its weight as the shape of the man's knee pressed into the mattress, pulling the sheet tight against my bare legs.

By the time his other knee dented the mattress, his two legs straddling my backside, my struggle between here and sleep was in full swing. I became entangled in my bedclothes. A stifled scream floated to the top of my dream, the bed sheet cinched tightly around my waist.

I eventually twisted myself free from my nightmare. Shot up in the bed, my legs tucked into my chest before my screaming could cross over into the visible world, chasing the intruder from existence, my bed sheet returned to its normal weight against my skin. Gram's bedroom as empty as the day she left it, leaving me once again sleep deprived.

THREE

THREE

Invisible Theory

I find when I look down toward my own feet, I see the top of my head as a child, my spirit seeming too small, too light for the size I've grown to be. But the spirit grows in due time. Not up and down like the body grows. The spirit twists into corners previously unthinkable, never fully recovering at times. Like gum on your shoe, the effects of which lessen with time but never fully subside. Even when the outward signs have grown imperceptible, the spirit still knows where you've been.

None Too Simple —

I used to wish I were invisible. Not overlooked and dismissed as was the case, but really invisible: rub a cream over my body and disappear. I didn't talk the first eight years or so of my life. I walked and ate and controlled my bodily functions like any normal eight-year-old should. But I never spoke.

I could communicate. I'd point or gesture, nod my head in response to a question that required nodding, but for some none too simple reason had made up my mind it was best I save my words.

It didn't help that I couldn't stand the sound of my own voice. It was too gruff for a child's voice, like a stuck pipe preparing to fire. Before long, I decided I could get along fine without words, sparing my neighbours the occasional barrage of startling backfires. This affliction afforded me a certain distance from other kids my age. I rode a special bus to school, spent the entire day in a special classroom. My classmates and I ate lunch at a special time set aside for us in the cafeteria. I wasn't the least embarrassed by my set aside status. I relished the time spent alone in speechless bliss, even if it was feigned.

With time, I outgrew my bout with silence. I started talking slowly at home, then at school. Never too much and never too loudly, but I was talking. When kids realized I could talk but had decided not to, they labelled me strange, oddball strange. Somehow choosing not to do something seemed to them more peculiar than not being able to do the very same thing.

Only Herald Grimes didn't find me strange. Herald knew strange and I was no stranger than Herald. The kids used to call him Charmin. Not that he was squeezably soft. Herald was sissy-soft. They say he could hold his head between his legs and lick his own thing-thing. I suspect it wasn't true, but didn't care if he could. To me, he was Herald: peasey-headed, crater-faced, bug-eyed beautiful wrapped around a magnificent soul. The two of us became best friends and each other's saviour.

Herald lived with his great-aunt on the top floor of our building, my saviour always in easy reach. I could climb the stairs to his great-aunt's apartment, rap alongside the hallway next to his bedroom and Herald would meet me in the basement next to the janitor's closet. I don't know why we sneaked. It just seemed that a pair of oddballs ought to sneak. The other kids teased us mercilessly when either of us was alone. Being seen together would have invited an onslaught of abuse, the effects of which neither of us could have withstood.

Yet the one time Herald needed me, there was nothing I could do to save him. That afternoon started like any other. Some of the neighbourhood dregs were assembled in the alleyway shooting dice—renting beer from the corner store, relieving themselves against the red brick of the adjacent building to make room for another quart. Herald was standing watch at his bedroom window—like any freak would, peering out at a world that wouldn't allow him an easy way in.

The man kneeling at the head of their circle leaned away in disgust, his hand paralyzed above his head from his last roll. He watched as the dice careened off the alley wall then peered up at him—*snake eyes!* His cries to the heavens caught Herald at his bedroom window, the shine from Herald's black skin pulling back into the shadows. A quick survey of the man's stubble-faced comrades revealed a fellow gambler returning his limp member to its zippered shut confines, the man's high-top sneakers soiled with back-spray from the brick alley wall.

It hadn't been Herald's intention to leer. Even more, he hadn't meant to be seen. The math of four squares— four windows up by four windows over—led the men to his great-aunt's apartment. Herald had the good sense to bolt the front door. But, owing to an unscrupulous landlord, was flushed from his nest anyway.

He squirted out the front door flailing. He made it all the way to the next landing of stairs, the men seeming to prefer a chase. A long arm caught him before his hand could disappear from the banister, reeled him in, his legs still wheeling in flight. I screamed for them to stop, but my voice was lost in a frenzy of thundering blows. I stood as they bashed him against the wooden banister like a rag-doll in oversized kid hands. They stopped once one of them noticed Herald was bleeding. Even a man who will stand in a stream of his own back spray knows to fear a freak and whatever disease he might be carrying.

They left him in a crumpled heap outside his doorway. He pleaded for me to leave him, wanting someone of bigger consequence to find him than another oddball freak. I dragged him into the bathroom, hoping to spare him the last indignity of admitting he was different, as tossed up inside as out. Got him cleaned up and changed before his aunt could return. She would never know the peril she left him to, the burn of a light that forced him forever inside, the glare of his black skin sentencing him to a lifelong house arrest.

Favour —

Herald longed to be good looking, wished beyond anything to be looked upon with favour. Left to himself, which was most often the case, he developed a keen ability to see beyond his physical limitations. Peered into a mirror that peered back, unaffected by the catcher's mitt he had been given for a face, the colour of deep rubbed shoe polish turned up at the edges until his forehead and chin stood out in profile beyond the rest of his features, his bent nose included. Wary eyes sat behind folds of loose skin, their yellow bulbs boiled in blood like two rusty sparks spread out on a bumper car nose. When he blinked, you'd see a car backing up, the glow from its taillights bleeding into reverse.

Herald's limp voice and frail ways likely originated from the need to compensate for his grotesque appearance. Not that he was deformed in any way. He was instead the product of two painfully ugly folks who one dreary night made love beneath a sky bent against this kind of union. They say his momma was his daddy's older sister, his great-aunt and his grandma crammed inside a single person, though great-aunt was easier to explain.

At street level, Herald was stared at, both of us were. Or whispered behind like an awful secret that plagues the onlooker until the secret has been told, the lie passed like a disease to its next carrier. That's when I most wanted that cream, to rub it over Herald and me so we could both disappear, never to be heard from or whispered behind again.

We came to life in the basement. The high-waisted woman in 3-B owned a collection of movie soundtracks that she kept stored in a cubby, lined with chain-link fence. We didn't have a record player down there, but we studied the dust jackets until their images filled the basement like our dank quarters had been part of the original movie set. Carmen Jones was our hands down favourite. Harry Belafonte was everything Herald wasn't. From his square chin to the smooth expanse of his bronze forehead, Harry was someone to gaze upon with great adoration.

My Dorothy Dandridge required long preparation. Unbridled sex appeal was the only requisite for my choice in attire. I had a pair of pinstriped Capri pants and a yellow halter-top that tied at the back of my neck. Momma's eyes would chase me from the apartment with suspicion whenever I wore that ensemble. *'Girl, you're in love with that getup.'* I was in love with the man who loved me in that getup. Didn't matter whether it was Herald or Harry, I was lost in illusion.

We sang song lyrics we had only seen printed on the jacket covers. Danced to tunes we'd never heard played out loud, holding one another like we were lovers, a love neither of us had yet to experience above ground or below. One time, we got so carried away that Herald grabbed me up, took me in his arms and kissed me, his tongue poking around inside my mouth, unsure what advance the rest of his body was attempting. I wished for a moment I hadn't been born a girl so he could kiss me with his full tongue, wished I could love him in a way that would make him love me back.

Thinking quickly, bright as a light, I undid my halter-top, letting it fall around my waist before Herald could squeeze away. He slithered down my belly, still locked in character, his lazy eyes blinking glances back and forth between my ripe-hard nipples. Ravenous lips wrapped a thick tongue around my titty, stroking like my breast might release its spasm for him, gasping long and warm down his deep throat—thick mother's milk sent to nourish an aching soul.

A creak along the floorboards above our heads jolted Herald back to the real world, his eyes scrambling from the realization that my swollen breast couldn't produce the nectar he desired, the ram of steel not there to send him gurgling and dizzy across an irretrievable threshold. He pulled away, his third leg running long against my hip. Then he wouldn't kiss me. I wasn't who he wanted.

Reality poked a huge, gaping hole in our basement existence that day, letting in a light too brilliant for either of us to ignore. Had we left well enough alone, not tried to erase that tiny bit of distance between us, we'd still have had those few precious moments alone in each other's company. Could have rested within the confines of our safe haven where the two of us were free to act without reservation, as though we both belonged.

Left alone in the darkness, whatever little bit of Dorothy Dandridge he saw in me led Herald to believe he could kiss me. Seeing traces of her smile reflected in my face provided the bit of assurance he needed to allow bold ambitions of rubbing himself full with Harry Belafonte type good looks run free in our basement hideaway. Disguised as Harry, Herald was no longer a freak. Held close inside his arms, I was no longer a freak either.

From that day onward, a rap alongside the wall connecting Herald's bedroom to the hallway went unanswered, my saviour unable to spare himself a lifetime of crippling shame. He'd never succeed in contorting himself to fit the image held inside his head of Harry Belafonte, my Dorothy Dandridge falling far from his desires. In the end, my Herald didn't want me in that way. Didn't possess the right makeup in his DNA.

By the time I left for Picayune, Herald had grown into his sissy-soft ways, had learned to use his loose walk and shrill manner of speaking to keep people at bay. He chose deafening individuality over silence to mask out the world. I wished for the moxie to do the same. Even his light bulb eyes took on a new slyness—look into them wrong and they'd likely cut you if not swallow you whole.

Blue Eyed Brown

Me and Miss Spinnaker became fast friends, only friends in the way she and Gram had been friends—she was there if ever I needed her and I would be there if ever she needed me. We just worked hard at not needing one another. Though, if it weren't for her reaching out, I might have left Picayune. I thought for a moment I would, that I would take what I could from this experience and return to more familiar struggles. In the end, I decided my leaving would disappoint Gram more than anything I might think to do, running from one difficult circumstance only to face another, the turmoil awaiting me in New York far more crippling than a lifetime of solitude in Picayune.

I contemplated a handful of dim possibilities—wallowing amid the incessant back biting inside the hair salon, my feet stuck in mud, or resigning myself like Miss Spinnaker to remain alone for the rest of eternity. I set out in search of companionship instead. I studied the faces I encountered, stacked their interests up next to mine. I thought about the things I might share with someone my own age, weighed that against the insight many a talk with the likes of Gram or Miss Spinnaker had afforded me over the years. Maybe another lost soul would get off the bus needing to find her way. I'd be there for her in ways no one had been for me. Would help her steer clear of the pitfalls I had managed to hit full stride, each wrong step sending me reeling more unsteadily than the last.

But, at the end of the day, even a lost soul will have family to return to come nightfall. Night-time isolates all creatures to some extent. If you're alone already, night-time casts a shadow so dark even a spirit less brittle than mine might break. Any trouble seems a hundred times bigger, any need you have all the more desperate.

Curtis had awakened something inside me. It was the same something that Herald had stirred, only the thing stirring inside him was too much like the thing stirring inside me for our two things to find more than passing interest in one another. I had learned to silence my thing, for long stretches need be. But once awakened again, it wanted all the more to make up for the time spent silent pretending it wasn't a thing.

By day, I thought about having a friend. But, left alone at night, I longed for the touch only a man could lay on me. The trouble was, men like Curtis didn't grow in abundance around Picayune. The men in town were rawhide: rough heads, rough hands, rough hearts. The most you could hope was that some stranger might blow into town and carry you away. Eventually one did.

Though I had yet to meet him outside my dreams, he was all I could see, standing on the periphery of my conscious mind waiting to know me, to see me, subconscious thought at work inside his head rehearsing how to pronounce my name. I left him resting beneath my pillow when I headed out in the morning, rushed to bed each night anxious for him to visit me again.

See Through Sanctity —

The outside air took flight, a light breeze giving life to everything in its path, connecting folks to one another even if they were unaware why they were feeling this way. A low rumbling started outside, like somebody pulling a toy wagon along the sidewalk. I listened for the sound to pick a direction as I tippy-toed across the front room. I spied him from behind the screen door, my dream lover in the flesh, pulling two suitcases up the walkway. He was dressed in a soft butterscotch suit, his tie the colour of freshly dipped caramel popcorn. I hadn't seen a suit so fine in all my days, the ribbon above the brim of his hat matching the caramel-corn handkerchief peeking out from his breast pocket.

The man inside the suit was extraordinary too—more man than you could take in with a single glance. I watched through the screen door as he removed his suit jacket, rolled his shirtsleeves up to the elbows. The heat had raised the veins on both arms, forming a relief map to where he'd been that day, this lifetime even. I wanted to press a palm against the screen and study the raised contours on the back of his hand, finger a path and see where it might lead. But I held my composure, restrained by the see-through sanctity of a latched screen door.

I caught him as he reached to knock. "We don't have any rooms to rent."

"Thank you just the same Ma'am, but I'm not looking to rent a room," he replied, bobbing his head, one hand shading his brow periscope style as he tried to make out who was lurking behind the screen door. His blue eyes were nearly as bright as his smile, his face brown and full from the sun though the creases around his smile suggested that this was no year-round brown. His colour came and went with the seasons, a consequence of whatever sun he'd endured.

"Then why are you carrying your luggage with you?" I asked.

He adjusted his necktie to let the words flow more freely. "This isn't my luggage, Ma'am. I'm selling it." He pushed his hat back to reveal a layer of perspiration before dabbing his brow clean with his handkerchief, a ploy as I've since learned to pull an invitation inside.

"Why are you sellin' somebody else's luggage?" A brand-new raindrop would be less naïve. I told him I wasn't in the market for new luggage but asked him in anyway. It was the least I could do after having him drag those suitcases all the way up the walkway dressed in a full-on suit, especially on a day like that, the sun hot enough to melt age-old concrete.

He introduced himself using all three names at once: *August Horatio Gossett*. He apologized for the name, claiming it didn't suit him. Having never met a man named August, or a woman for that matter, I didn't know how one should look.

I soon became conscious of my staring, was surprised to find him staring back. "You're not from here, are you?" he ventured.

I attempted to retouch my hair with my fingertips. I feared what kind of creature might be standing in front of him, having spent the morning straightening the kitchen cupboards. "What makes you say I'm not from here?"

"I've darkened many a doorstep around these parts," he offered. "You don't seem like the typical Picayune girl."

"What makes a girl from Picayune typical?" I asked, suddenly realizing how little interest I had left in wanting to be typical.

"Something about her look," he replied with a wink, some of the salesman in him still at work behind sparkling eyes. "The way she'd rather frown than smile, stares defying you to say something then dismisses you with her eyes just when you might think to speak. You know—*typical*. I don't get that from you. You're different somehow." My whole life I had strived to fit in. Now it was different that would spare me any ordinary fate.

"I grew up in New York," I confessed.

"Meaning you're grown?"

"Not any more grown than I appear to be," I replied, labouring to control the stammer stifling my tongue. "What I mean to say is I lived in New York before coming to Picayune."

"Meaning you used to be from New York? I used to be from Towson, just outside Baltimore," he explained, sensing my lack of familiarity with the place. "Now, we're both from Picayune. At least for today."

He didn't talk like your typical door-to-door salesman. His conversation lacked sufficient pace to keep the exchange one sided, left too many holes for the inevitable, '*thank you, no,*' followed by a polite door slam. Still, he was a riddle with words, his conversation always on the edge of pretence, making it hard to discern the person behind the smile. Fortunately the wrapper seemed worth the effort.

A few long gulps of lemonade and he dropped the sales pitch, settling into more normal conversation—where he had been, where he was headed, where he hoped someday to be, that kind of talk. He described how he started selling luggage to escape his family's business breeding horses—that explained the fine suit. Said he didn't have anything against horses, just believed in making his own way in life.

"It would have been easy to stay, prepare myself to take charge once Granddad retires. But there's a big ol' world out there I want to see first. Having never been especially proficient with my hands, I'm content making a living with my feet instead." He bent to wipe the front of one shoe with his handkerchief. His shoes were the only things on him that showed any signs of wear. Then even they were quite unlike the mud flat boots I was bound to run across traveling the streets of Picayune.

"I met a salesman one day on my grandparents' property, the front man for this French luggage company just making its push stateside. By the time he left, not only had he sold me a set of steamer trunks, he convinced me that selling door-to-door would be the perfect escape from a lifetime ferrying horses.

"Mind you, a thoroughbred horse is a magnificent creature, but connecting with another human being is what makes the world go 'round." He was beaming, a wayward comet flashing a twinkle across his eyes, the full warmth of the sun having taken command of his smile. I don't know how much luggage he sold, but to be out there selling seemed to fill him with an excitement, only a fraction of which could transform my outlook permanently.

I found myself smiling at him, the way you smile at someone who you believe will smile back. Then it delights you when he does and it seems the whole world can breathe again. I could breathe again too, my latent desires having finally found their mate.

Slow Motion —

That first encounter played before me in slow motion whenever I found myself in a restful state. Like, by remembering slowly, I could make each moment last forever. I could kick myself for failing to take his suit jacket, missing the opportunity to feel the weave of its fabric as I carried it to the coat rack Gram kept by the front door. To handle his Panama style hat, tempted the whole while to rest the hat on my head before setting it on an open hook. Instead I let him sit, his jacket folded over one knee, his hat resting atop the other, the pair serving as a constant reminder that time would eventually come for him to depart.

This is how I fall. Most people interest me. I study their ways, fret over their most trivial concerns. Seldom does my interest in a person spark genuine intrigue. Once intrigue takes hold, there's little distance for me between the first prick of curiosity and the unrelenting pound of desire. I was a few short hours from having met this man, yet thoughts of him were swimming inside my head.

I sat down to dinner that evening still distracted by his presence inside Gram's house with me. I could see the arm of the chair where he sat from my place at the kitchen table. The bass in his voice echoed from the far end of the room, disrupting the staid familiarity I'd grown accustomed to expect inside these walls.

The food on my plate went invisible, replaced instead by a meal far more sumptuous than anything I might prepare for myself alone. My mind set off in search of butter and brown sugar, molasses and syrup, biscuits and jam. Smothered pork chops and whipped potatoes, a generous helping of cobbler resting beneath a mountain of vanilla ice cream. An entire box of chocolates, that first sip of wine.

I found myself standing at the wide part of the river, staring across at the far bank like getting there was an easy step, as though anyone had invited me to attempt the leap. *August Horatio Gossett*—I was beginning to get used to the sound of his name on my tongue. I wondered would he have stayed had I invited him for supper. Had he stayed, would I ever want for him to leave.

The front room on the other hand seemed inconvenienced by the intrusion, like it needed more time to get used to this much company, due in large part to the fact that I'd entertained a grand total of no one since Gram's home-going. Meanwhile, the kitchen stood by in a state of full-on jealousy that we hadn't spent more time in there, August having dipped into the kitchen only momentarily to deposit his glass in the sink before heading out the front door.

I'm able to relate firsthand with the kitchen's regrets, feeling myself like we hadn't spent nearly enough time together. Still, remembrances of him lingered everywhere I turned. I shadowed his gaze as he studied the pictures Gram had hung around the front room: photographs that over the years had grown invisible to me, a lifetime of memories transformed by time into a jumble my mind's eye no longer bothers to see. He remarked at length on the fine detail Gram had embroidered into the doilies that adorned the arms of the sofa, which for me signified yet another chore to do—straightening those doilies each time I put up the hideaway bed. It's as though he'd spent a lifetime inside Gram's house and I was the stranger encountering the place for the first time.

I sat helpless as he shifted restlessly in his seat, working to catch a draft from the paddle fan that waved lazily down on us from the bead board ceiling. Gram and I had battled countless times over my having turned that fan on too high, burning up all her electricity. Now fully trained in her system, I was able to offer my first real visitor the most meagre of accommodations, the two of us left to swelter in a heat dictated by indelible memories of Gram's penny pinching.

Our exchange eventually grew playful as the fantasy built inside my head. I imagined him showing up at Gram's house one day, tossing his hat into a vacant corner, then dancing me across the front room—my Carmen Jones making her long awaited comeback appearance. When we sat, I would take the place of the suit jacket resting on his knee. He would stare the same stare at me, only this time his eyes would hold my gaze when he catches me staring back. With time, his suit jacket would find a home in the bedroom closet rather than hanging all by its lonesome on the coat rack in the front room. Before long, all of his belongings would take up residence inside Gram's bedroom closet, filling in the jagged-tooth smile of empty hangers with one fine suit after another. With that final gesture, his life packed in next to mine, my fantasy of having him was fulfilled, my desperate yearning for him locked deep inside the walls of an overactive imagination.

I attempted to regain a hold on reality as I cleared away the few dishes I'd managed to dirty with my meal. I didn't know this man from a can of paint. But sitting across from a can of paint didn't cause the backs of my knees to ache, the pull of desire churning on the inside rendering my physical self nearly powerless despite outward attempts to remain unaffected. Looking back, several years removed, I now understood the mystery of Pandora's box. Only it's demons inside my box he had yet to unleash.

My thoughts continued to wander as I drifted off to sleep that night, a spare pillow pressed tightly between restless thighs. I slid my hand beneath the pillow as the warmth of my body spread itself ever so slowly across the bed sheets, released the demons stirring inside me— once, twice, three times that night. Oh, how I needed for this man to want to open that box.

Alien Sighting —

By first light the next day, the desire for simple companionship had spawned the possibility of romance. With
no further contact between us to discourage my fantasy,
the possibility of romance blossomed into fully articu-
lated lusting. I was drowning in the thought of this man
touching me, my subconscious consumed by the feel of
his hands on my skin, his tongue reaching any place his
hands alone couldn't satisfy.

I stayed extra-long at the hair salon the following
Saturday to soak in every last bit of conversation,
hoping to catch some hint of August's whereabouts
around town. Nobody had seen him firsthand, but
everyone had heard the tale of this suit wearing, dream
of a man inviting himself inside people's homes, sitting
up in their front rooms, big as life. You'd think they
were talking about a creature from outer space, only
one whose company you wouldn't mind keeping if the
opportunity presented itself. And there I was, the only
one able to say how the creature looked up close, could
recall the scent of his cologne stirred ever so slowly
with each turn of the paddle fan. I nearly peed myself
trying to keep from spilling the details of my secret,
especially those aspects conjured inside my imagination. But I wasn't prepared to give up the fantasy just
yet. For the first time in the longest while I had a leg up
on the rest of the world, a privilege I was in no great

hurry to relinquish.

It wasn't another Saturday or two before somebody stepped inside the hair salon claiming to have seen the creature with her own eyes. As time wore on, one person after another began to report having enjoyed the pleasure of his company, my make-believe lover having spent time seated next to them on their living room sofas. One of the shop patrons eventually got to talking crazy about how she dreamed of fish the night August came to call on her, signifying the two of them were meant to wind up together. Miss Thula wanted to know whether she ate the fish or did she see the fish swimming around in her dream? Cause, if the fish in her dream were swimming along beside her, it might suggest that she and August were meant to be together just as she had hoped. If on the other hand, she cooked and ate the fish, it meant she was going to have a baby and no one in the salon was willing to believe the luggage salesman had paid her that kind of visit.

Thankfully, Lamar was there to set things straight. He remarked how a woman's fully capable of falling in love, falling out of love, then going right back to being in love again without the object of her desire ever knowing a thing about it. I didn't know whether he was remarking on the sad state of romance in the world or how low a woman might stoop to disguise how lonesome this life could be. Either way, his commentary succeeded in silencing the woman's crazed fish-talk about dreams of my man.

I wished to speak with no one outside of August when I wasn't lost inside my head talking to myself about him. As strange as it may sound taking such fascination in the mere possibility of a man, the thought of him wanting me back never once crossed my mind. Still, he had yet to distance himself from me, had yet to make some choice that would keep him from darkening my doorstep again. I especially liked when things were tossed up this way, that period of uncertainty, usually short-lived inside my head, before reality anchored the outcome of something I wanted hopelessly outside my reach.

I made a solemn vow to ignore August. Meanwhile the rest of the town began buzzing around him like bees turned onto a new kind of flower, one whose pollen tasted sweeter than the rest. Not that any of his virtues were lost on me. I simply refused to cast myself after his scent along with the throng of swarming bees. If I was meant to see him again, it would come to pass without my having run behind him. That's what Gram would have tried to convince me had she been here. It's what I eventually managed to convince myself, landing me once again on the outskirts, a resident alien in the place where my momma and daddy's eyes first met.

The Lonely Season —

As hospitable as this town had grown to be, it could still at times draw that none too subtle distinction to remind me that we would never truly be family. I called it *the lonely season*—a stretch of time that started with Thanksgiving and lingered well into the Easter holiday, the entire town wrapped up in kinfolk, leaving strangers like me on the fringe of any close-knit ties.

At long last, Easter Sunday was upon us. I started the morning as I normally would: lying face up in bed, contemplating how to spend the rest of my day. Attending Sunday service would be the natural thing to do. But having never been to church, not a single time since arriving in Picayune, showing up for the first time on Easter Sunday seemed too hypocritical. I'd made a conscious effort that week to steer clear of the hair salon, a decision I was beginning to regret. Even a dinner invitation offered out of pity would have given me someplace to be.

Still, the day was too perfect to stay cooped up inside, even for a gloomy Gus like me. The sun hung in the sky just so. Even the few clouds that bothered to show up were just enough to punctuate how bright the springtime sky could be, their oblong shapes outlined in varying degrees of shadow and light against an other-wise endless expanse of blue.

I took the bus into town to feel like I was going

someplace, then continued the ride home never bothering to disembark, seeing how desolate the Easter parade cleanup had left the streets. I thought about the lost soul I hoped to befriend as the bus crossed Sycamore on its way back toward Richardson. I spotted August strolling in the opposite direction alongside the roadway, his suit jacket flung across his shoulder. He looked as pitiful as I felt. The thought moved inside me before my mind could protest. Still, I had to force my feet to go, had to urge my hand to signal for the next stop, landing me square in August's path.

The bus left me in a thick cloud of exhaust fumes. I found the solitude helped to quiet my nerves as I waited for the air surrounding me to clear, for the sun and clouds and springtime blue to install themselves in the sky again.

It's unclear which of us was more surprised to see me standing there, having temporarily abandoned my circumspect ways. "What are you doing out this way?" he asked. I might have asked the same of him.

"Just coming from town," I replied.

"Is there something going on in town I should know about?"

"Not a solitary thing," I offered, conceding defeat over my sunrise ambitions. "It seems the whole world is wrapped up in having not a single thing to do." I listened for a bird chirp before pressing further, to make certain mine wasn't the only voice sounding off in the universe. "Where are you on your way to?"

"No place in particular," he replied. "Just whiling the time away."

"That sounds like an awful waste of a perfectly wonderful afternoon." *Steady, nerves. Steady.* "How about I take you around a bit, show you the Picayune I've come to claim as my own?"

"I can't think of any better thing to do," he said, shifting his jacket to a new position on his shoulder as he motioned for me to lead the way.

I would always head for the river whenever I was feeling especially forlorn. It was the one place I knew where nothing mattered outside of what I allowed to matter. At least part of me felt memories of that place belonged to somebody else, from a time long past. But with Curtis having moved away for good, our history together dashed to bits, I had assumed ownership over any good times spent at the river's edge, past or present, to do with as I pleased.

You had to navigate a dense patch of forest to reach the river. It initially seemed an awful lot of trouble to escape the rest of town. The closer you got, the more you suspected your guide had gotten off track and led you both astray.

"No one ever comes out this way," I said, invoking the same words Curtis had used on me as I pushed my way through the first thicket of honeysuckle. "It's like there are two Picayunes: one resting outside these trees meant for the uninitiated, the other reserved for those willing to let their souls wander more freely, where the movement of the river echoes our connection to some distant land." The words sounded even more contrived coming from my lips than they had on Curtis's tongue. August graciously pretended not to notice.

A dapple of sunlight slipped in every now and again, the space in between tree branches growing narrow in spots before bursting apart with a twinkling of brilliant light. I allowed myself to forget momentarily that I was the repeat visitor. Split time between tourist and guide as the first few glimpses of the river's gleaming skin began to show through. Opening new eyes to some hidden splendour appealed to the adventurer in me, awakened a spirit honed from many a childhood adventure exploring the farthest reaches of some city park, my sisters and I glued to the heels of our father's shoes. I carried on like he would, pretending I had been the one to discover the place, this our first landing despite the path well-worn with feet.

I was reminded how the view leapt in scale, the span of the river swelling with each stolen glance between thick foliage. The wall of massive tree trunks gave way to sedges and long flowering grass as the ground grew soft beneath your feet. The path eventually dissolved into an endless expanse of unspoiled blue sky. Just when you thought the trail might run out, the scene exploded before you, this little slice of heaven suddenly too vast for the image conjured within the confines of your mind's eye.

I reached for August's arm as we emerged from the last line of tree cover to amplify the sensation that, with the slightest misstep, one or the other of us might tumble headlong into oblivion. "Watch your step," I warned. "Lose your footing here and I'll wind up watching you somersault, all the way to the river's edge."

Our feet eventually found the path that marked a gentler slope down the riverbank as I proceeded to point out the few birds whose names I still remembered, trying to impress August with the little bit of local knowledge I had picked up.

Somehow, the trip failed to energize me the way I thought it might. That was another of my daddy's traits: tasking the world around him with upkeep of his good mood, like he had no say in the matter. A gray sky signified a gloomy day for him. Sunshine and bright blue overhead meant he was in store for a string of bubbling good fortune. Seldom did the sky cooperate in that way, sunshine and rain showing little concern for how your day was going.

I ventured a glance to gauge whether August had picked up on my melancholy. He seemed wrapped in a depression all his own. Being a relative expert in every conceivable strain of sad emotion, I sensed something more at the root of his despair than having nothing to do on a lonesome Sunday.

"Something wrong?" I asked. "You seem a hundred miles away."

"Nothing I'd want to burden you with."

"It's no burden," I replied, hoping whatever was bothering him might shed some light on who or what had put a damper on my sunshine. "I've found talking through your troubles helps to put things in perspective. For what it's worth, I'm a terrific listener." With that I managed to bring a tiny grin to his face, one that lasted shorter than a gnat's breath.

I sensed his mind shifting in search of a suitable excuse to conceal the true source of his despair. "I'm just finding it hard to break in down here, to work my way into the rhythm of things." I couldn't tell whether he meant slow luggage sales or difficulty managing his personal affairs. I suspected the latter, but not knowing him outside of a single porch visit, I assumed his drowned mood had more to do with things that preceded his arrival in Picayune, the same way the root of my melancholy stretched all the way to New York where Easter parades and family gatherings were undoubtedly in full swing.

"You know your trouble?" I asked, studying his frown, my face twisted in a way reminiscent of one of Miss Spinnaker's pained expressions as I tried to conjure a cure for his depressed condition. "You don't belong here."

"Where would you have me go?" he asked, mild

intrigue reframing his gaze.

"I wouldn't have you go anyplace. I'm only telling you so you'll know. It's helped me a great deal to realize just how out of place I am. It's a sad truth, but I can tell just by looking that you don't belong here either."

"Who's missing you?" he asked, setting me back on my heels. "I find it hard to believe somebody's not standing by at this very instant, desperately needing to see you."

"Nothing would delight me more than someone longing to see me again. But I can no longer tell who, if anyone, needs me."

"How is it that you have no place to go today?" I resisted his attempt to turn the tide on our conversation, digging deeper into my despair.

"Who's to say this isn't where I'm supposed to be?" The grin on his face lasted two gnat's breaths this time.

August accompanied me back to the spot where the bus had left me. I hoped he might choose to wait, but could read in his affected smile the need to attend to the matter that had him stuck inside his head our entire visit. I understood that need from the inside out. Besides, I'd gotten all I bargained for and then some, stepping off that bus on a whim. We hadn't connected how I dreamed we might, but we had managed to kill a good portion of what otherwise promised to be a thoroughly dreadful afternoon. I was still left alone at night to wrestle with pillows beneath my bed sheets, but that chance encounter on Easter Sunday sealed a bond between August and me, our alien status in Picayune an excuse for us to relate, to seek each other out whenever we found a dull moment.

August had begun visiting on a regular basis despite my having made clear the limits on my ability to afford any fancy French luggage. Outside Gram's front room, we maintained separate existences. I stuck to my ordinary routine while he worked one block after the next, peddling his wares. He had created quite a stir, my blue-eyed brown having become somewhat of a minor celebrity in the neighbourhoods surrounding downtown Picayune—a kind of pied piper soothing eyes sore for the style and sophistication the image of a man in a suit can't help but convey. McGreggor's Department Store would have done themselves well to set their entire summer lineup around the suits he showed up in, week in and week out, never wearing the same ensemble twice.

Sitting alone in Gram's front room, I was like a teacup turned cold, waiting for the warmth of August's smile to perk me up again. Through him, I had come to appreciate the difference between being alone and being lonely. Alone was a temporary condition. After meeting August, never once had I had to wait long to see him. I simply wished to see him then he'd turn up, looking bright eyed and wonderful as ever.

At first, I thought a black man shouldn't have blue eyes. I fell into Miss Spinnaker's kitchen conversation that his complexion alone, a dollop of coffee dipped in fresh cream, was sufficient evidence of how recently his lineage had been compromised. But the more I looked into those eyes, the way they danced with all the wonder in the world, the more I determined a man shouldn't have eyes any other colour, even one whose complexion was cream-coffee brown.

Twisting Colours —

The blue-black sedan pulled up on my luggage salesman, the sun twisting colours on the car's hood like a basket of slithering pythons. August adjusted his tie against the tint of mirrored glass, an opening line at work inside his head as the window lowered.

"How's tricks?" a voice asked, conditioned air mixing with cigar smoke from deep inside the car's interior.

"Beg pardon?"

"How's business?" the voice continued to press. "Makin' many sales this way?"

"Doin' what I can," August replied, the salesman inside telling him to distrust the pitch. "Something I can interest you in?"

"Where I send folks, I don't need any luggage." Mr. Graves paused to add emphasis to his openly menacing intent. "Been to see Miss Penny lately?"

"Miss Penny's a tough nut to crack."

"Maybe there's no sale to be had there. Might be best to let it alone. Let her call if she finds she needs something. Everybody'd be better off that way." He eased off, his window raised before August had the chance to respond, August's door-to-door sales pitch no match for the caretaker of departed souls raised from this earth in a fiery mix of smoke and hot ash.

184

Penny Stamps —

I was in line at the post office a few days later, waiting to buy a book of penny stamps, when a commotion started on the sidewalk across the street. It was my luggage salesman out to meet his constituents.

He greeted one smiling face after another: Missus Bell whose husband owns the appliance repair shop, Agnes Hines and Dorie Miller, both of whose husbands work at the paper mill. You'd have thought from the way the crowd converged on him that he was a politician on the verge of reelection.

I looked on as he made his rounds up and down the sidewalk, touching hands and kissing cheeks the whole way. He eventually disappeared inside the diner, bringing an end to the commotion on the sidewalk, but I could only imagine the blushing cheeks awaiting him inside.

Again, I vowed to keep my composure, to refrain from asking about the women I'd seen tugging on him from the post office window. But a woman's desire is a jealous cat, especially one that hasn't been fed. Then, after three straight days of not a single word from him, my emotions got the better of me.

"I saw you the other morning in front of the diner." I turned away from him, the jealous cat in me unable to look straight into those blue eyes. "I was across the street waiting in line at the post office."

"You should have come over. I would have appreciated the company," August said smiling, not as yet having picked up on my salty mood.

"Looked from where I was standing like you had plenty of company: Missus Bell, Agnes Hines, Dorie Miller. Sounds like plenty company to me."

His smile faded. "Is that what this is about, which customers I visit with?"

"What you call customers, I call company, fawning all over those women out in the street for anybody to see."

"Why, Miss Penny, I do believe you are jealous."

"I'm not hardly jealous of any Agnes Hines or Dorie Miller." I tried to hang onto what little self-restraint I had left. "I just don't know how to take you at times. You visit me all the time, yet I don't recall any hand holding or cheek kissing."

"That's just something you do to be cordial," he said, dismissing the notion. "I didn't mean a thing by it."

"You don't owe me any explanation."

"It sounds like the opposite is true," he replied, his patience waning. "I'm a great fan of people. I thrive on their energy. I especially enjoy the company of a woman. I don't deny any of that. But, what do you suspect I do when I'm away from here? Spend idle time with every housewife in town? Sure, I'm going to be friendly with whoever I meet out in the street. But, I assure you my sole interest in any of those women is getting their husbands to buy a set of my luggage."

The sound of Gram's voice was ringing in my ear: *'find yourself a man who loves you with equal strength. That way the weight of either of you being in love won't lean too heavily against the other person.'* Try as I might, I couldn't keep my weight off him.

"Is that what you're being with me, cordial? Just not so cordial to want to kiss my cheek?" I asked. "You're in my front room anytime it's convenient for you to get by here, yet you walk past me on your way in like I'm part of the screen door. Then you're all hugs and kisses out in the street."

"Is that what you want, for me to kiss you?"

"That's the least of what I want, but I'll settle for a kiss." And, just like that, he kissed me. All matter of fact. No idle glances, no pause of anticipation. No long embrace afterwards to seal the kiss. A pat on the head would have been more befitting the level of intimacy his kiss was meant to engender.

He seemed lost momentarily, his attention focused on the expanse of floor that had opened up between our feet. He offered some excuse about business he needed to attend to then headed for the doorway, promising to get back this way again soon. He kissed me a second time before he left, partly to make the first kiss appear less awkward—one on the way in followed by another on the way out, as though he had intended either kiss.

But mostly he kissed me because I was still standing in the doorway, blocking his escape.

I latched the screen door behind him feeling I'd once again blown it. Squeezed something I desired so tightly it needed to squirt away, chasing the thing I wanted straight out of existence.

One Hundred Miles Running

It took some doing, but August and I eventually managed to mend the peace I'd unsettled between us by rushing him to kiss me too soon. He stopped by one evening, his eyes wide with excitement. "Come with me someplace." "Someplace like where?" "My grand-daddy's birthday in Birmingham."

It started as simply as that, the spark that lit the flame that launched the rocket ship between us. I thought to say no, should probably have given more weight to the popular suspicion concerning my new beau's whereabouts away from Picayune. The self-appointed keepers of all gossip in the hair salon had wanted to know whether he was married. When I had finally screwed my nerve up to ask, he said he was whatever married is. I still didn't know what that meant.

"I'd be delighted!" I replied, the ease of his invitation giving my answer confidence, the complexity surrounding our visit failing to fully register with me.

Everyone in the hair salon had her own theory on how to take my luggage salesman. Miss Thula mostly kept her opinions to herself, but cautioned me not to get my hopes up. "Men are like bookends, fallin' in love on both sides of the relationship—on the way in then on the way out, messin' you over the whole time in between." I recognised this as a direct reflection of her circumstance. Still, I took her warnings seriously having witnessed with Curtis those bookends played out in reverse.

Lamar, the only seemingly straight male hairdresser in the state of Mississippi, was there to lend a man's perspective. "Ask him what you want to know. If he kisses you before answering, it means he's struggling to find a way to answer without hurting you unnecessarily. If he answers first, then the kiss is his way of asking forgiveness for the lie he's just told." He waved his curling iron at me magic-wand style to underline the significance of the wisdom he had just laid on us.

Miss Thula's niece, Cecile, was all for the idea of a mystery romance. "With little practical experience to go on, I've determined the best kind of man to have is a traveling man." That's how she started most conversations, by first acknowledging the limits of her knowledge on the subject, then advising how to proceed despite that admitted lack of insight.

"First, a traveling man is made of fast money, mostly unaccounted for, looking for a reason to spend. Next, he's always on the move. I tell you, a man can be hard working, church going, and law abiding as long as somebody's watching. But catch him in the crease, and he's bound to do most anything. A traveling man is always in the crease."

She wanted to know what kind of outfit he was planning to buy me for our trip. I couldn't understand what would compel a man to buy a gift for me to celebrate his grandfather's birthday. Cecile was quick to remark how every occasion should be celebrated with gifts, bestowed on her by any man she was even loosely connected to.

My connection to August was growing intense despite a mutual disregard for gift giving on off occasions. Miss Thula and her niece both warned me not to let my expectations get ahead of me. Things may not wind up the way I had hoped.

I didn't share their concern. I met August with the ease of a summer's breeze, breathed him in, thought of him on the inhale then exhaled to find I couldn't get him out of my head. Where he'd come from, how he landed in Picayune in the first place, was no concern of mine. Besides, he had chosen me. Any prior obligation, complications his showing up with me might present, only he was conscious of. And about this getaway, he didn't flinch.

West Side Grille —

I primped and prepped myself best I could not knowing where he was taking me or who we might encounter once there. August's only concrete instruction was to carry an overnight bag, in case the party ran late. The word overnight hung long in the air like the tail of a shooting star.

For months, I had watched my door-to-door salesman schlep suitcases up and down Picayune by foot. This time he showed up in a car, a man's car: deep voice, hood rattling enthusiasm, fenders bulging with muscularity. The engine roared in anticipation of the road ahead, flexing its deep muscles to shake the cobwebs from its long winter's rest. I felt like Cinderella—if Cinderella were competing in a road rally strapped into the passenger seat of an open top roadster, the wind screaming in her face.

We arrived at a place decked out for celebration. Even the flowers seemed to have come out in honour of his granddaddy's birthday, bees buzzing among them with all the excitement of flight, newly rekindled for spring. Crape Myrtle bloomed in vast abundance, violet and brilliant pink, marking the entrance to a wrought iron gateway flanked by a wall of stone stacked shoulder high.

Gossett Estate hung high above the gateway, thin streams of metal twisting one letter into the next like a flow of molten lava frozen in time by frigid winds. A gravel driveway made a ceremonious oval past the house before exiting the gateway. My eyes followed the landscape up the hillside across the carefully manicured lawn leading to tall grazing fields. Stables ranging in size from small to big-as-all-get-out dotted the grounds interspersed by a series of fence encircled training pens, the soil inside the pens dark with the mincing of thoroughbred horse manure.

We pulled up to the house to find his grandpa sitting on the front porch. He was fair skinned like August, only he'd seen even less sun. Seated beside him was a woman who initially struck me as his grandfather's caretaker based on the fact that he seemed to need caring for. That plus she was dressed too plainly for a birthday celebration. As we climbed the porch stairs, her age and relative state of care became more apparent. Only heavy dollops of rouge saved her cheeks from disappearing into the lapped contours of loosely folded skin swimming up past an invisible jawline before rippling back down her neck. Her eyebrows were drawn on in the same muted shade that painted her lips, setting off the ruby-red tip of her nose all the more.

Gram had instructed me to admire any woman who wasn't ashamed to show her flaws, principally as a way to excuse her own lack of vanity. I took to this woman instantly despite the circus clown appearance, subtle references to Gram alone sealing an inherent kinship.

Only August's grandpa seemed worse off. He smoked a chain of cigarettes, one eye squinted like the smoke afflicted that eye only. Inhaled dragon's breath till it seemed his chest might turn inside out, his lungs bulging beneath a crisp, white T-shirt. Then a trace of smoke emerged like some tiny factory was at work deep inside him, using dragon's breath to feed the twinkle in his un-squinted eye.

"You from Picayune?" he blurted out at no one in particular. I nodded, realizing I was the apparent target of his question. "I've been there. That's a place you can go to get your grits fried."

"Ain't no such thing as fried grits," Miss Estelle, as his companion was eventually introduced, interrupted, attempting to rescue me before his foolishness got into full swing.

"That's what I'm saying. Folks in Picayune so eager to please, they'll fix you something they don't want they own selves. Make you nervous all those folks running around askin' what they can do for you. Got myself out of there before I figured what they were hopin' I'd ask for."

"This is a beautiful estate," I said, attempting to sound even less impressed than I was. "Did you always have ambitions to breed horses?"

"I used to think I wanted to box. I was a fair to good fighter in my youth. It just so happens I'm a better horse trainer. Nearly won the Derby three times. Then I won it two times. Been more or less retired ever since." Gram's claims of semi-retirement sprang to mind. If only she'd had more time to enjoy the fruits of her labours.

"How long have you been in the horse business?" I meant my question as a show of polite interest, took care not to come off as prying too early in my getting to know August's people.

"Training horses is a way of life before it's any form of business." He stared at the lit end of his cigarette then blew on it to make sure it was still burning. "What you mean to ask is how I made such a living training horses—pure by accident." He let a minuscule whiff of smoke go in the direction of the far end of the porch.

"My pa used to train horses. I grew up in his footsteps. Reared more good horses than I've known bad people and I've known some folks, let me tell you." He took a long pull on his cigarette, his squinted eye held tight through to the exhale.

"Once time came to leave my daddy's house, he arranged work for me with Mr. McHenry. Mr. McHenry used to board horses though he weren't no horseman. Couldn't tell a high-stepper from a nag. But he was wise enough to surround himself with men who knew horses. Courted my daddy for years to come work on his ranch. Settled by taking me on as an apprentice instead.

"My job was to get the horses settled in for

boarding. I'd walk 'em, talk to 'em, stroke 'em between those river-glaze eyes. But I never rode 'em. My daddy taught me that much. Any animal worth taming can never truly be tamed. A horse that's broken is just that, and won't anymore be whatever you saw in him before you broke him.

"From him I learned to approach a horse the same you would any living creature—you strive for some level of mutual respect. Can't gain a horse's respect from behind his ears. Any attempt to do so would imply a level of subservience that places man above beast, a beast so strong can carry ten men yet wouldn't harm a flea. No other creature on God's green earth is as powerful and docile at the same time. But gain a horse's respect and you can harness that power in nearly any way you'd like. If that respect someday inspires your horse to run for you like he will no one else, consider yourself lucky. Making a horse run though, who doesn't choose to run on his own, should never be a trainer's aim."

"How do you bring a horse to want to run?" I asked, my initial show of polite interest giving way to legitimate curiosity.

"I teach 'em to outrun the sound of they own thunder, just like my daddy done before me."

"Let's get you inside." Miss Estelle touched his arm, hoping to put an end to his rambling. "The humidity is going to work up your angina."

"You know I don't like no bought air. I'm doing fine

right here talking story with my new friend." I felt he had befriended me. It wasn't clear why. But, still unsure about the other guests yet to arrive, I appreciated any show of familiarity.

"Any trainer worth his snuff will tell you the toughest part to training a budding racer is getting the horse used to the sound of its own kind running. This I used to my own personal advantage. A lone horse running has nothing more to contend with than the cadence of its own hooves pounding the dirt. Ya' hear it: ga-lup, ga-lup, ga-lup? Sounds almost rhythmical. Now you take a whole field of horses running, it's like man-made thunder when the field passes you by. Imagine if you were forced to run alongside all that commotion. You'd find a thunder that has no ending.

"It was never my aim to rid a horse of his fears, mind you. Instead, I worked to have him outrun the sound of the other horses beating inside his eardrums. We'd start on a track outside the normal training pen. I'd have one of the jockeys run the horse opposite the field. Have the horse pick its own pace as the rest of the field approached, all hell and damnation bearing down on him from the opposite direction. Won't be long before that horse learns the swiftest way to distance himself from the sound of thunder is to pound his hooves in the dirt and run, like he never before dared dream he could run." Visions of the horse running danced in his eyes.

"By the time that horse rejoins the field, turned in

the proper direction, outrunning the sound of thunder will have become second nature to him and you'll have an award-winning thoroughbred on your hands. Once he figures the sound of thunder is nothing to be frightened by, he'll be so much faster than the rest of the field, it won't matter he ain't scared no more." He leaned into me to keep the next part of the conversation private.

"The science behind my daddy's technique was lost on Mr. McHenry. He lacked the patience, not to mention the proper disposition, to comprehend the notion of mutual respect. He kept horses out of love for the kind of money they attract—old money, long as your arm. But money can't buy horse sense. It only buys horses." He leaned away again, returning his voice to its normal, constricted tone.

"Most of the folks who brought horses for Mr. McHenry to board didn't know a thing about respect either. Took a long time for their animals to get comfortable. But once they did, weren't no more trouble than a foal who had been reared here." He lit another cigarette with the one between his fingers.

"My big break came on a trip up north. Mr. McHenry had been at war for months with this used to be, high roller from Memphis stuck on an endless streak of bad turns and failed opportunities. Having finally hit rock bottom, he was forced to sell off most of his stable. He left this year-old colt behind as collateral while he tried to drum up the funds necessary to make good on his unpaid boarding fees. Mr. McHenry said he didn't expect to see any part of that money. Seems Mr. McHenry didn't respect human animals either, even a fellow wannabe horseman.

"Mr. McHenry tried for months to sell that colt, but didn't have the proper paperwork. Kept the horse out of spite, that plus sheer inability to dispose of it in anything other than an unseemly manner.

"I took to Sully's Debt like no horse before him. That's what Mr. McHenry called the horse, laying claim to the money Sully Kearns still owed him. Sully's Debt was pure athlete—a thoroughbred among thorough-breds. He started out ungainly and lame like most colts do, but the condition lingered in him longer than most. I took special care to look after him, given his crip-pled state and all. But once he started running, ran like lightning incarnate. But only when I was watching. How that horse loved to show off for me.

"Mr. McHenry took him on one failed outing after another before realizing I was the one could get him to run. Didn't matter what pint-sized maniac he had atop the saddle, whip in hand, peppering Sully's hind parts.

"Sully won the first race Mr. McHenry took me along to see, went all the way to Baltimore—Pimlico Race Park. I left the racetrack that day with fifty thousand dollars tucked inside my shorts, scratchin' my public hairs."

I looked over to see whether the remark had drawn

Miss Estelle's attention. Not a flutter, use of the term evidently part of Grandpa Gosset's everyday conversation. He waited for me to lean in again before resuming. "See, Mr. McHenry's distrust for humankind taught him to hand over his winnings to the lowliest person in sight, a stable boy as was the case in my situation. No one would suspect me to be carrying if we ran into trouble. Having never been to the big city, my sense of trouble was foggy at best.

"Mr. McHenry, along with one of his business associates, decided to get away from the buzz of the track. Sully's Debt had by all accounts stolen the race. No sense partying with a bunch of spoilsports. We headed toward the edge of town, believing the threat of danger would subside the further we got from the city's tall buildings and dark alleyways. Made sense at the time to a couple podunks from Alabama. Being a podunk too, I sat in the back seat of Mr. McHenry's friend's car quietly observing the scenery that passed my window, not knowing how little regard trouble had for the city limits.

"We found this little bistro—*West Side Grille*, spelt with an 'e' at the end and everything. The barkeep spoke fast like there was a gang of folks waitin' in line to place their orders behind ours. 'What you'se havin'?' Started pourin' before Mr. McHenry could get the words out good. Mr. McHenry and his associate ordered one scotch after another. I ordered me a bushel of those steamed crabs Maryland's so famous for and a cheeseburger to work up the strength to deal with those crab shells.

"Not long after my food arrived, Mr. McHenry and his friend had an entire bottle brought over for the two of them to share. I set up in a corner, spread a piece of brown paper across the table and dug in—after relieving Mr. McHenry of his pistol that is, another part of the ritual developing between Mr. McHenry and me—once he got a bottle in his hand, it was best I hold his winnings *and* his handgun.

"Just then a couple fellas entered the bar and moved directly to the back. Didn't find it odd at first. Continued with my food, rinsing the burn of Old Bay Seasoning with one too many iced-teas. Before long, I had to visit the john. But these two fellas was still back there. Didn't make me no never mind. Those fellas were out in the hallway. Besides, the bathroom door closed most way.

"On my way back to the table, I overheard them talkin' about how they were planning to rob Mr. McHenry and his friend. I could have shit a pile of nickels."

"Fiodore!" Miss Estelle shot him a look, his choice of words having after all exceeded her tolerance. "Mind your language, please."

"My apologies. To you too, dear." He gave my leg a pat, then continued with his tale.

"I found myself in the middle of a cat and mouse affair, and I'm just a block 'a cheese, rootin' for the cat. Seems these two fellas didn't recognise me and Mr. McHenry were together, my ethnicity binding me to disregard their scheming as a condition of my share in their brown skin. My knees quaked, my heart leaped to the top of my throat, the details of their plan loose in the air as I passed. I laid a twenty-dollar note on the bar to cover my tab then headed straight for the front door, never looking back at the mess of crabs I'd left uneaten.

"I thought to run, wanted more than anything to get out of that place, but my legs wouldn't carry me. I looked up and down the block for police before deciding to lay low till things blew over. I started for the alleyway when I heard the door creak open. Mr. McHenry and his friend stumbled out singing some tune contemplating what might cause one or the other of them to Go from Rags to Riches. They started toward me, joking how they'd begun to worry that I had run off with the purse. I wanted to bash in both their skulls myself before they got us all killed.

"Then it hit me. I removed Mr. McHenry's pistol from my waistband just as the door creaked open again. Saw the same two fellas step onto the sidewalk from the corner of my eye. I stuck the gun barrel between Mr. McHenry's ribs, then told him and his friend to hug the lamppost like their lives depended on it. Half-drunk plus stunned by my sudden shift in attitude, they did as they were told.

"I glanced up as the men passed. It took all my strength to steady my hand against Mr. McHenry's ribcage, but I met their stare. Looked deep into the eyes of the predator I was pretending to be, saw a flash of comprehension. Fortunate for us all, my ruse proved effective, pushing the men to look for easier prey. The closer of them nodded to me as he passed as if to say, *'Nice kill.'* I nodded to him in reply, *'Better luck next time'*."

There Went the Bride —

His story ended in a heap. Within minutes, a dozen party guests descended on the front porch to offer well wishes for Mr. Gossett's birthday. The din from their conversation pushed me inside the house where I found Miss Estelle again, seeming to have sought refuge from the crowd herself.

"That was some story," I offered as I pulled the screen door shut behind me. I was reeling from the harrowing escape his story seemed to portray, the wheels still turning inside my head to make the connection between his success in the horse business and the deed he'd done to save Mr. McHenry's hide, his own hide too.

"He'll tell you a million foolish tales if you let him." She seemed disappointed to be shut inside, cut off from the celebration taking place just a screen door away.

I took a seat next to her on the sofa facing a wall adorned by a floor to ceiling painting, a brightly coloured mishmash of vague swirls that reminded me of food—messy on a plate and deeply satisfying. We sat, pretending to be oblivious to the clamour filtering in from the front porch.

Eventually, I had to ask, "Why are you cooped up in here?"

"Oh, I can't take the heat any better than he can. The humidity works up my bursitis something awful."

She rubbed an elbow that until mention of bursitis hadn't seemed to ail her.

I understood her plight. There's something about being cast outside the familial circle that can leave you lonely, even in the midst of celebration. We sat clinging to one another like a couple castaways adrift inside the house amid a sea of merrymaking out on the front lawn. We passed the time surveying the stream of guests, Miss Estelle sparing nothing in the way of commentary as they strolled up, our whispers held safe by a closed windowpane.

Most were business associates offering warm hand-shakes while their companions feigned kisses in the direction of Grandpa Gossett's pale cheek, hanging the whole while from their escorts' arms like accessories meant to mark whatever status their men had achieved. We observed one man continually manoeuvring himself to the end of the line, hoping to greet August's grandpa uninterrupted. He bent and gripped Mr. Gossett high around the shoulders, eventually pulling his wife into their embrace.

"That's Ford McHenry and his wife, June." Miss Estelle waited for my eyes to question. "Yep, Mr. McHenry's son. He's with the State's Attorney's Office. He and Fiodore have done remarkable things for this region, creating opportunity for people who would have had none if not for their perseverance.

"They 'bout like brothers, Ford having grown up in

Fiodore's shadow. The McHenry's property backs up to this one, just over that ridge." She motioned toward a window not easy to see out from our place on the living room sofa. "They still board a few horses on the estate, though the McHenry's are no longer in the horse business." The last part she whispered like it was a matter of national security.

August's brother arrived with his bride, just returning from their honeymoon to the Florida Pan Handle. August announced the newlyweds, then offered a toast in their honour. She seemed sixteen if she was a day, pregnant to the gills and glowing at the prospect. August's brother can't have been but a year or two older though he carried himself with the demeanour of a man several years his senior.

I rejoined August on the front porch. We watched as his brother nuzzled his newborn bride. August seemed happy for him in a way he couldn't manage to be happy for himself. He talked at length about Octavius on the drive up, preparing me for the introduction. I couldn't understand why, of all people, August was most concerned with my meeting his younger brother.

"That boy was born to breed horses, is cut from the very grain those horses feed on." His words carried a deep familiarity, like he was talking about a part of himself, separate in physical form yet connected deeply to him. "I thought for a brief while I was jealous. But that can hardly have been the case. I mean, you're not supposed to envy your little brother. Besides, he and I never wanted the same thing. He'd rather twist a blade of grass between his toes out behind the stables than make his way to a corner of the world as remote as Picayune, a town full of new people brightening my day." August shot me a look from the corner of his eye that made my knees quake a little.

"What I most admire is how seamlessly he fits in with his surroundings, how easily he moves in well-conjured circles. To achieve with effort half of what he's accomplished without even trying would be remarkable. Like the first time I noticed my brother could play the piano. That he had practiced the same lessons I ducked at every turn, only now he can play. Make love to the keys and stroke your eardrums, the notes swirling around the room in physical form. But, being your little brother, he shelves his talent feeling you won't appreciate anything he's accomplished ahead of your lead, considers your pride over his own ambition. And all I can be is jealous." Octavius nodded his head in August's direction, the mutual admiration between the brothers plain to see.

"When my grandfather first took ill, everyone looked for me to step in. I gave it my best effort despite having never shown little more than passing interest in the horse trade. Eventually, it became evident that what Granddaddy needed, what the whole estate needed, is someone whose passion for the business was surpassed only by that of Granddad himself. Even our father has taken a back seat, moving to Maryland to maintain ties with the east coast tracks—by that I mean sipping cocktails with snobs who thumb their noses just as high at Alabama as he does, leaving me on my own to fill impossible shoes.

"I stayed on for a bit to serve as co-superintendent, a title manufactured to ease the embarrassment of having been bailed out by my little brother. From there, I headed straight for Picayune—well, mostly straight."

Before long, a woman appeared unaccompanied. Miss Estelle and I were back inside the house, watching from the living room window. "That's Fiodore's first wife," she explained. "She can be cordial, but we don't speak none." The woman held onto Mr. Gossett's hand a long while, said little, then turned and headed back down the front steps, conscious the whole while of us lurking behind shut glass though seeming not to care. I followed her with my eyes, as far as the closed screen door would allow, as she moved out into the yard to greet her grandsons. I suspected she wouldn't have made the party at all without them in mind.

She stayed a while longer, taking turns around the yard on each of their arms. She too was separate from the crowd, except the isolation in her case seemed to be of her choosing. Then as quickly as she had appeared, she was gone, through the crowd and into the back seat of a car left waiting at the far end of the driveway. I wished to slip my feet inside her shoes, become one with her locomotion, my arms swaying in time to her rhythm, her back so straight, shoulders proud, not looking for anyone to lean on.

I searched the crowd for August's blue eyes, but he was nowhere to be found. His grandpa was gone too, the wind having taken up residence on the front porch, keeping Mr. Gosset's chair rocking in his stead. Eventually, Miss Estelle joined me on the porch again, the condition affecting her bursitis having left the premises.

"I wonder where that goes." She gestured in the direction of August's brother fawning all over his new wife. "That overpowering urge to surround himself with her, to spend every waking moment as close to her as time and circumstance will allow. She doesn't know how good she's got it, how bad it's going to get." Her sympathy seemed directed at all mankind, not just the teenage bride who sat on the verge of making her and Mr. Fiodore great-grandparents.

"You seem to have it pretty good."

"Let me tell you, it took some doing. I used to accept things as they were, leaving me to sort out the ups and downs of the good and bad of whatever was going on between us. It wasn't until I realized I had some choice in the matter that things began to improve. Trust me, if you expect nothing of a man, nothing is what you'll get. Expect too much and even a good man trying will never measure up.

"If he loves you, he'll try his best not to hurt you, but breaking hearts is like a reflex reaction with some men. If history is any judge, you'll be made to endure a half dozen bad relationships before you even know what a good one looks like. The only hope is that your chances improve with each failed attempt. Just be careful your spirit doesn't get broken along the way. There's a whole gang of lonely people out there who just got tired of trying before they came upon a workable situation." Her eyes said all there was to tell about the depth of circumstance surrounding her seemingly simple account of fleeting romance.

"Once you find true love, it's a lifelong affliction. But keeping that love, matching actions to the level of commitment those feelings would seem to engender, is like catching raindrops with the tip of your outstretched tongue. The success rate is hit or miss. Then even the hits you get are few in relation to the amount of rain falling out there, the love you manage to hang onto small compared to that either of you has to give. Find a man who's generous with his feelings, and even that small amount of loving you will seem immense."

Eventually I caught sight of August and his grandpa leaning against a lone stretch of fence that appeared to have been placed there for the sole purpose of leaning against. They were smoking cigars August had purchased for the occasion in between sips of whiskey his grandpa had brought down from the house. Swapping stories from the looks of things, the deep creases of August's smile affecting his whole face when he laughed, the long lines of his torso rumbling beneath the crinkled fabric of his soft linen shirt.

"Look at him," Miss Estelle offered, interrupting my daydreaming. "He smiles like an athlete." I couldn't say how an athlete should smile, but understood the sentiment that only a woman in deep like can convey to another woman in deep like.

"You can judge the depth of a man's passion by how quickly his face moves from smile to frown then back to smiling again," she proceeded to explain. Just then August raised his glass in our direction, winked one of those twinkling smiles at me.

"Why has he brought you here?" Her abrupt shift put me on the defensive.

"Oh, we're just good friends."

"Honey, friends don't carry friends across state lines for their granddaddy's seventieth birthday celebration," she assured me, seeming to consider me naïve.

"I'm not one to throw stones. I consider myself lucky to have hung in long enough to see Fiodore slow down, outlasted the turmoil some men can't seem to escape in their relationships to have landed at the top of the heap. And I thank my lucky stars to be here despite the bumps and bruises my ego took along the way." The good fortune her story was meant to convey seemed hopelessly lost in the ache of buried heartbreak.

"Time heals most wounds, but the scars remain. Fiodore and I are friends as well, wonderful friends. But there was a time he left me too, the same way he left somebody to be with me. The ordeal still has me more than a bit devastated. Perhaps I'll recover before I'm dead—perhaps I will."

She seemed to be crumbling on the inside, her emotions held silent behind dry eyes. Gram had often warned that bottling your sorrow inside eventually drowns the soul, washing away your capacity to feel in a pool of unshed tears. I wished for some collection of words to comfort her, tried to recall some conversation with Gram for a single thought that might comfort either of us.

It's from Miss Estelle that I needed rescuing, a distraction from the doomed fate she seemed to predict for August and me. I reached for his hand as he climbed the porch stairs. I wanted to taste his cigar, wanted to press my mouth against his and chase the trail of spent cigar smoke with my tongue.

He pulled me in close as though able to comprehend the need percolating inside me. He wrapped his arms around my ribcage, pressed the heat from his body together with mine. Then he kissed me. Not like the time he kissed me in Picayune—too dry, too thin, like a kiss trying not to be a kiss. This time he kissed me with the warmth of all creation. It was all I had anticipated.

The smell of his skin, so fragrant from a distance, became lost among the scents of the night's escapades. The whiskey he'd drunk hit me first, filling me with surrogate intoxication. The roasted smell of smouldering cigar tobacco came next, like train smoke hanging long at the entrance to a tunnel.

As our tongues slithered deeper, the cigar smoke gave way to sweeter tastes: ice cream and cake from the birthday celebration, followed by the swallow of champagne he'd taken in toast to his granddaddy's good health—*'Here's to another year,'* he said. *'Many returns.'*

By the time we let go, we had relived all the day's events as far back as the sun-soaked drive in his roaring convertible. I can still taste that first real kiss if I hold my mouth just right, lean my tongue aside to make way for his gentle probing, long and deep inside my imagination. I count that summer's eve on his granddaddy's front porch among my fondest memories, dreams of countless days together drifting toward the heavens like threads of light smoke, twisting away from the bamboo lanterns lining the front lawn.

August and I went to bed that night separate yet bonded. I was set up in the guest room, the only bedroom on the main floor of the house. August slept upstairs alongside Fiodore and Miss Estelle, their movement evident above my head long after the house had gone dark.

I allowed my head to sink into the goose down

feathers filling my pillowcase and nestled myself in the sounds of a house settling down for the night: the rustling of sheets, the clearing of a throat that doesn't intend to speak, followed eventually by the hushed rumbling of people snoring—men snoring. When last had I gone to sleep to the sound of my daddy's snoring, any man's for that matter?

I imagined myself small inside my father's arms, small in a way that made me feel safe, not insignificant. I got that same held safe feeling inside August's arms, the pounding inside his chest thumping in time with the beating of my heart. That's the warmth I missed when I was alone at night, the friend I hoped to find each morning still content to rest beneath my bed sheets. That night I slept with the ease of a child, nothing on my mind outside a collection of butterflies flitting about a vibrant expanse of wildflowers, toy balloons floating in an endless sea of blue sky.

I was awakened the next morning by a light commotion coming out of the kitchen. I covered my nightclothes with a matching silk robe, both of which I'd inherited from my grandmother's side of the closet. I tipped over to the kitchen to find Grandpa Gossett standing over a hot stove, preparing breakfast: fluffy omelets, bacon and sausage, home fries and cheese grits. Exchanging gossip with Miss Estelle was one thing. Holding court with August's grandpa was something I hadn't prepared myself to do.

He greeted me with a boom in his voice. "Grab yourself a plate. Got some eggs 'bout ready to serve." I stood stuck to the door frame. "What, surprised to see an old man in front of the stove? I cook plenty. Can't make no scratch biscuits like Miss Estelle can, but my pancakes are legendary."

I took a seat at the bar surrounding the cook top. He dropped a platter of food in front of me piled high enough to feed a small family of elephants. Instinct told me to wait, suggested that it would be impolite to eat ahead of the rest of the family. That's when Gram's voice popped inside my head, *'How are you gonna be too polite to eat?'*

"Dig in," he told me, silencing the debate brewing inside my head. My aim was to keep my mouth full with food until somebody else ventured downstairs to divert attention from the two of us.

Mr. Gossett didn't seem to mind the silence. He deftly cracked another egg, splitting the shell between fingers and thumb, never involving the other hand. He whistled as he poured the runny mess into an egg pan, whistled the way only someone who's working can whistle. Had I whistled, my whistling would have given voice to my anxiety, would have lent body and mass to the silence looming between us.

His whistling stopped at a point I couldn't eat another bite. Still, I felt obliged to strike up conversation. I'd seen graciousness and little else carry Gram through many an awkward situation. I made my best attempt at impersonation. "I want to thank you for letting me crash your birthday party."

"The more the merrier," he responded. "I'm glad August brought you along."

"He's awfully fond of you."

"There's nothing awful about a boy being fond of his grandfather." My cheeks grew flush from my apparent misstep. "I feel the same about him. Couldn't be prouder were he my firstborn son. But then I suppose I wouldn't appreciate his talents the way I do. They say we have kids to break our hearts and grand-kids to even the score. I wouldn't change a hair on his pointy head."

Just then August entered the kitchen, winked at me, then proceeded to the other side of the breakfast bar. He massaged his granddad's shoulders, eyeing the food on the stove before helping himself to a plate. This was a man who knew how to fill a silence—by simply going about his business like whatever conversation preceded his arrival was no concern of his. "Don't let me interrupt," he joked, "unless of course you're talking about me."

"Boy, if your head gets any bigger, won't be able to fit inside this kitchen to gobble up all my food." Granddad winked at me this time, imitating his grandson. "Sleep well?"

"Indeed, I did."

"That's news to no one in this house. Could'a cut

down a whole forest of trees with all the lumber you were sawing."

"I'm surprised you could hear my snoring over yours."

"It's a well-known fact, by everybody except you it would seem, that a man can't be accused of snoring inside his own household," Mr. Gossett explained. "Must have been somebody else you heard snoring." August and his granddad turned toward me, returning the flush of red to my cheeks.

"It must have been somebody *outside* the house I heard snoring," August offered in a half-hearted attempt to come to my defence, both of them seeming to take pleasure in seeing me squirm.

"Must have been. Now eat your breakfast, Mister."

Splendid. Every moment of this trip had been absolutely splendid. With expert aim, I couldn't have thrown myself in the middle of a more spectacular dream. Gram would tell me to hold my arms open wide for everything I wished to attain and all life's bounty would eventually come my way. For the first time, I believed that was true.

I could hardly brush my teeth for all their grinning. Caught myself playing peekaboo with my washcloth when I reached to clean my face, surprised to see eyes so alive smiling back at me in the mirror. *'Girl, what's got you so happy?'* That's what Momma would have asked. But Momma wasn't there and happy was what I aimed to be.

And Never Let Go —

Soft tunes from the car radio replaced conversation on the ride back to Picayune. The roadside was bursting with colour, wildflowers blooming to show their worth. The wind tossed my hair until I could no longer make out whatever style I had attempted that morning, why I'd bothered to fix my hair in the first place.

I tried to remember a time I'd felt so free. "I bet we could fly if we set our minds to it. Not any cape wearing, super hero flying. I mean lift your arms over your head, stand on the tips of your toes, then step out on a fast moving gust of wind."

The words were out of my mouth before I could catch them, not that I was in the mood to halt anything I was feeling that day. I turned the spotlight on August before another outburst could take command of my tongue. "Tell me something a person wouldn't ordinarily know about you."

"Something about my past, something I would be embarrassed to admit having done?"

"Tell me something only someone who knows you might understand, some part of you that you'd want me to see."

"I believe the best I have to offer still lies ahead of me. That despite anything I've accomplished, I still consider myself largely undone. Tell me something you wish to have," August said, turning the spotlight back toward me.

"A crystal ball." The idea seemed silly sounded out loud. "Not to look way into the future. Seeing too far ahead might prove intimidating to the point I'd never take another step. No, I'd reserve use of my crystal ball for the closing moments, right before something is about to happen, to determine whether to move ahead or stand still. If I am to move, should I turn left or right? Should I continue straight ahead?"

"How about you?" he asked. "Tell me something a person wouldn't ordinarily know."

"I take my time with everything I do, yet I always get where I'm going."

"And do you always know where you're headed?"

"Usually not, but I never let that keep me from enjoying the sights along the way." I winked a smile at him this time.

"You're an odd mix. You know that?" My look must have indicated the need for further explanation.

"I mean it as a compliment. Anytime I look at you, I never see the same person twice. You have an easy way about you, yet your eyes are alive with an enthusiasm I only hope to match. You come across as sweet, delicate even, but look like you could toss an elephant on its ear if ever it came to that. You can be simple or sophisticated, shy or seductive depending on the circumstance thrown your way."

I told him that didn't sound much like a compliment,

but had long admired the same qualities in Gram. That I tried to emulate those qualities whenever boxed into a situation whose outcome I couldn't predict. I had been left on the outside far too long to not eventually find ways to conduct myself once the world allowed me an in. Gram used to say that no one was ever going to climb her stairs for the look of her front porch, but they would never want to leave once they'd experienced the warmth inside her home. I knew she was talking about more than her decorating style but identified with the sentiment behind her words just the same.

Gram's most powerful skill was indeed her ability to use outward appearance to whatever advantage most suited her. With the right shift in attitude, she could open herself up. But only to someone she wished to let in. Then once she let you in, it was your opportunity to lose or keep. It was never Gram's way to beg anyone for his time. She was completely content with any amount of attention shown her seeing how she had her hand on the spigot the whole while.

"You'll see soon enough. There's much more to me than meets the eye," I said, directing a shoulder shrug at the empty space between us.

An infectious grin started sideways in his mouth before spreading across his face. "You're some kind of wonderful."

"Now that sounds more like a compliment." I returned his grin with a look from the corner of my eye. "I'm every kind of wonderful, only you don't know it yet."

One of his smiles turned to frowning right in front of me. "How will I find you if ever we become disconnected?"

"What do you mean disconnected? Where will I be?"

"I can't begin to imagine where either of us will be, that's why I'm asking."

"Meaning without question you'll want to find me again?"

"Without a doubt."

With that I decided to let silence soak away the miles that lay ahead, not wanting to risk another ill-timed inquisition spoiling what had otherwise been a thoroughly remarkable time together. August, on the other hand, looked like he needed one or the other of us to whistle to break the silence between us. Yet, he too seemed to recognise how whistling would set loose his anxiety in a way that would spoil the moment.

When he eventually did speak, his upbeat mood seemed to have returned. "My grandpa was quite taken by you. That's something he and I share—a fondness for truly genuine people. Be shy if you're shy, just not shy to the point your shyness is all anybody ever knows about you. When you finally do speak, say something worth having waited to hear. There's nothing Granddad dislikes more than somebody talking for the sake of hearing his own voice in the room. Getting him talking though, about things he's seen or done in his lifetime, that's the fastest way to Granddad's heart."

"You might have shared some of this ahead of time to be certain I'd make a good impression."

"I was sure I wouldn't need to." I couldn't decide whether I found it sweet or pathetic that he could read me so easily, that he could predict how I would come across in his grandfather's eyes.

"My brother liked you, too. But he once ate a live frog thinking it would be filled with jellybeans - because of the bumpy skin and bulging eyes and all. So, his opinion doesn't count nearly as much." He let out a stifled laugh under his breath, then went back to looking like he needed to whistle.

My turn to break the silence between us: "So then, how taken are you with me?"

"To the point my jaws ache from too much grinning. Seeing your face in the morning is a wonderful start to any day. Breakfast and sunrise have little over you." I should have let the rest of the ride go by without another word, should have wished to expire in that moment as fulfilled as any one person deserved to feel.

Gram says each of us has his or her own compulsion. Mine is pressing at the edges of my good fortune to see if my upturn in circumstance is real or imagined. The greater the fortune, the more difficult my compulsion is to contain.

The thing he'd said—'*I am whatever married is*'—
visited me again with exaggerated force. I didn't more
know what it meant to be married than I had known
what it would take to raise a child until Curtis's seed
was already planted inside my belly.

Even the memory of August kissing me the other
night couldn't silence my curiosity.

"What price will I have to pay for knowing you?"
I asked.

"Who says there has to be a price to pay?"

"This is the closest I've come to flying. To land
gracefully would require I give up the flight willingly.
To crash land is my only sure fate. I only hope I survive
the fall."

"Suppose I promise to catch you if you fall?"

"Let's not make any promises you aren't prepared
to keep." His eyes seemed to understand my meaning.
Thankfully his lips knew better than to attempt a
response, resuming the silence between us. I let better
judgment prevail over my tongue as well, allowing the
car radio to carry us the rest of the way to Picayune. In
the end, I surrendered to the wind as it erased the last
traces of style from my hair, let myself fly even if I was
destined to crash land.

Last Night's Kisses

We made love for the first time in full view of a half-lit moon peering down on us from outside my grandmother's bedroom window. I never considered how something so distant could appear so enormous, how such a silent encounter could speak so directly to my soul.

He concentrated on every ounce of my being that first night like my flesh might slip away if not for his kiss, his touch, the strength of his embrace. I held onto him afterwards to keep his flesh from slipping away. I hoped his mind would stay of its own accord. I thought of the many splendid ways we might see each other in the morning as I drifted off, my back curled into his chest, of the tenderness we'd feel toward one another, the deepened knowledge we had shared. I pressed my eyes closed to hold inside the rush of emotions until I could visit those thoughts with a clearer head.

Then he was inside me again, this time more energetic than the last but still silent—like the sky giving way to the darkness of night, a half-moon providing stark contrast to judge the edges of night by, the depth and expanse of which seemed otherwise beyond comprehension. I visited that space whenever we made love, that brief glimpse at eternity where our love might last forever. Wander back to a place when my trust in him was beyond questioning, back to a time before his feelings for me needed examination in light brighter than that from a half-lit moon.

Gram claimed you could trace your entire existence with a man in the span of your first night together. How he made you feel, inside as well as out. She never told me how that feeling would persist long after he'd finished kissing me. How the feel of his hands on my skin would linger long after he'd left my side. His touch was like air—I felt self-conscious without it. Yet in the morning he wouldn't kiss me. My eyes pleaded, 'But you kissed me last night.' Eyes unable to meet mine replied, 'That was last night. Today, I can't kiss you.'

Insistent hands reached for his. 'But you'll be right back here tonight, kissing me.'

His hands wrestled free from my grip. 'Be that as it may, today I can't.'

I should have known he would leave me. Should have recognised he'd eventually decide that leaving was the right thing to do. I'd reached the same conclusion a hundred times myself. Could have easily read, had I been paying better attention, how he'd been preparing me with the most delicate choice of words for the moment we'd become disconnected. After all, what we shared, no matter how sweet and warm or life affirming, was highly contemptible by any other account.

Legs a wobblin' —

I had begun sleeping in Gram's bedroom on a regular basis, planting each heel firmly in her persona before letting up on the last. The crease of her crisp bed sheets seemed to distrust August's presence. The slant of the lampshade on her bedside table cast a disapproving glance. It was the same look Lamar gave me the next time I visited the hair salon. He claimed among his numerous talents, the ability to see a woman's disposition walk its way over from bubbling anticipation to genuine satisfaction. I turned in the direction of the most mindless conversation to keep him from asking what had me so satisfied. Not that August was with me all the time. Still, his presence was seldom far from mind.

"Why is it that you have to be married?" I asked after the next time August and I made love.

"It's not that I have to be married. I just am."

"Then how is it you love me so good, seeing how you're married?"

"A man should consider himself lucky to still have a woman by his side by the time he gains any understanding of how to love her."

Then he'd disappear again, turn the corner at the end of Gram's block, not returning until he felt comfortable lying next to me again. The better the feeling together, the longer he'd stay gone. Maybe it was the ache of being apart that sent him back to me, once being separated from me became more than he could bear. Either way, I was left on my own more often than not despite having a man who loved me in close proximity.

Detective Daugherty showed up again on one of those off days in between visits from August. He had been by to see me no less than a half-dozen times in the weeks following the death of Bunk's wife. Then his visits ceased, the trail between me and the murder investigation having gone hopelessly cold. By the time he showed up again, I had a keener sense of her dilemma, had my own Mr. Harrison on my hands, my own pile of lies coiling inside my head, a tenuous hold on the truth slipping further each day beyond my grasp.

"Miss Penny." The detective removed his hat as I pushed open the screen door. His look had grown no less stern since I'd last seen him. He had at least gained the familiarity of calling me by my own name. "I suppose you've heard the news?" he asked. "Tobias Booker's case has finally gone to trial. Bunk, I mean," he said, shaking his head to break loose the cobwebs constricting his memory. Bunk deserved as much as I did to be called by his rightful name.

Having distanced myself of late from the flow of gossip, I had to admit not having heard. "But, I thought he confessed. Why the need for a trial?"

"Oh, Bunk's fate is sealed," the detective confirmed.

"I've been tasked with working to determine what had Bunk pushed to the brink. The stories I've been told don't seem to add up. The judge has sent me to gather additional witness reports to help sort out whether there's any shared responsibility to blame, anyone else to call to account."

A lingering sadness welled up in me—for Bunk, his wife, for his older brother, Booker. But I couldn't afford to dwell on sentimentality what with the full attention of the law on my shoulders, his intent set evidently on leaning again into me. "So what concern is this of mine?"

"Just tidying up loose ends based on the testimony that's been given so far." His notepad magically reappeared. "Can you describe your relationship to Miss Thula?"

Miss Thula dismissed it when I asked about the concerns Booker had conveyed, insinuations about the role she'd played in sending his brother away. "Those are just idle ramblings of a man tormented by grief," she contended. "You can't assign much weight to anything he has to say in his present condition. Besides, who am I to send a man away from his hometown?" She placed her hands across her chest with all the virtue of a schoolgirl.

I persisted, explaining that Booker seemed to be under the impression that someone around here was supposed to help his brother—'to fix it'.

"You can't reach a man who's far enough gone to want to kill his own wife. There's no helping that kind of despair," she replied, the lie reflected in her eyes growing more crooked with each word past her lips.

Detective Daugherty repeated his question. "What's your affiliation with Miss Thula?"

"She does hair around town."

"That much I've gathered," he replied, the stern look on his face beginning to form a frown. "How much time would you say you spend in her company?"

Suddenly it felt like I was the one standing trial, my guilt implied by some untold chain of association. "Not nearly as much of late," I admitted. I had indeed slowed my visits to the hair salon. Finally having something in my life worth gossiping about, I couldn't risk a slip of the tongue giving folks in the shop any fuel to feed on. Besides, having witnessed enough backbiting to last a good little while, I didn't feel as strong an urge to seek out the kind of company I found in the shop regulars. I missed Lamar and our private talks together, tucked in close next to his station. At the same time, it was his scrutiny that I most wished to avoid, concerned he might read in my sunny disposition all that August and I had grown to be.

I elected to keep from Detective Daugherty the reason for my having curbed visits to the hair salon, preferring not to give him anything to ponder that wasn't already written down inside his notepad. "I get by there every other month or so."

He asked whether Miss Thula and I had discussed Bunk's situation. Whether she'd said anything about dealings she might have had with Coach Harrison, prior to the murder or since.

"Not that I can recall. Is she in some kind of trouble?"

"That's not my call to make. I'm just here to gather information." He closed his notepad then turned back toward me, his final question meant to be asked off the record. "Are you in any sort of trouble?"

My mind raced through a flood of random episodes, times Detective Daugherty might have spotted August and me together. Worse yet, a time he may have caught August leaving Gram's house at some ungodly hour, his face stricken with guilt. I brushed past him to open the screen door again then answered, shading my eyes beneath a loose tangle of hair. "No, sir," I said. "I'm not in any kind of trouble."

"I hope to see you keep it that way, Miss Penny. It might be best to give the hair salon a rest. Leave Miss Thula to clear her own name if ever it comes to that. Besides, a young lady as pretty as you doesn't need that much time in the beauty parlour." His stern look started to fade, any knowledge he may have held concerning August and me far from mind.

"You have a pleasant day, detective."

"You have yourself the same, Miss Penny," he

replied, letting the screen door slam shut between us. He carried his Stetson loose in one hand as he lumbered down the porch steps. He folded himself back inside his putty coloured sedan, backed the car out of Gram's driveway then eased down the block, hopefully gone from my life forever.

Round About —

August showed up on Gram's front porch one day, mid-afternoon, early for the routine we were working to establish. He seemed edgy, fidgeted with his tie for the longest while before managing to utter a single word.

He started roundabout. "Ever had a deadline, a time that you needed to finish something only to earn the chance at doing that very thing over again?" My silence indicated that I hadn't.

"I'm not talking ultimatum, a choice of this or else. I'm talking obligation, just something you were supposed to have done. Should have been doing all along." Still, I failed to follow his meaning.

He eventually cut to the chase. "See, I gotta sell two dozen sets of luggage by Tuesday after next."

"How many have you sold so far?"

"How many have you bought?" I got the gist of his dilemma but didn't understand the reason for the long-winded explanation, all his fidgeting.

"There isn't much market here for the wares I'm trying to peddle. The kind of folks to need French luggage move in different circles, horse-breeding circles." He managed to get his fidgeting under control, though the words still eluded him. "I spoke with my grandfather the other day. He suggested another trip to Birmingham. Offered to introduce me to some folks

232

who might help get that luggage sold."

I prepared myself for the invitation, rehearsed an answer inside my head so as not to come away sounding overly anxious: 'I'd be delighted,' 'It would be my pleasure.' But the invitation never came.

"I'll be back in a couple weeks. I'll call you first chance I get." Then he was gone, off to wherever he parked his little man car, on his way back to Alabama—without me.

Miss Spinnaker's voice rose inside my head. *'Certain things will break your heart but they won't succeed in killing you. You'll only wish you were dead.'* Suddenly it occurred that loving this man would eventually crush my spirit, the hurt a hundred times anything I experienced with Curtis. I liked Curtis beyond measure. That for the moment Curtis seemed to favour me made it feel like we were in love. But love was still miles ahead for either of us.

This man I wanted on first sight, from my insides out.

I showed up at the hair salon later that week, all my emotions spent, to find Miss Thula sitting alone in her vacant chair.

"What's eatin' you, Miss Penny?" She said my name long and slow, *Pen-nee*, like two separate names pushed together by a lazy tongue. "Man trouble?" My eyes trailed past her in the direction of Lamar's station. It too sat empty, his broad smile having yet to come bursting through the doorway.

I had yet to acquaint myself with the ritual of disclosing nothing but dread and misery in the hair salon. It was like the air in there contained a truth serum that only revealed itself in times of misfortune. To listen long enough to the tales of woe told above the hush of over-the-head hair dryers, you'd think men and women weren't meant to be together in the first place. Only Lamar seemed capable of holding a steady relationship. Then he had a salon full of bad experience to consult whenever things got out of sorts with his woman. That plus he never discussed his private affairs in open company.

He cautioned me privately against mixing my issues with the gossip in the hair salon. "From far enough off, your problems might seem like their problems—same soup, different spoon. The most any of them can advise is what they would have done in your shoes. But your future is brighter than they can begin to comprehend. Don't foul it up by adopting their dim outlook." For a straight man, Lamar had a sure grip on human emotion.

"How do you keep love strong?" Once again, I'd asked a question and raised a gun, everyone in Picayune careful about anyone digging too deeply into their private dealings.

"What bearing will my circumstance have on your situation?" he asked, the calm in his voice beginning to waver. "What appears right on the surface might not be all it seems. But wrong is still wrong no matter how you slice it."

"Well, I've seen wrong between two people. What you have is the closest thing to right I'll ever hope to know. All I'm asking is how to maintain what you have regardless of who's judging right from wrong."

Lamar contemplated a response, his anxieties recovering from a false alarm. "Share with your man all your worldly desires. Just make sure he's capable of at least meeting some of your needs. Then forgive him his shortcomings for any desire that goes unfulfilled."

"What do you do to stay strong?"

"I remind myself each day how small my world was without her, how bright my outlook became once she invited me in, how knowing her has opened my eyes to new possibilities. No care in the world is big enough to matter if you keep those few simple truths in mind." He put the final touches on a tucked under curl. Spun his chair around to face mine then continued, his voice lowered to keep the conversation private.

"But keep in mind, love is a two-way street. Your man too has needs. No different than a woman, he wants to be desired. Not needed like a handyman with his assortment of tools. Not even loved. For us, we find love in how much our woman appears to adore us. Even when the fires have burned down low, a man can look back on how his woman has wanted him over the years to know how much she still loves him. And, for that, he loves her even more."

Lamar was the kind of man you'd want your man to be, one who'd gotten past the notion that he had to exercise his might, to be strong in front of you all the time. The kind of man who made no apologies for his ways, refused to judge himself by what the rest of the world saw. Had learned to accept the good and bad in himself with equal compassion.

"What a man most wants from a woman is that look, that she can't get enough of him even if she tried." Miss Estelle sprang to mind, how she looked at August's grandpa, like nothing in the world mattered outside of sitting there on the front porch, her man by her side.

"To hear Miss Thula tell it, love can't help but burn itself out eventually," I said, hoping Lamar might have some light to shed on what about this notion felt so dissatisfying.

"I wish to be so lucky to stay with a woman long enough to wear out the love between us, to use it all up," he admitted. "What Thula neglected to tell you is what happens when the love is tired already, doomed from the outset. Tired love is bound to wear itself out regardless of what you do to stay strong."

On top of being the most level-headed person in the hair salon, Lamar was also Miss Thula's most accomplished stylist. You could go to Lamar with the most outlandish transformation in mind and he could get it done. Would take the notion fantasy had planted inside your imagination and make it sprout on top of your head on only the vaguest description of the look you were hoping to achieve.

I'd given up trying to figure what to do with my hair. Had begun to allow the style of my hair dictate how I wanted the world to perceive me. I took my turn in Lamar's chair determined to unearth my true, inner-self.

"What do you see when you look at me?" I asked, hoping to appeal to the person as opposed to the accomplished stylist in him.

"I see a little girl princess, looking as darling as can be." Being a man, I found Lamar far too often fell back on flattery to boost the ego of whomever he had in his chair. He erased years with his words, caused the creases around an aging smile to recede, crow's feet to disappear from around tired eyes. Rather than express his own heartfelt opinion, he told a woman what he felt she wanted to hear.

"Lamar, you can spare the sweet talk for one of your middle-aged mistresses. I'm not in here looking for flattery. Besides, I don't need to appear any younger than I already do. Tell me what you really see."

"I see a little girl who feels she has to wait on a prince to come to her rescue. I see a girl who has yet to realize the woman she might someday grow to be if she can only find the strength to rescue herself, to make herself whole whether or not she has a man in her life."

"And, how would this woman look?"

Lamar stepped away from his station, spun the chair around slowly to square me in front of him. He brushed his hand against my cheek, gathered the hair from around my face to reveal the full length of my jaw line. He studied my features like a sculptor about to do work against a massive hunk of wood. "She'd have an elegant, long neck like yours, high cheekbones, delicate ear lobes. Only she'd be bolder in her approach, would proudly show off her features. She would flaunt her elegance with quiet dignity. "

He touched my cheek again with the back of his hand as he retook his post behind the chair. Let my hair fall around my ear, his fingertips brushing my skin as he straightened the loose ends falling across my shoulders. I felt goosebumps rise on my forearms. Wished to be the woman Lamar sensed stirring inside me, lurking beneath the surface.

Unfortunately, Lamar hadn't shown up for the day, his first appointment not scheduled to arrive for another couple hours. To make matters worse, Miss Thula had already dusted off her lecture on the hopelessness of all hope before I had chance to sit down good. "Love starts out like a fire engine, red and glowing. You find yourself rushing about proclaiming, *I'm in love, I'm in love, make way for my new love.*' But love can eventually set on you like a well-cooked meal. You're grateful for the nourishment it's brought you, but who bothers to stir the pot once our stomachs are full?

"The trouble with falling in love with a man is how to keep the love after you've fallen. See, there's no continuous act of being in love. You fall in, you fall out, trying to hang on the whole time in between. It's like everything is at work except love, jerking you every way but straight. Even straight ahead will leave you on the outs despite being in love. But it's the quickest path to resolution, some ending, albeit a bitter one."

Sounded deep. To the untrained ear, it might appear Miss Thula had some real insight to share. But I'd heard this same elixir applied to every sort of ailment between woman and man where the only predictable outcome was the illusion of help to keep the crowd in the hair salon coming back for more.

I eventually elected not to wait—too many hungry eyes beginning to show up around the salon for me to consult Lamar's advice in private once he did arrive. That's when Missus Graves and her circle of hens showed up in the shop again—the venerable keeping of acrimonious housewives making their appointed rounds in Picayune.

The women piled out of Missus Graves' chalk white station wagon, smoothing the hems of their skirts like they'd driven a long way to get there. They sampled the air with their noses raised to the sky like the weather might have changed since folding themselves into Missus Graves' car on the other side of town. You'd see that car parked next to the blue-black sedan whenever she and Mr. Graves showed up in the same place together. It's like the sun had robbed her car of all its brightness then shone the left-over colour on his paint to avoid it going to waste. Lamar liked to joke that the whole of her station wagon would dissolve in a cloud of dust if it got caught out in the rain just one more time. I sincerely believed it might.

Missus Graves greeted me as I stepped through the doorway to leave, "How do?"

I detected a touch of New York slickness in her *how do*, something dimly lit, off-block menacing inside her words, meant to gauge friend or foe, to determine whether she and I were on the same or opposite sides in the world.

I returned her greeting with all the warmth of Picayune behind me, "I'm tending to mine. How are you?"

A couple hens in her circle started cackling. "Tendin' to yours, mine, and everybody else's what I hear."

Gram's most determined gaze took command of my face. "What gives you-all the right to judge me?"

Missus Graves stepped to the front of their circle. "I'm not judging you any more than you're judging me," she said. "I know what you're thinking, that I've got my head so high up in the clouds, I can't see the world around me, don't know the wrong it's done me."

I looked at her through Gram's eyes, responded to

her the way Gram might have. "I wanted things in my life, too. Have accepted that certain things may never come to be. But that doesn't change how I see myself. I have learned to love myself. With any hope, the rest of the world will follow suit."

I left those women to contemplate the same words that struck me as they fell off Lamar's tongue: *Who am I? Who can I rightfully claim to be? Who is the woman I want the world to see?*

Love-Hate, Same as Yesterday —

I headed home thinking I'd be better off soaking away my troubles in a hot bath. I was interrupted by a knock at the door before I could get the water running good. A knock I feared might come eventually.

We stared at one another, knowing and not knowing, the truth as either of us had come to believe it recoiling at the sight of the flesh and blood rendering looking us in the eye. The cosmos would not be so kind as to place August on the front step with us, his fully-married-self left on one side of the screen door to answer to his wife while his less-than-married self scrambled to clean up the mess he'd made inside.

"Is he here?" she asked.

"I'm afraid he's not," I answered.

"Don't believe for a second that I'm oblivious to what's gone on down here." She bore into me with her staring. "I get it. You want to believe that you matter. But you couldn't possibly matter to him at all in the same way that he matters to me. So, I could care less who you are. At the end of the day, all I want is to have him back home with me, to forget that anyone like you ever did exist."

I shut the door between us before the tears could get to rolling, swelled to fill my lashes before streaming down either side of my face.

I lay awake late into the night, waiting for August to return. Hours of wait became days. Days of wait became weeks. Eventually, the years slipped past.

I searched my memory for one instant, a single gesture that might still suggest he loved me. He came by one morning on his way into town. The sound of his luggage on the walkway took me back to the day I first laid eyes on him. Though we had already been intimate, his touch that day took our intimacy to new heights.

He stopped me at the doorway, pulled me to him without a single word. He focused all his attention on the shape of my face, the pout my mouth made whenever he'd been gone too long. He kissed me, his lips barely parted, each kiss planted with noted emphasis: solid, lasting, like a champion athlete might kiss the winning trophy, or a mother her newborn child.

He began slowly, my face in his hands, depositing kisses on either side of my nose. He rested his mouth especially long on the fleshy bulge defining my cheekbone before making his way back to my mouth. From there his kissing grew desperate, his teeth tugging gently at the edges of my lips: grasping, pulling, holding on. I had never been on the receiving end of such intense desire. Oh, how I believed in those kisses that this man loved me.

I saw him in town later that day. I couldn't manage to leave him alone, to maintain the quiet distance we had agreed to observe in public upon returning from his granddaddy's birthday party. The next time we kissed, he managed to hold his desperation at bay. The burn of desire was still evident, only his passion for me was less targeted, his intensity spread thin over the full expanse of my skin. I need that kind of heat, too. But I'd trade a hundred days of straight love making for another minute's time of him holding my face in his hands, covering my mouth with kisses.

I was invisible again, thrust backward into a sea of nameless faces, just another doorstep he'd darkened, a customer he'd called on as one in a long list of things to do. Miss Spinnaker said a person's spirit died a little each time her heart missed a beat. My heart stopped twice the day August disappeared. Once on its own, when his wife showed up on my front step asking to speak with him. I attempted to stop it myself later that night, focused physical strength on arresting the beating of my heart as I lay in the darkness fighting back the possibility that August might never return to me.

I cursed his name, tore to shreds every tender thing he'd ever said to me. I vowed that day to never again fall in love with a man who wasn't prepared to stand by and love me back. How I love-hate, hate-love that man.

That night, a little part of me died inside, true in form to Miss Spinnaker's old wives' tale. That small piece of hope held in reserve for my most precious desires expired, resurrecting in so bitter a form that I needed to hold my heart still to keep it from taking command over my entire being. It was the same hatred that rooted itself inside Gram the night my baby died, the same ugliness she wished to aim back at someone whether it served in bringing any relief to her suffering.

Iron Bones

I usually dream in colour. Whether that makes me lucky or unlucky depends on the kind of memory my subconscious mind has chosen to unearth on any given night. The way I see a person in my dream depends on the future that might still exist between us. Gram I see as I always knew her, only I'm aging around her like a tree trunk forming around a metal railing, like she'll always be central to my existence. I see Curtis and me stuck at the age we were when we last knew one another, believing we could make a life together. I usually don't recognise Herald until I think back on the things that occurred in my dream, things only Herald might know about me. With August, I dream that I'm lying next to him, at every age I can ever imagine reaching. I close my eyes and pretend that he's off someplace inside his head, dreaming the same dream about me, for all eternity.

I had accepted that August and I would never be together. But I hadn't counted on not ever seeing him again, never once seeing in those eyes the sorrow he must be carrying. Never receiving any word of his whereabouts or any explanation for why he left so abruptly, whether I was due one. I was left to wonder, against the most hideous shadow of doubt, what he had hoped to gain knowing full well he had somebody back home who still wanted him badly enough to show up on my doorstep and tell me as much. Why, of all people, he had done this to me?

I found comfort in the most unlikely of sources— Booker. Bunk shooting his wife wrecked summer that year, everyone around town left to make sense of what might push somebody they believed they knew to the point of taking the life of the one person he found he couldn't live without. It took the seasons changing to return any sense of normalcy, the wind turning colder, the sun spending less and less time in the sky each day, the clouds taking on an unfamiliar hue, the mind's eye having long ago buried any recollection of the onset of winter's gloom.

The roadside was littered with the colours of fall by the time I managed to put my concerns to rest about the possibility of another encounter with Booker, the haunt of seeing him push his way through the row of cypress pines, looking to accost me again, buried beneath piles of fallen leaves. I didn't mind any longer that he might approach. I'd never get any sense of what it is he wanted from me otherwise, what Gram was supposed to have done to fix his brother's situation.

I'd begun seeing Booker on a semi-regular basis driving his truck past the bus stop outside Gram's block. I hid my face the first time I saw him pass, pretending best I could that I hadn't seen him. But it's certain that he had seen me, watched me out the back window until his truck reached the next bend in the roadway. Checked for me again through the side mirror once the gentle winding of curves allowed him another view of the bench where I was seated.

With time, I found the composure to meet his gaze. Questioned with my eyes where he was headed, why he had begun passing this way with such obvious regularity. After seeing him pass countless times, invariably on his day off, it occurred that he must be on his way to visit his brother, Bunk, taking the road through Richardson on his way to the interstate.

Weeks in, after exchanging glances enough times to make approaching me outright appear less threatening, he stopped his truck in front of the bus stop. Having long ago labelled Booker harmless, just troubled is all, I was already on my feet to greet him by the time the sidewall of his front tire bumped the curb. "How's Bunk managing?" I asked, having to stoop to make eye contact through the lowered truck window.

"Why don't you ask him yourself?" He swung the truck door open, patted the seat with the flattened palm of his hand. Something moved inside me again, Gram perhaps mixed with my own muddled feelings of regret. I was in the truck beside him before I fully understood where he was taking me.

He corrected me when I asked how long a drive it was to Natchez. "Bunk isn't in Natchez any longer," he informed me. "All the death row inmates are held at Parchman Farm." The words *death row* got caught in his throat someplace, this being a phrase he would never get accustomed to repeating with any fluency.

I'm ashamed to say, but I couldn't will myself out of the truck on my first visit to the state penitentiary. Passing through that gate, the weight of all my sins bearing down on me in a way no impromptu church visit ever could evoke, church folks, much like me, still a lifetime away from standing judgment for their trans-gressions. I feared Bunk on the other hand might see straight through me, might judge me in a way, though not entirely unfair, was certainly unkind for the limited role I'd played in his despair, only learning of his strug-gles second and third hand after he'd already committed his crime.

I wasn't prepared to answer to him, to make amends for any way he might come away feeling like Gram had failed him, for the way Miss Thula had dismissed him, sent him away without the slightest thought. For the things I'd done that in any way paralleled his wife's seemingly hardhearted betrayal. Gram's spirit moving about had gotten me this far. It would take more than a feeling to get me inside to confront Bunk face-to-face.

Booker didn't stay long, having sensed my anxiety spike as we left the main road to enter the prison compound, the pavement beneath the truck giving way to loose gravel. He had accurately read the look in my eyes when he pushed open the driver's side door to see if I was planning to follow suit. Maintained an even stride as he walked through the prison doors knowing my feet wouldn't be on the worn path behind his, needing to catch up.

He drove me back to the bus stop at the end of Gram's block without a single word said between us. I stepped onto the curb before swinging the truck door shut behind me.

He waited for me to look back then asked, the lilt of a question barely registering on his tongue, "I'll see you in another week?"

"I'll see you next week," I replied, the burden of guilt resting its full weight on my chest.

On our next trip to The Farm, I managed to make it inside the visitors' waiting area but couldn't muster a single word outside of a muffled hello.

"Who's she?" Bunk asked beneath his breath, the three of us left alone in a room filled with hard to bruise surfaces, able to withstand years on end of public abuse, making it hard not to eavesdrop.

His brother put a reassuring hand on Bunk's shoulder. "That's Penny Hill, Miss Evelyn's grandbaby. She rode up here to pay you a visit." I was grateful to Booker for sparing the bit from our previous visit where fear had kept me outside in the gravel lot. Still, an eternity passed before I was safe inside the cab of Booker's truck again even though the time spent with his brother this visit was even shorter than last time around.

The next time I jumped into the truck next to Booker, the world didn't feel the same. The same shadow of guilt hung over me, but I didn't see it the same. Discovered instead a sudden ability to peer through my shame, like a light fog sent to distort my view though not meant necessarily to destroy my outlook. Even Booker's dusty old truck seemed to recognise the shift in attitude, moving up the highway with unusual ease. We'd just celebrated the Thanksgiving holiday, allowing folks to save up their visits another couple of weeks, waiting for Christmastime or New Years to take to the roadway again.

We arrived at the sign-in station early for the scheduled visiting hours. We took a seat on the hard, laminate chairs and waited for Bunk to be brought to us. It was the first time I'd seen Bunk standing, struggling to move against the weight of iron bones—elongated ligatures in steel chain shackling his ankles and wrists together before being locked tight around his midsection, intended to make any attempt at running an ill-fated endeavour.

Bunk would later talk casually about his internment, detached even. He likened those chains to an extra skeleton worn outside his clothes to remind a man sentenced to death of the fate that awaits him. He remarked to his brother how liberating it felt to break those bones after each visit before being returned to lockdown, his sense of emancipation short lived. Their visits together were bittersweet in that way. On the one hand, Bunk got to see his older brother. At the same time, he had to endure the shame of sitting across from his closest kin, chained to himself like a runaway slave.

I pushed my chair off to one side to allow the two of them a few moments' time alone. Eventually Bunk motioned me over, his two hands clasped together to quiet the movement of chains binding his waist and wrists together. He mentioned Gram, told me how sorry he was for my loss. Apologized for having offered his condolences so long after the fact.

Said he wanted to thank me for all that my grandmother had tried to do to ease his anguish. "She wouldn't allow me to hate my wife, kept me from crushing the feelings I still have left for her. She comforted me, telling me over again how certain she was that Lorraine still loved me. That love does crazy things, at times causing a person to act in a way that's hard for anyone to explain." He wrung his hands together, remorse for what he'd done pouring from every ounce of his being.

I touched a hand to his face, pressed his cheek together with mine. "I can't begin to understand how you got here, how you reached the point of doing what you did. But that's done now. There's nothing any of us can do to change that." I allowed Gram's words to channel through me. She like me would have been unable to find in her heart sufficient disregard to throw Bunk away even after what he'd done.

"I won't claim to fully comprehend the feelings your wife had left toward you. The fact that she came to Natchez shows her sincere desire to at least try, to make a clean break from whatever wrong she'd done and start over again with you. That she ultimately failed in her attempt doesn't mean she stopped loving you," I assured him. "But Gram was right. Love is a far from perfect emotion. It'll trick you, it'll fool you. It will leave you broken hearted more times than not. But that doesn't necessarily mean that love doesn't still love you."

The sound closest to my ear was full with the loose rustling of chain pulled against the weight of iron shackles as he raised a hand to touch my skin, pressed our two cheeks closer together. He told me that love still loves me too, suggesting Booker had somewhere along the way told him a good deal about my despair. I was moved by the gesture, especially given how small my worries were in comparison to his. Bunk told me that he had gotten in the habit of weighing every concern, big or small, as a way of seeking solace.

I suddenly felt at ease in his company. The even tone of his voice, the gentle touch of his hands on my skin, revealed that he had begun working to forgive himself.

At some point, Bunk had allowed anger to rule his fate, to root itself so deeply inside him that he needed to silence his most precious desire, strike it from existence to spare the pain of seeing her each day, reminding him of how much he'd lost. No one still harbouring those kinds of demons could exude such tenderness, could let go of all his emotions in the arms of a stranger, distant in relation to even his closest kin.

My cheek was wet with tears when we finally pulled away from one another, part his, part mine. Even Booker's cheek had gotten wet from clear across the room, the older of the would-be twins—one chocolate brown, the other's brown skin continuing to rub off in places—having refrained from joining in our embrace. I said an extra prayer for Bunk as the truck left the prison yard making its way back to solid blacktop, *'May God have mercy on your soul.'*

Booker and I drove the whole way back to Picayune in silence as had become our routine—he drove, his eyes lost in the distance down the roadway, while I let the world outside slip past my window, each of us lost in a blur of private emotions. The weight resting on Booker's shoulders stemmed from brother-love, the bond the two still shared, the one thing that would ultimately succeed in taking his brother from him. The source of my distress was caught in a tangle of mother-love, grandmother-love, sister-love. August.

Booker and I exchanged our customary farewells as

I stepped down from the truck, agreeing to meet again the following week.

That night I slept with the warmth of a dozen doe-eyed kittens, just days old, piled on top of one another as yet unaware how cold a place the world can be.

FOUR

FOUR

Slow Train

How long must the same lie be told before it becomes the truth, before the events surrounding the lie conspire to make the lie appear true? It's like a slow train coming. You sense its approach from miles away, measure the beat of its rumbling beneath the soles of your feet. Live for years in full knowledge of its movement, the tempo of the train's rhythm riding up and down your spine to remind you of its proximity.

Yet you elect consciously to stand firm once the lie reaches your ear, vowing to never step aside despite the weight of that train bearing down on you, the lie threatening to consume the whole of your existence. Neither do you blink or flinch, recognizing how this would give up the lie, would draw attention to all those blameless faces going around living the lie like it was gospel truth, placing you at odds with everyone to have perpetuated the lie before you.

Instead, you adopt the same unwitting stance and let that train keep rolling on you, knowing full well the power it possesses with its locomotive to crush everything you hold dear. After enough time pretending, the lie lurking behind the slow blink of your eyes turns true, claiming your existence among the shattered ruins of those to have fallen in the train's path before you. Given enough time, it may come to pass that the *real* truth, about which no one ever dare speak, never did exist.

Raising Korn

Another stranger showed up one day, his arrival in Picayune not nearly as stirring as my luggage sales-man's. He stepped inside the hair salon and announced where he was from like someone had asked the ques-tion—*Naw'lins*. His tongue grew muddier with each new use of the word: how we were the prettiest women he'd seen since leaving there, how he wouldn't get a decent meal until his return home.

A noticeable amount of time passed before anyone would acknowledge his presence. Then, without prov-ocation, he started talking, irreverent talk, talk that lacked all self-consciousness, like a wind rushing through him, the words slipping into his nostrils before whooshing past his lips with little time in between for conscious thought.

He talked like anybody or nobody might be listening. Either would suit him just fine. Started in about boiled crawfish and sewer rats followed by a lengthy discourse on the spoke rims he'd bought for his new Cadillac—not new from the looks of things, just new to him. Explained how he could just as easily have settled for the forty-eight spokes, but the ninety-sixes set off his whitewalls better.

I scanned the shop for the slightest interest in what he was saying. All eyes were bowed, everyone focusing more attention than usual on their hands and feet like the lack of eye contact might disconnect them from the sound of the stranger's babbling.

I felt some kinship toward him. It was not long ago that I too was a stranger in Picayune. I wanted to throw him a bone, an *uhuh, you don't say* to keep him from feeling estranged. But even I was struggling to find interest in his conversation.

He spent the better part of the next hour standing in the shop doorway. Split time talking about himself, his car, the clothes he was wearing, how much he had paid. His accent raised an extra tinge as he talked about the bit-off town he grew up in, especially to my New York ears. Eventually someone had to ask, "Bit-off?"

"Just a bit off the road that runs out of Naw'lins on the way to Slidell. Too small to be considered a town in its own right, so we refer to it as bit-off: a place that fits inside your mouth, small enough to chew."

With that he seemed to run out of things to say, eyed the doorway again as if contemplating a means of escape. That's when he blurted out what he had undoubtedly entered the shop that day with the sole purpose of asking: "Anybody know where I can get some fresh korn?"

I caught Lamar's eye on my second scan of the

room. Always the cynic, Lamar stood glaring, arms folded across his chest, refusing to let the assault ruminating inside his head escape his lips.

I wish I had possessed the same cynicism. Wish I had observed the same silence. "My grandma used to raise corn," I said. "That's what she tells me."

Everyone seemed startled by the sound of another voice in the room. The stranger from Naw'lins leaped at the chance for discourse. "Then she's the one I need to speak with."

Miss Thula was out from around her chair before I could explain that Gram was no longer with us. She took the stranger by the arm and led him toward the backroom where she kept all her business affairs. "Let's see if I can't help find what you're looking for. Get you on your way."

I caught wind of the stranger's cologne as he crossed the shop floor, became ensconced in his smell. Saw it wavering behind him like a spectre, a dense fog of aroma reminding you of the path he'd taken on his way across the room.

I stopped my breath as he approached, held it flat between inhale and exhale to quarantine his smell. Filled my lungs with just enough air to postpone the need to breathe again until the last trace of his smell had disappeared from the air around me. By the time Miss Thula directed the stranger to a chair in the corner of the backroom, suppressing the urge to breathe again required all my attention.

I exhaled sharply as the office door swung shut. Waited another half-second for the air surrounding me to clear before taking several long pulls of cologne free air to get myself back on the road to normal, everyday breathing.

I studied the door frame. Examined the narrow spaces the door failed in its job to fill properly, hoping in those few dust-filled columns of light to catch some sense of the conversation taking place back there. This time, unfortunately, my eyes and ears failed to connect.

The shop seemed vacant without the sound of the stranger's blathering. Suddenly I felt eyes crawling all over me, gnawing at my skin. You'd have thought from their stares that I had dropped drawers in the middle of the shop floor and blessed them all with a fully spread moon. But I couldn't figure what I had done to offend any of them.

"It ain't right enticing folks from outside the circle." Miss Bynum spoke like she was using her voice for the first time, faint like her voice might break if she applied too much force.

"Outside what circle?" I asked.

One of Miss Thula's nieces chimed in. "Girl, I told you she ain't know."

"You'all go on about your business." Miss Thula returned and broke things up before the wrong hen got to cackling, stirring things up more than they needed to be stirred, the way certain folks around the shop had a tendency to do. "Ain't nothin' none-a-y'all need to know about. Get right on off it. Ya' hear?"

I left the shop feeling I had hurt her personally. Had blundered across some invisible line and crushed all her toes.

Hand-Me-Down Ruin —

Later that afternoon, I saw Miss Thula approaching Gram's house from as far away as you could see a person approaching. Something inside my head knew she would come. I had crushed her toes, dropped drawers in the middle of her shop floor or had in some other way put the wind behind her.

I watched as she turned the corner with those long, deliberate strides, an extra giddy-up in her step. I measured the weight of the message she was on her way to deliver, her unbroken stare trained in the direction of Gram's front porch. Meanwhile, I had yet to realize the consequence of my outburst. Had yet to recognise how that tiny misstep, a mere slip of the tongue, had created the opening Miss Thula had been waiting on to relieve herself of her burden, no matter how worrisome, and leave it for me to carry in my grandmother's place.

I opened the door without her having to knock. She entered the front room without my having extended an invitation. After a few nervous laps around the coffee table, she got to talking. She always had a direct to the point, matter-of-fact way about her. What alarmed me was how congenial she started out, tender even.

"Time has come for you to fully understand what's going on in the world around you," she said. "This should be coming from your grandmother, but I suspect time ran out before she had chance to tell you.

"There are things that go on in Picayune that are hard to tell straight out, hard to take the first time you hear them. Things between folks you encounter every day, folks no different than you, except they've got this thing between 'em. Most everyone around here do.

"Mind you, what people do amongst themselves is their own private business. How they do it, how they manage to get by with it is a matter of broader concern. I can best describe it as a series of arrangements made to protect the interests of folks around town who'd prefer to know nothing about goings-on of this sort."

That's the first time I'd heard mention of the term— *arrangements*. What she meant to speak about was a series of extramarital relations conducted all over town, connecting one household to another, seemingly without end. Affairs arranged between folks who lived and worked and socialized right around the way from each other. Maintained ties to one another, intimate ties, despite a host of conventional commitments each of them had at home to keep. The arrangements were made to conceal the affairs, to keep from harming any innocent bystanders.

"So these arrangements you speak about, Gram was party to it?"

"Your grandma was responsible for keeping a record of the arrangements made, obligations that needed to be kept. This wasn't any pen and paper record, just a rough tally inside her head of who went with who,

267

when and where. Most especially she was there to ease any hurt feelings whenever a particular arrangement seemed to get out of sorts."

Unlike Miss Spinnaker, whose conversation lay riddled with an endless string of infernal pauses, Miss Thula didn't leave much time in between thoughts for me to get my head around the last thing she'd said. She kept rolling over me with her words, one Mac truck after another flattening me deeper into the pavement.

She recited countless tales of couples affected by the brush of scandal in and around Picayune. Live one place. Sleep someplace else, the whole town a giant collection of swinging doors, Gram's role in the affair to keep the wrong doors from swinging into one another. To maintain a loose schedule of arrangements to ensure that no two doors opened up on a compromising situation, a circumstance that might disturb the balance needed to sustain the arrangements taking place all over town.

But that was only the surface telling to the story, a long history of entanglement whose roots as I've since learned even predated Gram's involvement. "You might think an arrangement like this wouldn't need regulating, everyone more than willing to accept his role in the affair," Miss Thula wondered out loud. "Quite the opposite is true. A man can sleep with another man's wife easily enough. But to look into the eyes of the man who's been sleeping with his wife will just as fast turn his world inside out. Your grandma was there to prevent that from ever happening, and there to sort everyone out if ever it did."

To hear Miss Thula tell it, Gram never took part in the affairs, just provided the coordination needed to make the affairs possible. "Every so often, some previously unsuspecting mister or missus would stumble across what his or her spouse has been up to. Your grandma was called in to intervene, having inherited her daddy's easy hand in dealing with folks caught in the midst of turmoil. Her efforts were instrumental in helping maintain an air of freedom to indulge as you please with the right amount of discipline to remind us all that certain boundaries must still be observed. The whole town owes her a debt of gratitude for all she's done to keep the peace around here, pays that debt in whatever fashion is most practical."

Images of Bunk flashed inside my head, his limbs bound together by a jangling arrangement of iron bones. I saw his wife again, slumped over the wheel of her car, the sound of sweet music spilling from her head. What debt did either of them have left to repay?

I pressed my back into the hard coil springs of the sofa, folded my arms across my chest like I'd seen Lamar do earlier that day to broadcast my contempt. "Cecile was right what she said—Gram was a kept woman just by no man in particular, the people in her life little more than back scratchers eager to return some deed she'd done?"

Miss Thula shifted her weight, pressed an elbow into the arm of the chair. "Are you going to talk or are you going to listen? 'Cause I'm not about to sit up here and tell you something you aren't prepared to listen and hear." Her congenial tone started to fade. "I can only tell you the truth as I know it. I can't believe it for you. You just let me know if I'm wasting my breath in here 'cause I've got plenty else I could be doing."

She waited for a response from my side of the room then continued undeterred, my body language having failed to communicate how little interest I had left in anything she had to say.

"Like it or not, this is as much a part of you as I am a part of it. You can click your heels three times and still find yourself right back here in the middle of this conversation, needin' to hear what I'm trying to tell you."

I wished Gram was here so I could direct my thoughts at the right pair of eyes, wished for a moment to see Momma busting through the door to send Miss Thula on her way. I didn't expect her to flee Gram's house the way Miss Spinnaker had on the heels of another run in with my mother. But I wished more than anything that Miss Thula would recognise my need for her to pack up her tired conversation and leave me to sort things out on my own.

Unfortunately, I have my father's eyes, can't hide what was rumbling inside me. "Say what you're feeling,

Penny. Spill it."

"How am I supposed to feel? Walkin' around here feeling better about myself than I deserve to feel. All this messin' around the only reason I've got a roof over my head."

She resorted to her matter-of-fact ways. "Your grandma ain't need nothin' from no one, ever. Done what she did out of obligation, responsibility she needed to keep. And you're one to talk about messin' around. Laid up here all last summer with that travelin' salesman when he's as married as I am. Tell me now how you're so different than any one of us." Now my toes felt stepped on.

I decided to listen again, convinced myself that I needed to know how this thread connected me to the rest of Picayune. I felt another chasm about to open, sealing off the path I would have preferred to take had I been aware of the need to choose, my ability to predict fate woefully inadequate absent the insight Gram might have provided.

By the time she started in again, Miss Thula's talk had shifted in the direction of Gram's father. Her tale picked up where Miss Spinnaker's seemed to have left off, with my great-granddaddy renting houses to GIs returning from war, more often renting to their widows according to this more recent account.

"The war left us struggle-stretched to the thinnest collection of men Picayune has ever seen, at a time when a woman couldn't easily maintain a household alone. What your great-granddad set out to do started with the simplest of intentions. Not having enough houses to go around and little land left to build more, he resorted to pairing migrant workers up with one of the widows to sublet from, the rent usually too much to make on their own once their husbands' military benefits ran out.

"It seemed odd at first, workaday field hands living among the townsfolk who might otherwise have held themselves in higher regard. But this was a simple matter of one hand washing the other, ensuring no one went out on the streets. They might have predicted how things would turn out.

"A woman left alone can only fill her bed for so long with thoughts of a dead husband. Workaday field hand or not, a live man is better than not having any man at all. You didn't parade your man around town during daylight hours, but you held him tight each night, one makeshift cot getting far less use than the others the woman had set up in her spare room. But, as the seasons changed so did the field hands, making permanent ties difficult at best to forge."

The ends of her logic didn't seem to connect. "That only explains the despair of a few unfortunate widows. How'd the rest of the town get so tangled up?"

"It started isolated enough. But a thing like that's bound to catch fire before long. The men the widows didn't choose needed something to fill their urges. As sure as the sun will shine and on occasion a bit of rain must fall, a man needing someplace to lay his head will eventually find somebody needin' him as badly as he's needin' her, even if she's got someone at home already. Won't be long before her man's feet set to rolling, shuffling past somebody else's back step.

"Things got out of hand once the ratio of makeshift boarding houses outgrew the number of committed households this side of town. The same land your great-granddad set aside to raise corn soon became a fertile hotbed for undercover affairs, lovers changing hands month in and month out till it was never clear who belonged where. He never did get around to planting that crop. Left this earth half-hero for the many existences he helped sustain from one little piece of dirt and half ruined for the mark it left on Picayune.

"Your grandma put an end to all that mess. She came up surrounded by folks on the brink of destruction. Having witnessed her daddy's good will transformed into rampant disregard for any human commitment, how it crushed his spirit, she put folks on notice that all that door swinging was about to come to an end. Word got around pretty good once she put the first few folks out of her daddy's houses, sending them across town looking to pay twice the rent for half the accommodations."

I'd heard similar hero stories about my

great-grandpa, minus the unfortunate aftermath. Usually told by folks too young to have known him, the lore of him bigger inside their heads than his flesh and bones could have sustained had they witnessed his story firsthand.

The thought sickened me, realizations of the role our family's history had played in creating the mess left on Picayune's hands twisting knots inside my stomach. "Evidently, Gram's warnings didn't stick."

"You ain't never lied." Miss Thula acted as though we had struck some newly formed kinship, like it was okay again to be congenial.

"Half the town never managed to settle into the notion of normal pairings. Most everyone else found themselves paired with someone they wouldn't have picked had they known the lights were about to come on leaving them standing wherever they were, stuck inside a permanent situation.

"It didn't take your grandmother long to realize the only sure way to regulate this kind of goings-on was to charge for the privilege of doing it on her daddy's land. You want to lay up someplace, you'd better leave more behind than the smell of your stinking feet to cause you to think before laying your head someplace else. Don't sit up here acting like the world ought to be grateful you're spending time in it. If you find yourself in a position that paying direct would draw too much suspicion, rake a yard two blocks over, mend a fence somewhere around the way."

It would seem everyone had a role to play, each person keenly aware of the debt he had to repay. Even the women weren't without obligation. One baked, one sewed, one looked after everybody else's kids. Evidently, one did hair. I asked Miss Thula how she found herself caught up in the circle as I now understood it to be known.

"Many separate paths lead to the same destination. Some folks are born into it like you were, had no choice in the matter. Others fight the pull their whole lives but wind up here anyway despite their best intentions. You're taken by a man's broad shoulders only to realize he won't carry you anyplace. Then he's drawn to the twinkle in somebody else's eye, failing to recognise how those eyes look down on him, step on him every chance they get so they'll look better by comparison.

"Others still wind up here on their way someplace else. Set out looking for one thing to find this is the thing that suits them best. I stayed inside my marriage for years believing what I had at home would suffice. Hoping what I had to offer could stick him to me. That's when they mess you over. Once he's told you a million times how much he loves you, you don't notice after a while how bit-by-bit he begins to treat you differently. I caught on to what folks around me had been preaching—what's good for the gander, the goose may as well go ahead and try."

"And you don't wonder none what he's been up to, where he goes at night?"

"You cook and clean for a man, wash his dirty drawers, and there's not a whole lot left to wonder about him."

I used to keep Miss Thula separate from the rest of the women around the shop. I pitied her for reasons separate from the reasons I pitied them. Her story was no less sad. But she kept the sordid details of her heartache locked deep inside herself, took more pride than to air all her business in the hair salon. Now even the veneer of self-respect was beginning to wear off.

"How can you claim to love a person then not care where he goes at night?" I asked.

"Loving someone has got little, if anything, to do with the fairy tale notion of living happily ever after with that person. I made the mistake of believing love is all it takes, that love can conquer all even when love doesn't treat you like he loves you anymore. Countless stars must align for anyone being in love to wind up staying in love, 'til death do you both in forever."

Her talk brought to mind Miss Estelle's endless stories of despair, the doomed fate she rightly predicted for August and me. They had both evidently reached the age where the vast difficulty of things began to outweigh the meagre possibility that anything would work out in their lives the way they had hoped. I wished to never reach the age where anything in life worth having seemed better off doing without.

"Seeing the possibility of wedded bliss dangling hopelessly outside my reach, I set my sights on attaining happiness in shorter stints—weeks and not years, hours and not days. Focused all my happiness on those fleeting moments when you close your eyes hoping he'll kiss you again. I ain't felt messed over since."

I could still at times close my eyes to feel August kissing me. He would start out pretending he didn't intend to kiss me when we both knew full well that eventually he would. But I couldn't afford to stand there in front of Miss Thula, my eyes closed waiting to feel August kissing me again, the brush of his cheek warm against mine. She'd think I'd gone soft in the head.

Before she left, she told me to rest on what she'd said, give myself a chance to get right with things before deciding what course to take. I had yet to contemplate the scope of responsibility my new-found insight seemed to heap on me. My spirit took leave of my body again, eased across the room, peering back at the person I used to be—unwashed, wallowing in the filth of my own ignorance. I wanted to disappear inside myself, to flee arms flailing above my head to the innocence I'd once known. But, short of losing my mind all together, innocence once lost is seldom regained.

Mouth, Eyes, Nose

Here's the thing about secrets. The more you amass, the easier they become to keep, one secret piling on top of the other until the whole lot of them is immovable, like stones packed into the riverbed as time passes you by. The first little lie you tell gnaws at you. You suspect everyone has caught on to the lie, is able to read every thought to cross your mind. Every smile you offer wants to tell the lie, every frown to utter a confession.

The biggest lie I ever told was that I had stopped loving my mother. I told myself I had stopped, knowing full well that I had kept on loving her. Loved her the way a reluctant smile turns to greet the first blush of sunshine, warms to her touch, smiling at the vague recollection of sun-shiny days. I loved her even after she turned her back on me, cast me from her home to live out in the world. She couldn't have known my grandma would die so shortly after placing me in her care. Still, she shouldn't have put responsibility for my upbringing on my grandmother's shoulders, shouldn't have tasked her with taking me on. I was her burden to keep, her daughter to raise. And still I loved her, even as the lie cut loose inside my head, masquerading as though I never had a mother.

Then again a lie is not like a secret. A lie is something you tell, a secret something you hold deep inside your subconscious mind.

My big secret was that I slept with a man, not a boy in my class, not a lover, not my best friend from back home. A man I let have me for no better reason than to feel like somebody wanted me. Not a strange man, but still someone whose acquaintance I might not otherwise have expected to make. That my mother had conducted herself in a similar manner, had lain down with a man, given herself away in an effort to feel wanted, offered little consolation. I watched our paths crisscross on one another, my way in life plagued by the same snags she found impossible to escape. And still I let the lie spill from my tongue as I worked to convince myself that I didn't love her anymore, that I no longer needed her to be my mother.

Overages —

I avoided the hair salon the next several weekends. For me, it represented the worst kind of deception. The shop sat alone at the centre of one gigantic conspiracy meant to keep me at the butt of everyone's joke. The folks in the hair salon weren't sole proprietors of the joke hanging over my head, but they had befriended me, grinned in my face each day knowing I was their fool anytime they needed someone to gossip behind.

Shame soon gave way to curiosity. I took to the streets again. Set out to test the bounds of responsibility Gram's departure seemed to have left me with. Nothing was any longer as it seemed. Each new face I encountered revealed another secret. Each secret revealed begged another question. And most especially—no longer was I invisible.

Nobody walked the streets at night. No phony names were given at cheap motels. Children went to school each day, yards were kept, church choirs continued to sing. The only evidence of strange happenings around town was the string of overages exchanged on top of everyday transactions. But you needed to watch carefully to see it.

You witnessed someone purchase an extra loaf of bread at the market, two cartons of eggs. One parcel he took with him, the other set aside to be delivered someplace else. Then you saw the same few cars pass the full-service pump two and three times a week. Pay over and over to fill a tank that, for a stretch of road just long enough to make a bus ride through town worthwhile, ought to still be full.

The cashier knew, the box boy knew. I suspect many of the store patrons knew as well, but nobody batted an eye. You were either in the circle, decidedly on the outside, or highly oblivious to the arrangements going on beneath your nose. I wished I could return to being oblivious—an act no simpler than making the wind blow in the opposite direction, the river to flow back on itself, turning upstream to down in the blink of an eye.

I made the grand mistake of consulting Miss Spinnaker, thinking she'd have some sense of the hornets' nest I'd gotten myself into. "Get over the fool notion they've been feeding you that folks around town don't know what's going on," she growled. "This town ain't bigger than nothing. How are we not gonna know?

"I knew all along. Felt him slipping further from me with each lazy excuse offered in response to yet another broken promise, watched him grow more distant with each day that passed where he wasn't by my side," she grieved. "But I never wanted him in the first place. Stayed with him seeing how it's easier to have a man you don't want than to lay up here pining away for someone you never could possess." This I took to mean she was decidedly on the outside, wouldn't have taken part had the opportunity presented itself.

Having been separate from August a good little while, talk began to resonate of little worth in a man who won't stand by you. That after all, something had to be better than nothing. In the end, what I got was sorely less than nothing.

Affliction —

One of Miss Thula's nieces entered the shop one day in a fluster. She had a date to keep, but her real man, daddy to the babies she was hoping to have someday, was scheduled to return early from a job down in Houston. Erecting oil rigs off the coast of Texas while Sharaine was back in Picayune, raising korn.

Sharaine's man didn't know a thing about what she'd been doing to fill the time. She wanted to keep it that way if she could. And her date didn't know she had a steady man who was about to bump him from the spot he'd held twice weekly since her man left town. Two separate lies set on a collision course right outside Sharaine's bedroom window.

In the middle of the shop floor, with all those lurking eyes, I refused Sharaine's offer to have me stand in for her, shrugged off her suggestion that I might enjoy myself, that I was just his type. I tracked her down once outside, my regard for what curiosity had done to the cat hazy at this point in my life, though I had yet to admit to anyone in the shop, Lamar especially, that I'd gone through with it. I couldn't take the look he inevitably cast on most everyone who frequented the hair salon, wished to maintain in his eyes my set aside status even if it was a lie.

Sharaine hugged me like I'd saved her life when I finally

caught up with her a safe distance from the shop's front entrance. She launched headlong into how the evening was to unfold. Her date, heir to a vast shipping legacy, was a college professor. He returned each summer to spend the school break at his family's holiday retreat on the north side of town. She couldn't impress on me enough how particular he was. I had to dress just so, act just so, and, above all else, arrive promptly at the time requested.

I set out on my way after receiving word from Sharaine that her date was all right with my taking her place. The sky was lined in gray velour, its surface brushed this way and that so no two parts of a cloud appeared the same. Every once in a while, the moon would poke through, a vague sliver of light that came and went with each new shift in the swirling cloud cover.

His house sat on a lonesome hilltop, his family's history of success isolating their home from the rest of Picayune. I followed the instructions Sharaine had given and let myself in. I climbed the stairs to his bedroom, first door on the left, knocked once before entering, then closed the door behind me.

He waited for silence to settle in the room before attempting to speak. "Did you find it alright?" His house or the bedroom, I wasn't certain. Either way, the answer was yes, I had found it alright.

"Come, I want to look at you." That was the point,

had I been a guest, he would have invited me to sit, would have offered some refreshment, engaged me in a bit of small talk. I would have inquired about his family, how he was enjoying his summer. He'd eventually get around to asking about my day, how I was feeling. Somehow this small exchange would succeed in lessening my anxieties, would ease my shame at having been placed in unfeeling hands to conceal somebody else's wrong deed.

In the end, I wasn't a guest. The purpose of my presence in his family's household was clear, my flesh and blood offered in exchange for a few gallons of gasoline, an extra loaf of bread. Every other aspect of my being left outside his doorway to await my return to more mundane circumstances, as close to oblivion as I would ever hope to come again.

He emerged from the shadows darkening the corner of the room to meet me at the foot of the bed. Not especially tall, not especially good looking. When I replay this instant inside my head, he looked like any man I've ever encountered—*mouth, eyes, nose*. Nothing off-putting. Nothing extraordinary either. And an incessant movement of hands. Hands that couldn't seem to hold still yet didn't know how to touch me either.

He set my overcoat on the bed then proceeded to undress me without the slightest thought as to whether this was okay by me. He wrestled my dress over my head then began tugging at my undergarments, pausing with a pat and a squeeze to examine each new bit of flesh left revealed by the last article of clothing. I wanted to squirm away, to fit myself into a corner of the room and wait for him to grow tired of me. But that's when the realization took hold: I had already conceded nearly anything he would have me do by simply walking through that doorway.

I turned my skin to glass so his touch wouldn't leave an imprint. Sealed off my senses best I could so his smell wouldn't smudge my memory of more pristine encounters. Somehow, I couldn't see his eyes—in the right place yet entirely the wrong colour. In my dream, he doesn't have eyes, sees me instead with the backs of his hands, his palms, his fingertips. Sees me like a blind man sees, the surface of my glass skin walled off to his touch.

When he enters me, I become the room. Leave my body all together to test the view from behind the drapes, from inside the wall sconce, through slats of wood framed to form the closet door. I see him full inside me, his face and lips and eyes pressed against the walls of my glass skin, bulbous and grotesque in places where the contours of my body curve outward, and stretched vapour thin in places where my curves go the other way.

This is where I leave him. Each time I dream the dream, it ends with him motionless inside me, neither of us more than scarcely aware of the other's existence.

I returned from the dream to hear his breathing

growing heavy inside my ear, the weight of his pushing more insistent. I imagined the huffing noises coming from deep inside his throat were the chug of a train sounding off in the distance. I closed my eyes and waited for its whistle to blow.

Afterwards, I lay still in the darkness not wishing to speak. He seemed struck by the same affliction. In another moment's time, I would be back on the street defying every basic instinct to remain inside whichever arms would have me. I was pushed outside by the sober realization that the more shallow reaches of a man's being lord over his desires. And once those desires have been spent, the arms generally let go.

The clouds had taken on the consistency of apple butter by the time I began my descent from the hilltop—deep copper brown and thick with contour-adding weight to the sinking feeling welling up inside me. I thought about August on the walk home. Images of his blue eyes slipped from my memory, teasing my consciousness. I wished to study the creases in his smile, see what kind of sun he's endured. To look into those blue eyes and see how much they had missed me, how much longer I'd be missing him.

False Truths —

I should have heeded Detective Daugherty's words: *give the hair salon a rest, let things sort themselves out.* Now, I'm the one in trouble. Initially, I baulked upon hearing the family name, upon learning from the name that it was not one of us but the other whose company I was to keep when I'd never spoken more than a passing word to any white man. Sharaine assured me we're all the same under the cover of darkness. Black is still black and anything short of black falls near enough black to be considered black itself—another false truth untold.

Had I reminded him of someone, somebody he once knew, his advances might have been more tender. It wouldn't be me he was making love to but at least there'd be love in the room. Had his approach been less detached, I could have traced the encounter back to something I'd experienced with Curtis, anything August and I had shared. But even August's cream coffee brown was black as night compared to the harsh, trembling ways I experienced love making that night in a stark room alone on the hilltop.

I thought of Gram taking the reins under similar circumstances, standing wobbly legged inside her daddy's shoes, only a faint ghost of explanation to guide her. Had she tripped on the same crack in the sidewalk, hiccuped the way I had trying to gain her footing?

I am Gram tonight asleep inside her bed, her flat gray eyes burning beneath my closed lids, trying one last time to peer out at the world. Companionship at the hands of a stranger comes at too high a cost. Relationships I'd prefer to keep lost in the exchange of overages between folks whose separate lives just happen to exist in close enough proximity to make co-mingling the way they do plausible, necessary even if you believe the likes of Miss Thula and her nieces. My need to share a deeper connection with one special someone cast hopelessly outside the circle, an inevitable casualty of everything loose and easy and seemingly wrong about the goings-on in Picayune.

The next day, the sky went on a day long drunk. Endless rain poured through clouds already heavy with moisture. Pissing in its own beer is how my daddy would have described it had he been there. Then right at the bitter end, just before the sky went dark, the sun staggered in and made a half-hearted appearance through a haze of mist and fog, the clouds raining toward heaven and earth in both directions at once.

The sun blinked a blood-soaked eye down from the heavens, colouring the sky just long enough to let everybody know it had been there, that the sun hadn't been entirely derelict in its duties. Then it slid beneath the clouds again, back into its drunken stupor, the last bits of lingering glow disappearing among a distant band of trees, a silhouette of their towering trunks cast in stark contrast along the horizon.

Love Gone —

Miss Thula's birthday came and went without the slightest flutter of change in the daily routine around the hair salon. It fell on a Thursday. I didn't know her birthday had come until it had passed already. Till things in the shop had slowed to the point Cecile and Sharaine needed to call on the inauspicious events surrounding the passing of their aunt's birthday for amusement.

"Where'd he take you?" Cecile started in first, always minding somebody else's business.

"He didn't need to take me anyplace. We stayed in."

"He cooked for you then?" Sharaine's turn to stir the pot, a stifled laugh half choking her words.

"I heated up something he had in the fridge."

"You mean to tell me he fed you a TV dinner?" Sharaine and Cecile had the whole room on the verge of busting at this point.

"It won't no TV dinner. We ate leftovers from earlier in the week."

"Leftovers? And on top of that, you had to fix 'em. On your birthday."

"Ain't that a shame?" Miss Thula was the one who got to laughing first, put the punchline on her own joke. Lit the already burnt candle on her own birthday cake.

My birthday had come and gone too, several times over without notice. Then this past year, I went out to the front room to find flowers stuck inside the frame of my screen door. August—had to have been. Or some-body he'd sent to stick flowers inside my doorway. Calla lilies cut fresh, still firm with the fullness of life. But just that. No note, no card. No *how you do*.

A regular ring the bell and run. 'Who's there?' *'Love gone.'* 'Gone where?' I continued to press. I reached the front porch to find no one standing in August's place. Even the echo of a doorbell ringing had faded into the still afternoon air. Just two white lilies, their delicate heads pressed against the screen to say he'd been here, that my bell had been rung.

Pretty as those flowers were, as much as they acknowledged his connection to me, I didn't want acknowledgment. I wanted him, the real of him. I'd gotten past the idea of having him and not having him in the same breath. Had survived the urge to bust in on whatever he calls his life away from here, and drag him back to Picayune. Force him to choose, standing on his granddaddy's front porch—me or her, forever and ever more. No turning back this time to check on the choice you've made, both of us held in limbo while you and your decision blow in the wind.

"Why are you-all so set on being miserable?" Once again, I'd interrupted their monkey shine, bringing the shop floor to an abrupt silence. "Surrounding yourself with bits and pieces of a man that swept together still don't amount to anything worth having. Sittin' up in some other woman's house, eating her leftovers then

292

complaining how her man didn't take you anyplace. The whole bunch-of-y'all are pitiful."

I wished I hadn't started my tirade seated so far from the doorway. Didn't trust my ability to cross the shop floor, my legs trembling from years of ache, self-pity, loathing. I paused in front of Lamar's chair, took his hand in mine. Apologised without saying a word for all the lies I'd told in there, begged his forgiveness for all the things I said I hadn't done knowing full well that I had.

I left without acknowledging another soul. Went home to Gram's house and cried a river of blues into my pillow. Welled up a lifetime of sad songs then let them spill all over me, except none of those songs escaped to fill the room. They drowned my pillow but the room stayed silent. Eventually I fell silent too, alone again inside my grandmother's bedroom.

Silent Stir

I slept away the whole next day. I awoke in time to catch the sky settling down for the night. The sky looked like the sun had touched down on the backside of the earth and burst into a trillion tiny pieces. A persistent wind swept the flaming debris back across the sky, a reddish glow lingering along the horizon long after the last bit of sun had disappeared.

At long last this day had come to an end. The kind of day that leaves you in a heap, sleep calling to you as the last fragments of broken sun burned themselves out—if you could sleep. Me and sleep had again found ourselves on uneasy terms. On nights I was able to sleep, my dreams were haunted by one episode after another filled with countless human frailties sent to remind us that death is not an altogether bad thing. Most things we want in life we'll never possess. So much of what we have will eventually prove impossible to keep.

I was invariably shaken from my dream by an especially startling realization that things could still get worse, the ache I was struggling to endure a preview of things to come, callisthenics for the soul, meant to build my endurance as years more ache pile on. I would

be Miss Thula before long, Miss Spinnaker, with no
memory in life outside of the pain it had caused me. I'd
be my grandmother soon enough, dead inside a box, a
lifetime of untold regret lying in my wake.

Flesh and Bones —

I decided to take a bath before retiring again for the night, before lying in my grandmother's bed trying to coax myself back to sleep. I filled the tub halfway, letting my flesh and bones take the water to two-thirds full. I added doses of hot water over the course of the next hour as my skin grew used to the dissipating heat.

I got out once the tub reached the brink of over-flowing, threatening to douse the tile floor with splashes of lukewarm water. I could have let the drain out to make room for more heat, but that was one of Gram's superstitions: filling the tub while water drains out the other end is tantamount to tempting fate with the devil, heaven and hell coming face-to-face sloshing around the hollow bottom of a half-filled tub.

I thought about Herald as I smoothed cocoa butter over my skin, again wished to turn myself invisible. I prepared myself for a few solid weeks' depression. A singular loss was at the root of my pain—August. It didn't matter how folks around me chose to spend their time, even if sorting out their mess was my legacy to carry. It mattered only that the one thing left in life I truly wanted had turned to dust, as much ghost to me as Gram or my dead baby.

That's when the letter came, news from New York that my mother was ill. Had been for some time according to my sisters. Only she was sicker than they believed when they first decided to keep her illness a secret from me.

Knowing how stubborn my mother could be, I pictured Edelyn and Champayne having to drag her forcibly to the clinic, my mother scratching and clawing the whole way. She should have been thankful for their insistence. What started as a persistent cough lingered longer than made sense for any ordinary virus. Her prolonged listlessness was what eventually pricked the doctor's interest. A series of tests eventually yielded a proper diagnosis: hepatitis, contracted from some of the company she'd been keeping. I should go home.

I deliberated a half-second before recognizing this was an obligation I needed to fulfil. Dismissed and overlooked as continued to be the case, I was still her firstborn child. And she the only mother I was going to know. I called on Mr. Graves to arrange transportation. Certain things were still beyond my reach despite the bounty of overages afforded me in Picayune.

Blind Cats

Thoughts of home brought to mind an old nursery rhyme, usually told from the perspective of the farmer's wife. What would have happened had the mice in that story been born cats, better able to guard their tails, setting my sisters and me on a path separate from the one we're on today?

Folks called me shy. My sister Edelyn would have to come out of her shell several notches to even be considered shy. She was a shell, a cardboard cutout of a child meant to validate some aspect of my mother's determination to control everything in her midst even if she needed to defy all practical consideration to do it.

I believe she had me to thumb her nose at the world. To prove that she could—have me that is. What to do with me once I'd been had never entered the equation. When I was born not speaking, she pushed another baby into the world, a thin-skinned mannequin who, though able to speak, wouldn't know what to say unless somebody scripted it for her.

Champayne was born under similar circumstances— *look what good I've done now*. Only trouble is no one was watching, except for Gram of course who I believe loved us like no one else could. But Gram's opinion couldn't have mattered less were she and Momma complete strangers living at opposite ends of the earth.

I wonder how things might have turned out had Momma seen fit to stay, had she found some way to squeeze down her ambitions to the short list of possibilities Picayune has to offer. We'd all be from here then, raised here, mother and daddy living underneath the same roof.

Instead she drug herself off to New York then had us bit-by-drop, hoping to anchor our father's attention with the promise of new life. But that's a caged bird if ever there was one. He'd vacate the premises for months on end, returning with each birth. He and Momma would manage to hold things together just long enough to start another baby coming. Then he'd slip away again, back to a world of simpler ties, a life of fewer obligations.

That Momma and Daddy never married only added to the turmoil surrounding our circumstance, their relationship a simple means to an end, only different ends. Daddy needed Momma's help to get him on the path to New York, and she needed his support to stay there, would have had to swallow too much pride returning to Mississippi without him, living by the hem of her skirt, all of us on her back. Instead, she'd send one of us home whenever the burden became too much to bear, her pride suffering only a partial defeat.

Edelyn had already passed the age where I was sent away. She would be gone soon, too. Meanwhile, Champayne was by all accounts fast shaping herself into the same kind of misery Momma seemed to thrive on. Daddy once accused her of being stubborn as a fire plug—half the height yet twice as hard. He joked that if she weren't his own child, he'd paint her yellow and set her out on the sidewalk. Momma warned that if ever he laid a hand on her, he'd understand soon enough whose child she was—hers before his without question. (If asked to complete the survey, I suppose I belonged to him first. Edelyn they shared in equal proportion.)

Like Momma, nothing anyone ever did was good enough for Champayne yet she kept on asking, never willing to relax her expectations. And we succeeded in disappointing her at every turn, securing in her mind something she was loath to knowabout us.

There were times when my chief complaint was no more serious than Momma having failed to pick up the kind of cereal I liked. For never bothering to shake the box to see whether I had run out. After all, my cereal wasn't her cereal. And as long as we had plenty left of the brand she and my sisters liked, it didn't matter that I had run out. Other times, my disappointment was more pronounced.

But we can't pick fate. None of us can sift through the intricate turn of events that led to us being there, discarding all but those details we wish to build our history around. With the right shift in circumstance, we might not be there, fate and past circumstance colliding in a way that erases us all together.

Had my baby lived, there would be a natural procession of family back and forth from Picayune. The first trip to celebrate her birth, introduce her to her grandpa, followed by summer breaks spent with her aunties, then one grand reunion to celebrate her commencement from high school, her wedding ceremony, the births of my grand-babies. But I'm getting well ahead of myself. She would barely be through middle school at this point, no more woman than I believed I was the year she was conceived.

I sat contemplating what I might do with a nearly full-grown child, whether I'd ever get to hold a baby in my arms. Had a baby been born into this world (and not the next), perhaps the mother in me might have afforded a better understanding of my momma. Might have inspired the grandmother in her to consider how over the years she had disrupted my world, dedication to a shared task mending the broken line between us.

I tried to imagine my mother pregnant, her stingy flesh swelling to sustain another existence. I didn't see that in her, couldn't imagine her giving of herself in that way, though my sisters and I are living proof that she had, three times over.

Used-to-dos —

You don't realize how far you've come until you find yourself back home. Gram used to say that with three pebbles she could trace her entire existence on this earth. I needed only two: one for New York, the other for Picayune, my existence in either place spanning half my lifetime.

I returned to a jumble of unfamiliar cues cast against a smattering of vaguely recognizable background details. It was like someone had taken up the block to dust then failed to return everything to its original position. Anything I thought I remembered stood slightly off centre. Nothing different enough that I didn't recognise where I was. Still I felt lost.

That's when I came upon Businessman Bill, one of Morningside Heights' most recognizable icons. Though fully grown from my earliest recollection of him, Bill possessed the mentality of a child. Muddle-headed is how people described him. He had no obvious ties to the neighbourhood, no family to speak of. Yet, he'd turn up each morning, fresh off a bus from someplace, prepared to spend the day on our block tending his business.

But Bill was businessman only inside his own head. He earned the nickname on account of his attire: shorts and a T-shirt, high-top sneakers and black dress socks. And never was he without his briefcase, a beat-up black thing nearly rubbed through to the core at the edges. If the outfit weren't enough, Bill walked in an exaggerated skip-run, one knee locked stiff, his body turned slightly so that one foot never advanced ahead of the rest of his body. Like only half of him knew where it was heading and the other half was refusing to go.

Bill cruised up and down the block for the better part of a day, stopping occasionally to look inside his briefcase. Whether to check on its contents or to make sure the briefcase was still empty only Bill can say for certain. Then he would continue on his way only stopping again to explain his situation to the occasional passerby, seemingly in a trance, stuttering and stammering the whole while.

'Meeting. Must go. Late... Late. Meeting. Must go.' After the third or fourth rendition, you got that he was running late for a meeting. He'd stopped to pay you the courtesy of explaining why he was in such a hurry. At the root of his stammering was a simple social grace practiced at all levels of society—pretending to be in a rush to curtail any human contact. Though deep down you could tell Bill had only stopped to let somebody know where he was, to feel for a minute that he was not alone in the world, that anybody cared.

"Okay, Bill," I said, issuing a standard response. "We'll see you again real soon." Those few words succeeded in releasing Bill from his trance, sending him on his way. That he chose to engage me could only mean Bill remembered me—he would never have approached a face he didn't recognise as belonging to the neighbourhood. To his mind, I may never have left, might have grown up underneath his nose while he was away in a meeting, tending to his business.

Seeing Bill again reminded me of used-to-dos. I used to draw all the time, mostly on the sidewalk outside our building. I'd take a few coloured pieces of chalk and transform one concrete square after another into an entire village scene, raised in profile like you were seeing it in 3-D.

I closed my eyes and listened for the sound of girls my age jumping double-Dutch beside me as I drew, clapping hands with one another in sing-song unison:

> *Miss Mary Mack, Mack, Mack;*
> *All dressed in black, black, black;*
> *With silver buttons, buttons, buttons;*
> *All down her back, back, back.*
> *She jumped so high, high, high;*
> *She touched the sky, sky, sky.*
> *She didn't come down, down, down;*
> *'Til the Fourth of July, -ly, -ly.*

Eventually a group of boys would shuffle past, stickball and bat in hand if not dribbling a bouncing basketball. Without breaking stride, they'd step out into the street to avoid smudging my artwork with their high-top sneakers.

That's the only time people seemed to tolerate my strangeness, when I was outside their window creating a replica world on the sidewalk. The whole block looked on in fascination as I bent a new line into an already elaborate arrangement of cars and buildings, people intermingling in a scene reminiscent of the one surrounding my chalk mark creation.

But I lived a nightmare on this block, too. I can still feel the chill Momma's words raised up my spine—*'keep your fast behind away from around those boys'*. Nothing about me was fast. How could my behind have had any speed?

In the weeks before I was sent away, a creep plagued our block, lurking at night, peeping inside shop windows. It wasn't long before the creep was given a name: *Midnight Marauder*, on account of his only lurking after dark. With all the neighbourhood kids having to be inside before the streetlights came on, anything much past dusk may as well have been midnight.

I don't know how long he had been stalking me. How many nights he stood outside my window, watching me undress, watching me sleep! I might never have known he was watching me if not for the old China-man down the block who happened upon the marauder one evening crouched beside my bedroom window touching himself, his baggy sweat pants rolled down around his ankles. The thought still crawls my skin.

It turned out to be just another of the neighbourhood kids, a pint-sized teenager sent to spend summers with the grandmother on his father's side. I wished it had been a stranger. A stranger would be called to stand judgment for his crime. One of the neighbourhood kids being caught, on the other hand, was the source of all-around embarrassment. But, beyond the initial humiliation, the boy was never made to suffer.

By daybreak the next morning, he was already on his way to rejoin his family in Ohio. His grandmother never came around to apologize. Even the China-man's heroics weren't celebrated in the fashion I thought was deserved. Meanwhile, I was shipped off to Picayune, as far from family as I could imagine being. I still at times feel that way in Picayune, like we'll never truly be family. Other times, I feel more at home there than I do standing on the same block that raised me.

I longed for a piece of chalk. Thought about the scene I might draw today: two squares of concrete separated by a narrow bridge connecting Morningside to Picayune. I'd plant a bare foot in each square then spin myself around to twist my two worlds into one, make a whole existence out of two half-lives spent at opposite ends of the universe.

Long Lost —

Champayne appeared from around the corner as I returned from my nightmare, sped past me on tiny wheels that emerged from the soles of her sneakers, nearly knocking me into the street. She stopped at the steps of our building, resting on the un-wheeled part of her feet. She seemed to know who I was just not what I was: visitor, long lost, or runaway fugitive. I didn't know how to take this visit either, like a parolee returning to shake the rails of her former detainment. I tried to work my face into a smile as I started toward her but my mouth puckered in protest, unsure what emotion to portray.

She eased in the opposite direction as I drew closer, the tiny wheels seeming to emerge from her sneakers on command. Then, just like that, she disappeared around the next block. It's like I'd seen her and not seen her in between blinks of my eye. I stood at the foot of the steps wondering whether I should go up without her. That's when she peered out from around the corner. Stood to be certain she had my attention before darting off again. Eventually, I realized she meant for me to follow her.

It hadn't occurred to me that they might have moved. I fully expected the whole of their existence to have stood stock still while I was away in Picayune. I left Momma playing building superintendent, taking up the slack Daddy left behind in order to maintain the break in rent he'd negotiated once word got around that the former super was planning to retire and move back to North Carolina. I could hardly imagine my father holding a steady gig through to retirement even if the landlord were to drop the rent to free. That's the bird in him, forever unwilling to submit to the cage.

I feared the cage too, a cage that blunted my voice, shined a harsh light on my budding sexuality then succeeded in taking my baby from me. I felt the cage closing in on me again as we passed through the lobby door. Generous slabs of deeply veined marble lined the lobby walls. A multi-tier chandelier lit the entryway hanging in place of the customary glass bowl, its base lined with a dried medley of petrified bug carcasses.

A heavy weight settled on my chest as Champayne called for the elevator. She waited with the thinly veiled patience of a child, her eyes trained on the space above the elevator door, the numbers illuminating in deliberate succession as the car made its way back down to the lobby. She pushed the button to carry us to the seventh floor—of an eight-story building, one where you didn't have to walk eight flights of stairs to reach the rooftop, a far cry from the basement apartment I'd left them in.

I looked into Champayne's face to read the shift time had caused in her disposition, to see what emotion was tugging at her as we ascended to what for me amounted to the gates of hell. She no longer had the look of the devil's helper, a hell raiser in her own right. I studied her eyes as light swept past the narrow window cut into the elevator door before going dark again as we made our way between floors. I was reminded how wonderful it is to be a child, even my mother's child.

I braced myself as the elevator shuddered to a stop, held my breath as the doors slithered open—effortlessly, their movement silenced in quiet consideration for the turmoil raging inside me. I stood as the scene settled around me, my senses swelling with familiarity. I recognised their apartment from out in the hallway, smelled a lifetime of meals: rice and beans, chicken and collard greens served on a rickety table that shared space off the kitchen with the living room sofa. Heard babies crying, children bickering, grown folks conversing in their most hushed whispers, a building worth of tenants sharing a single address like socks in a drawer, our separate lives distinguished only by a number on the mailbox door, a row of buzzers on the vestibule wall the only means to summon us individually.

Champayne gave me a funny look as I reached to knock. "Let me," she said. "I have a key." I could no longer resist the compulsion to hug her, to embrace her the way I should have the moment we first laid eyes on one another again. She took my hand as we entered the apartment, knowing I'd need to borrow her strength to cross the threshold.

We stepped into a richly decorated room, the warmth of which was as far removed from my expectations as the street outside had been from my recollection of the old neighbourhood. Momma had always insisted on keeping a neat apartment. But never would you have accused any room in her house as conforming to a particular style. Things in our apartment matched on the odd occasion that they had been found at the same flea market or retrieved from the same rubbish heap. Now everywhere you looked things matched in that handpicked, meant to go together way a room with a carefully thought out decor ought to match.

The person sharing the apartment with Momma was different too—Mr. Rollins. Rollie as he corrected me to say, a big teddy bear of a man, the kind who invokes his whole body to tell a story, moving around the room to act out various parts of the tale. If this man is sick, it's locked way down in his pinkie toe. It would take a lifetime of disease to work through all that bubbling flesh.

I giggled at the thought of this meat of a man flattening my mother into the mattress every time they made love. I know we shouldn't picture such a thing, but the sound of my parents making love at night, room rattling love making, meant at least a day or two of peace between them. That was the only time Momma showed any outward sign of being even remotely contented. Had I only had images of her making love inside my head and the few days of peace that would ensue, I might feel more at ease seeing her again, might feel the tug of anything inside my chest outside of anxiety to get this visit over with.

The River or the Current —

Champayne led me past the kitchen toward a dimly lit hallway, all the doors pulled shut except for one. "She's back there," she said, passing my hand to Rollie like a baton in an indoor relay race. He was to carry me the last leg to my mother's bedroom, my head swimming in a sea of clashing emotions.

All the shades were drawn, the only lamp providing just enough light to make your way without bumping into something. "Come. Let me see you," she said, straining to lift her head from the pillow, her eyes taking extra time to focus. "Shucks, girl. Look at you. Left here thin is a rail. Now your body's got more curves than mine do."

She patted her hand on the bedspread. "Come sit," she said. I sat. "How was your trip?" I told her the trip was fine. "And, how are things in Picayune?" I told her things in Picayune were fine, too.

"Girl, you're shut tight as a clamshell. What's eatin' you?"

Over the course of my lifetime, I've bounced back and forth between having nothing to say and believing the next words out of my mouth were the most important I'd ever utter. For the first time, both feelings took hold of me at once.

I pressed a hand against the length of my clavicle, hoping to maintain sufficient composure to let escape only the emotions I wished to show. It was like I woke up in the middle of a dream where someone had called to tell me my mother was dying. Except this wasn't a dream. My mother's journey was fast approaching its ending, whatever thin layer of protection her being here had afforded me over the years about to evaporate from existence.

The part of me that wanted to say something was struggling between a deep-seated grudge and a gut-wrenching sorrow, my eyes welling with tears that this would be the last time I'd likely see my mother alive. I pressed my face against her sunken cheek, looked into eyes nearly swollen shut with fever and waited for another ghost to appear. At least she'd have the benefit of fair warning to plan her good-byes.

Ultimately, a lifetime of unasked questions broke the stalemate brewing inside my head. "Why didn't you ever send for me?"

"Sent to bring you back where? Here!" The notion sent a ripple of creases across her forehead, her eyebrows raised like that was the most ridiculous thing she'd ever heard said. "This ain't no place for you to be."

"You think I was any better off down there?" My eyes couldn't hide the hurt, causing her patience to wane.

"You make it sound like you had it so bad. Walked straight into your grandmother's waiting arms. Been down there so long, can't see yourself anyplace else, the whole town wrapped around you so tight they'll be the ones in need of counselling if ever you try to leave them. I only wish I'd had it so easy," she said.

"New York's the kind of place you can't sneak up on, sees you coming every step of the way. Then, after grindin' on you long enough, the city decides you might as well stay seeing how you're no longer fit to go anyplace else." She turned sideways on her pillow, leaned a bony hip into mine.

"I remember the thing your grandmother told me the night I left Picayune: *'you can't understand the river or the current until you've spent time rowing your own boat.'* You know how cryptic she could be, like she was standing beside God, handing tablets down to Moses. But, had she put it more plainly, the memory of what she said would have left my head before time came for the lesson behind those words to apply, once the consequence of some choice I'd made crept up to threaten the very existence I'd worked so hard to create."

I'd never heard my mother speak even remotely fondly of Gram, had long ago concluded they had grown to tolerate one another as a means of peaceable coexistence. Neither held any ill regard toward the other. But never would I have guessed Momma had taken heed to a single word out of my grandmother's mouth.

She kept on about the perils of life in the city. "New York is a kind of urban wilderness, overrun with wolves. I do believe your daddy is the only truly decent man I've encountered, but then he ain't from here either. Did by us best he could, would do for me before he'd do for himself. He cared about you-all even more than that. But, when it comes right down to it, there's nothing either of us could do to keep you from harm's way, wolves lurking around every corner."

"What's a girl at fourteen possibly got to fear?" I asked.

"A girl at fourteen has the whole world to fear," she grumbled, her voice creaking. "Only she doesn't know it yet, hasn't got adequate perspective to recognise the danger she's in, her curiosity fast outstripping the grasp she has on basic common sense."

"So, why'd you send me to Picayune?"

"For the same reasons I left. Couldn't step outside my own skin without somebody who knows my momma catchin' wind of it. Everyone on pins and needles whenever I come around, scared to cross paths with a girl whose momma runs the whole town, knows all their secrets, done read their dirt. Only your daddy was fool enough not to care who my momma was.

"Coming up, I witnessed folks pass by one another each day like nothing's ever gone on down there. Shared a classroom with kids who lived the lie every day, neighbour twins I call 'em, intertwined in age like clasped fingers living beneath separate roofs, alternating visits with the same man they both call daddy."

She bit her lip like she didn't want to let go all she

had to say in one sitting. "It's like being able to see in the dark while the whole rest of the world is pretending to be invisible. Like by choosing not to see, they can't be seen. But I could see 'em. Saw them, their shadow and their shadow's shadow." She had the energy of a windup toy, the brass ring spinning counterclockwise in her back, winding down as her conversation wore on.

"I suffered in silence as kids my age walked past me like I'm the one who's done something to be looked down upon. Meanwhile, I know things about their mommas and daddies that a child doesn't possess sufficient insight to comprehend.

"I used to stand around like a lamppost, waiting for somebody to beam his brightness back at me. See, I wasn't blessed with any of the gifts you and your daddy possess—those easy good looks, that quiet magnetism, able to lure people in even when you're not lookin' to pitch. There I am swimming in a sea full of wriggling fish, yet all of them know better than to find my net.

"I looked on as folks I grew up around fell one after another into the circle that had their parents so mixed up. Your grandmother wouldn't hear of any child of hers getting caught up in that mess, concocted all sorts of distractions to keep me apart from my classmates. I don't believe it was her aim, but your grandma's efforts succeeded in stopping the spell that had ruined our family's name dead still with me. Spent all her time trying to make right some wrong even her daddy hadn't intended." She seemed to have caught a new gust of wind, her energy level picking up with the stroll down memory lane.

"The role she played, attempting to organize the slew of co-mingling left on her hands only to wind up legitimizing things in the process, seemed lost on her. That I needed her to be my momma not the whole of Picayune's seemed lost on her, too. So, I boxed up my feelings and tried to overlook the fact that nobody ever wanted me. The whole town's spooning all over each other and I can't get the least bit of attention inside my own household.

"But, I don't fault her none. After all, she's my momma. Done for me the best she could. Ultimately, I decided love was a choice best not left to somebody else's choosing. First chance I had, I found somebody to love and got myself out of Picayune. Jumped into a river so swift, the man I hitched my wagon to nearly drowned—did drown depending who you let tell it." Her eyes went hazy again.

"It hadn't occurred to me that you might follow in your daddy's footsteps instead of mine. You've never been much at ease with your surroundings, but that can be a blessing in disguise. At the same time you're seldom overlooked, just like your daddy, neither of you even scarcely aware of the hold you have on people. Even that wouldn't be a problem if no one ever meant you any harm. But neither of you can tell a shark from a minnow, inviting your worst enemy over to sit down to supper. Long story short, I sent you to Picayune to keep you safe, believed no harm would come your way under your grandmother's watch."

Her eyes seemed to reveal that even she was no longer satisfied with this explanation. It seemed too simple an account to apply any longer. "I only wanted what was best for you. Wanted to give you the best chance I knew how to give, even if that meant we'd be apart."

Illness didn't afford my mother much latitude in expression. I had to channel my own trailing emotions to discern even the slightest shift in attitude before her face went blank again, needed to tunnel inside the darkest thoughts of missing my momma to have any sense of the anguish she must have been left to endure. I saw hurt on top of hurt, regret for any decision she might want to take back, any move she might wish to do over before her eyes could resume their vacant stare.

"What about my baby? What kind of chance did you mean to give her?" I asked, my question meant to knock her off balance so I wasn't the only one in the room struggling. She answered without pause, this evidently a question she had long anticipated.

"As women in this world, none of us is destined to mother a child. Yet each of us in some form or another plays daughter to our mothers. Have no choice in the matter." Her voice maintained its gravelly tone, the part of her that wanted to rest tugging hard on the part of her that needed to get through all she had to say despite what it might cost her in the morning.

"I've heard it said that a good man should raise a son. I suspect the same ought to apply to a woman and her daughters. But, I had little more to offer you-all in the way of advice than don't follow in my footsteps, don't let the mistakes I've made become your cross to bear.

"I found myself constantly pushing you out from underneath me with one hand while pulling you in close with the other, terrified of what lay in wait for you. Then here you come, trying to bring a baby into the world. It's a parent's worst nightmare, clueless what to do. Meanwhile, everyone's looking to me to make sense of the situation. My first-born child spreading roots while I'm still struggling to get my tree planted.

"So, I don't know what I wanted for you or your baby. I fought your daddy the whole ride down there what to say, fought the voice inside my head the whole way back that I'd done the wrong thing. By the time the New York skyline became visible through the windshield, the voice inside my head had me convinced how miserably I'd failed you," she said as she shifted in search of a new spot to lay her head on the pillow.

"Your grandma was my only saviour. I knew she couldn't leave well enough alone. Realized that I'd been hoping the whole while she might intervene. Would take matters into her own hands and keep her daughter from making the worst mistake she was ever going to make. It broke my heart what happened to your baby. Worse still that I never got the chance to tell you how sorry I was. Never can make up for the fall I nearly caused you to take." She ran her fingers along a crease in the bedspread, making room for my baby to lie down between us.

"I don't know how to begin to ask your forgiveness. But I hope with time that you will find it in your heart to consider how truly remorseful I am." I began to recognise that piece of me that was hers before anyone else's, her soft creamy centre that would have been better off had she stayed in Picayune. For the first time recognised the void we shared, the burden we together carried despite our long separation. I decided to let her be my momma again. I don't know what unseen force had kept us apart. But, since that day, whether or not she loves me is no longer in question.

"I need you to do something," she said, an added bounce to her voice. "I want you to take your sisters with you to Picayune, watch over them for me... just till I get back on my feet."

"Momma, ain't hardly room in that house for me."

"You've got room in your heart, ain't you?"

I was slow to recognise how difficult a thing this was for her to ask. Neglected the advice Mr. Graves had given on how to approach my return home: *'try to see your momma as she might wish to see herself, as the person she's aimed all these years to be, and forget for a moment any time she may have come up short.'*

"I'm not asking you to do it for me. I'm asking you to do it for them." At that point, I would have done it for her.

I sat by her side another minute, watched the brass key wind itself down in her back. Her eyes went vacant again, but her mouth mustered a thin smile, seeming to signify that my mother had managed what she set out to accomplish: making sure her babies were taken care of even if she no longer possessed the strength to care for them herself.

Black Haired Momma

I left my mother's room feeling I'd just met her for the first time, witnessed her turning ghost in reverse. As if, until that day, I had never known my momma.

That night, Edelyn invited me to accompany her and her boyfriend, Massoud, to open mic night at a coffee house they liked to frequent. I couldn't imagine anyone giving a child such a name. But, from the way he carried himself, blacker than black, mightier than Africa herself, I suspect it was a name he had given himself. It suited him well enough even if the name was the product of invention, cause and effect having been reversed, the man standing before us a consequence of the name rather than the other way around.

This would be my first time to a spoken word cafe, nothing of the sort having found its way to Picayune. My interest drifted in and out as I struggled to relate to the barrage of unsolicited grandstanding, a stream of verbal assaults hurled over our heads against an invisible foe from the safe confines of a dimly lit coffee gallery. I focused my attention in an effort to unravel the state of misfortune that had birthed the latest poem.

Each poet to take the stage had his or her own style

of delivery. One whispered, his eyes closed, like his poem was a secret he wasn't fully prepared to share. Most everyone else shouted about raising the roof or tearing it down, about imposing four-hundred years of misery on anyone who mispronounced their names, names that sounded as made up as Massoud's if not more so.

I was labouring to cosy up to the drink I'd ordered— chai laced with a hint of ginger (a delightful alternative for the non-coffee drinker according to our server. In hindsight, I should have pretended to want coffee instead)—when I heard my sister announced as the next scheduled performer. Only the emcee pronounced her name in the odd sounding way she seemed to prefer these days—*Eee'd-lyn Hill*, resting heavy on the first *E* then skipping past the next like consuming too many syllables in one sitting was somehow forbidden.

Edelyn had evidently kept silent the bit about her performing as a surprise for me. I couldn't imagine anyone exhibiting such grace having taken the stage spur of the moment on a whim. The mic served to transform her, her spirit melting into the crowd like ice cream resting atop a homemade dessert. She held the room transfixed with her solemn tale of a black-haired momma who was never gonna see gray. I recognised her plight firsthand.

According to Gram, gray hair is a sign of wisdom creeping in. She explainedhow the first half of a person's life is spent simple minded as can be, the second half trying to figure where the time has gone. Gram claimed she could count a gray hair for every mistake she ever made, for every time she was too quick to judge, for any time she failed to call on reasoning in her dealings with another human being.

Momma was just beginning to seek reason in her approach to the world, having only recently discovered the perspective a less combative attitude might afford. The tragedy was that time would likely run out on her before she could get any of it sorted inside her head. My cheeks were rolling with tears before my sister could get through the first stanza. By the time Edelyn passed the mic back to the emcee, there was hardly a dry eye in the room. After all, everybody's got a momma.

I was spent. *Black Haired Momma* served in pushing me further in my desire to curl up in a warm bed and click the switch closed on this day before Massoud had his turn at the mic. On Edelyn's insistence, I agreed to stay for his performance. I've never more regretted any single decision in all my years.

He prepared like the other poets before him, summoning the words from somewhere deep inside his core as the emcee introduced the title of his poem:

The Better the Bitch —
The blacker the berry, the better the bitch is
gonna make you feel.

324

*The sweeter the juice, the more you're gonna
come for real.*
*And you've got to come for real, or she's
gonna leave your ass, for real.*
*The bitter the bitch, the more she'll sweat
your game;*
*Catch you in the streets, forever callin' you
outside your name.*
*The better the bitch, she'll make your house
a home;*
*She'll cook your meals right and keep your
back tight*
squashin' your tendency to roam.
*The bitter the bitch, the more you're prone
to flight;*
*She'll work your least nerve and your last
nerve*
*Till you find yourself in the streets most every
night.*
*The better the bitch will take you at your
word;*
*The bitterest bitch ain't believed a thing she's
ever heard.*
*The better the bitch, she'll inspire you to
rhyme;*
*She'll be that rhythmic beat behind your
tightest verse*
making love in perfect time.

*The bitter the bitch can also infiltrate your
poem;
She'll be that off night behind your stage
fright wishing
you'd left her ass at home...*

I knew in my heart I couldn't do it, couldn't stand
in front of all those people and utter two solid words.
But, if I could stand there, if I possessed the nerve not
to mention the skill necessary to deliver a rhyme filled
message, I'd be sure to have something more to speak
on than the betterness or bitterness of a bitch. Even the
best woman by his account is still a bitch.

My sister could never be that bitch. No matter
how deep she managed to come across on stage, her
berry was not that black, her juice not sweet enough to
redeem a soul as bitter as Massoud's. She could wish
all she liked, but she could never stoop so low to be the
person he had in mind when this sad excuse of a tribute
struck his empty head.

Broke Bicycles —

We caught up with Massoud on our way out. I stood off to one side to afford Edelyn and him some privacy, my tendency to eavesdrop curbed by how little interest I had left in anything this man might have to say. Eventually their conversation grew boisterous, making their squabbling impossible to ignore.

"Do you at least know where you're going to be?"

"Home girl, I ain't gonna know that till I get there."

"Should I call you then, 'cause I don't mind calling if it's not convenient for you to call me?"

He mooshed her face. Placed the whole of his hand against the side of her head and pushed her aside like you would a broken-down bicycle or a worn-out couch, its springs no longer capable of supporting your weight. Not a hit or a smack meant to inflict physical pain. Only the emptiness of love lost in his touch, fatigue for a feeling he wasn't feeling any longer.

I waited another half-second for my sister to stand in her own defence but intervened in the end, fearing she might again ask whether she should call him. His chest grew large in front of me, the moniker of some just anointed clothing designer splayed before me in modern day hieroglyphics. I stood staring at the underside of his scruffy chin, past nostrils that breathed nothing but lies, a vapid stare at work behind vacant eyes making those lies out to sound true.

A simpler mind might have fled. But that would require I abandon my middle sister, Edelyn, reinforcing in her eyes that cowering before a man was an acceptable posture for a woman to take. For once, I refused to let anxiety dictate my will. No man was going to lay hands on my sister. Not on my watch. Even if she was prepared to swallow every ounce of pride she had left in exchange for the least bit of attention from him, allowing a man to dismiss her in this way was something I couldn't stand idly by and let my sister do.

I eased ever closer, unmoved by his chest puffing antics, stood as near to this man as I could afford without provoking a physical altercation between us. I wagged a lone finger at him. Spit bible and verse about how a man should worship his woman, should treat her with the utmost respect—bits and pieces of Gram and every other woman whose viewpoint I'd come to depend on rolled up in me at once. I left Massoud with a final warning: if he again touched my sister in a way she didn't want to be touched, I would meet him at this very spot, see he meets his maker.

I felt the crowd bubbling at my back as I stepped away from him, Massoud's entourage roused at the sight of him being bullied by his girlfriend's older sister. Eventually, Massoud decided to join in their laughter. Chose feigned amusement over rage as the more logical reaction to my threats, his eyes locked on mine conveying a litany of venomous intentions that more closely fit what I suspect were his true sentiments.

I stood steady on my word, prepared if need be to take him with me to hell. To spend the rest of eternity sitting up next to the devil, an eye trained on Massoud to make sure his soul is suffering.

Daddy's Little Girls —

Three days in New York and still I hadn't seen my daddy. We'd telephoned back and forth, but each time we talked, he explained how he was too busy to see me. The last time we spoke, I held the receiver pressed to my ear long after he'd hung up. Let the drone of the dial tone wash over me. It seemed the last person I could truly count on had deserted me, too. My daddy no longer wished to see his baby girl.

Champayne, who had grown to be as perceptive a creature as I've known a child to be, took the receiver from my hand and hung it up for me. What I hadn't factored, what intuition had informed her, was that Daddy couldn't bear to have me see him this way, against the backdrop of someone else having taken charge of his family.

She offered to take me to visit him at his night job the following evening. We exited the subway station then walked over a few blocks to a bus station housed beneath a vacant bowling alley. The place stood eerily still, the roll of thunder against a lightning strike of pins absent from the hall above his head. We stood peering through a wall of glass windows. There sat my daddy inside a security booth, double panes of glass permitting him only the tiniest sliver of interaction with the outside world. It was like watching him on a life-size television screen.

He tried once to get into the movies. Squeezed his way in with a group of extras cast waiting at a bus stop near 73rd, where Broadway and Amsterdam crisscross. He was made to endure a seemingly endless wait as the main characters walked up and down the sidewalk just short of where he was standing, perfecting their dialogue. Daddy used the time inside his head to work up the expression he might use, the raise of an eyebrow, a turn of his lip, to send a message to his little girls, to make sure we'd know he was thinking about us if ever we got the opportunity to see his scene played out on the big screen.

In the end, the camera cut away as the lead character cupped his hands to light a cigarette, the gesture inserted last minute to pull together the banter he and his co-star had struggled over the entire morning. Half a day spent and only the sleeve of Daddy's Parks Department uniform made the shot. To top it off, he lost his Parks job that day for being late (or quit, embarrassed to have wasted a sure thing for one he'd shown no interest in prior to the opportunity falling into his lap).

He once attempted to explain his proclivity to daydream, meandering from one fleeting opportunity to the next. He spoke as though talking about someone else. No doubt repeating something somebody had told him about himself, his wanderlust impossible to change even if he wanted to. It would appear his latest daydream had him working the night shift, sitting alone behind double panes of glass inside a downtown bus terminal.

Champayne and I watched as he stretched a loosely knotted tie peeking out beneath a collar that had no intentions of ever fitting his neck. Time had taken a toll on him too, only not how I had anticipated. You know the way a man gets as he grows bolder, broader, more full of himself. My daddy seemed to be shrinking down inside himself, getting smaller as the world grew large around him.

All his worldly possessions were arranged along the ledge just inside the double-paned glass: a comb, his wristwatch, and an open pack of Doublemint gum. The same man who denies himself the most basic necessities—a steady place to live, a stable home life, a woman who loves him beyond measure—anchors his happiness in the simplest of pleasures. How could I have failed to recognise his predicament: another man caring for the mother of his children, his woman lying in a bed, life slipping away for things he couldn't keep her from doing?

On the desk before him sat the remnants of a king-size Baby Ruth, a sure sign that he'd had a good day, an extra-long candy bar a treat set aside for this time of night. He turned the last two bites into four to prolong the satisfaction. The last bite brought a thin smile to his face, a lifetime of worry undoubtedly at work inside his

head. He shook the last few crumbs from the blotter
into the wastepaper basket and resumed his nightly
duties, waiting inside his birdcage for time to pass him
by, his fingers pretending to read a newspaper.

Champayne tapped the glass to get his attention.
"Somebody's here to see you." He sat for a moment,
struck by swelling emotion, before hurrying down
from his wooden stool to unlock the door to the ticket
booth. He came around to greet me. Had we shown up
midday, against the hustle of a crowd, he might have
been more self-conscious letting himself go in front of a
throng of people bustling past. But something about the
way he held onto me, like he might never let go, says
it wouldn't have mattered who was watching. Day or
night, he would have hugged me the same.

He stared long at me before turning to greet his other
daughter. Champayne and my father hugged like some
outside force had pushed them together, her affection
for him more obligatory than felt, she having witnessed
our father's neglect firsthand. Still, she cared enough
to orchestrate a meeting with his eldest daughter—*his
before hers without question.* She seemed to understand
the importance of the bond a daughter ought to share
with her father, even if that hadn't been her experience.
In some small way, this was a reunion for her too, the
furthest ends of her world at long last standing face-to-
face again.

A self-made philosopher, my daddy was seldom

know to talk straight. Conversation with him was invariably filled with wild speculation on endless possibilities. There he sat, working the graveyard shift of yet another dead end opportunity, yet he was more apt to talk to me about wonder and excitement, of all the things that still might be.

Something in his eyes indicated the need for me to speak first. "You look well," I offered.

"I look old is what you mean to say," he said, still beaming from the hugs he'd received. "You don't have to spare my feelings. I know how I look."

"Sometimes I wish I was old already. Can see how things wind up."

"Every day, I wish to be young again, to forge a new beginning."

"And, what would you change?"

"Not a solitary thing." His eyes were the only parts of him that seemed to believe the lie. The rest of him was in desperate need of change. But the eyes wouldn't betray their connection to his heart. "Besides, if you were to get old, where would that leave me?"

A nervous hand tugged at the scruffy end of an unkempt chin, his fingers attempting to mould his face into a new expression. "If I had my life to live over again, I'd start with the day you came along. Would hold you and your sisters tender in my arms 'til you were old enough to fend for yourselves. Would give all I had until you were strong enough to venture into the world on your own. All I'd want in return is that you find me when the journey starts over again. That you'll still be my little girls when we cross over into the next lifetime."

"Maybe next time we'll be butterflies, able to fly free of the cage."

"Next time we'll be the wind, set all the birds and butterflies free to escape whatever cage has its hold on them."

Before we left he ducked inside the ticket booth, rummaged around behind the counter, returning with a street lamp sized grin on his face. He handed each of us a single red balloon bounding at the end of a length of string. Champayne had evidently alerted him about our plans to visit.

Growing up, we used to take the D-Train to Coney Island, carrying with us a bag of toy balloons for one of the boardwalk vendors to fill with helium. He and daddy had worked together for the DPW, removing snow during a blizzard that winter. The man told daddy he could have all the helium he wanted come springtime as long as he brought his own balloons to fill seeing how the man who owned the stand kept closer account of balloons than he did how much helium had been dispensed over the course of a day.

We'd push through the crowds on the boardwalk, fill a dozen brightly coloured balloons, then head back toward the subway station, boundless expressions of hope bobbing along in time with our father's footsteps, my sisters and I close on his heels. The three of us felt like circus clowns standing in the centre of the subway car, bunches of balloons dancing above our heads. At the same time, we felt completely special, Daddy looking straight faced off into the distance like no spectacle was too grand to create for the benefit of his little girls, like this was part of our everyday existence.

Once back in the city, he'd lead us to an open expanse of park, empty of trees. From there we'd proceed with a make-believe game of cloud chasing, each armed with her own tiny bunch of balloons. The object of the game as Daddy described it was to release a balloon over our heads with just the right timing to see it collide with a passing cloud. According to his claims, clouds were filled with rain even on sunshiny days. Piercing one would cause it to spill a little bit of rain from the exact spot where our balloon had hit. He had us convinced that, with just the right aim, we could make our own private rain shower.

None of us ever managed to strike a passing cloud, the trip along the way the obvious intent of our journey, chasing clouds with a balloon on a string just an excuse to escape, to distance ourselves momentarily from the doldrums of our everyday existence. I'll always honour him for that—spending what little free time he had to brighten our lives by any affordable means. And I'll be forever in Champayne's debt for enabling him to be my daddy again, surrounded once again by the adoration of his little girls.

He gave us both a long squeeze then climbed back into his ticket booth. He sat staring into the distance long after Champayne and I had stepped back through the sliding glass doors onto the street, the newspaper he had been pretending to read no longer able to hold his attention, ancient curiosities stirred again inside his head.

Champayne and I released our balloons outside the apartment, against a sky filled with twinkling stars. I didn't wish to reach the clouds that night, my sights set on heaven instead, to cause an angel to spill some of her goodness down on my daddy provided I'm able to nudge her just right with careful aim of my string balloon. My mother lay on death's doorstep, fate steadily closing in on her. Yet I was more worried about my daddy, each moment of happiness costing him a lifetime of pain to repay.

That night, I lay still in the hollow darkness of fading memory and tried to figure what had gone wrong between my momma and daddy. I never once heard him say a bad word in her name. Momma never spoke too well of anyone. Still, she never cursed him openly in front of us, held that part of her tongue silent inside a mouth that at other times ran foul as sewer water.

They were by all accounts together of their own

choosing which you can't say about everybody you meet. Made a move on sheer determination to make their way in life together before any of us was even a thought inside their heads. Perhaps my sisters and I are the ones to blame—*step on a crack and break your momma and daddy's love making.* At the same time, he only seemed happy when we were around. She on the other hand seemed most agitated whenever left to deal with us too long on her own. I suppose you'd call that love.

My head was stuck on the last thing he'd said after he and momma sat me down to explain that they were sending me to Picayune: *'most disturbances will sort themselves out as long as you see fit to let them alone.'* Sounded like another of his monsters-beneath-the-bed theories, told to keep us from venturing beyond our covers after being tucked into bed at night. Daddy assured us no monsters would stir from their hiding places as long as none of us went poking around beneath the bed looking for them. The monsters hiding underneath our parents' bed kept to their hiding places, duty bound to remain silent so long as momma and daddy stayed put beneath the covers. Eventually, the places he'd disappear to, the company she kept whenever he went long enough gone were spilling from every corner of their lives together, lost time between them beginning to reveal itself with one disastrous consequence after another.

Mosquito's Buzzing —

I was still for the first time in my entire visit. Still, I was unable to sleep. I found the din from the outside world deafening, the street below my window teeming with activity long after the streetlights had flickered on. Sirens blared throughout the night as though ringing for their own amusement. No two square blocks could possibly house that many emergencies.

Picayune was a mouse hole by comparison, the only things stirring at night preferring not to be exposed for the rest of the world to see. Make no mistake. New York will always be a part of me, but the trip home had me convinced that my way in life was meant to pass through Picayune. I vowed on my return to bless every cricket's chirp, every mosquito's buzzing. Whether I wear out my bones in that place, breathe my last breath beneath her sky is left for God to decide. Until that time, I'll plant my foot each day on solid ground and hope to the heavens that I find my way, sideways or swift toward whatever fate I'm destined.

FIVE

Goodnight Sun

The sun burned a hole through the clouds, hung long on the horizon just for me. Turned its shape oval so I wouldn't miss a moment of its spectacle, took special care to ensure I'd be there to witness its final bow before disappearing for the night.

Momma liked sunsets too. Remarked how the setting sun succeeds in bringing an ending to any amount of turmoil in the world, returns everything to its proper place regardless of how unsettling a day she's endured. Daddy claims as his own the predawn hour, that time of day before the first car horn has had its chance to bleat, the first rush of people to take to the streets. Muted colours transform the landscape, sky and earth, land and sea coming together in an indistinguishable blend of blues and greys. Even the steepest hilltop appears little more than a pimple on the face of mother earth, the arrangement of streets and thoroughfares winding their way between clusters of towering structures reduced to mere creases in the vast expanse of her skin. Skyscrapers huddle against the first break of daylight to shield one another from the wind or rain or blistering sunshine, not yet knowing what the coming day will bring. Momma focused on endings, Daddy forever lost in the prospect of new beginnings, the three of us tucked neatly toward one end or the other in every meaningful regard.

I reserve this time each evening to pay homage to the setting sun, to thank the sun for being here, for delivering another day filled with warmth and light. I give special thanks for the sun having waited on me to show up on the back steps again, to bask in the warmth of her glow. To reacquaint myself with the pattern of light she casts special on the Mississippi Bayou.

Age and Wisdom

Edelyn and Champayne arrived by train a few short days after my return to Picayune. I couldn't have scripted a more perfect fairytale circumstance, all Evelyn Combs' grandbabies living again underneath the same roof. But, as fairytales tend to do, ours quickly lost its picture-perfect veneer. It never ceases to amaze me how one too many people in a room can ruin it for everybody.

Edelyn was on me from her first step onto the train platform, like some quarrel had worked itself up inside her head somewhere between here and New York's Penn Station that she needed to catch me up on. "What is it you call yourself doing down here, playing house? You're the mother hen and we're baby chicks sent for you to look after." She eyed me with the same contempt I had at one time or another felt toward our mother.

"How are you all of a sudden gonna try to play big sister? Ain't never once led a path for either one of us to follow," she said, dragging Champayne into our quarrel with a point of her finger. "Now you wanna stand up here and tell me how to run my life when it seems you don't have much going on down here yourself."

I thought for the longest while that I hated my sister

Edelyn, invented all sorts of cockamamie reasons to dislike her. She looked too much like me. Other times we didn't look enough alike, inviting me to pick on any feature of hers that was different from mine. There were times still where she tried too hard to shadow me, fixing her hair like mine then making a point to mimic the colour combination I was wearing whenever we went out, like a miniature version of me sent to get right any step I was destined to miss.

I believed at a time she had stolen my mother from me, came along at a point when Momma and Daddy loved me with equal strength. After she was born, it's like Momma didn't have enough love to go around. I can't explain why Edelyn's spells had no effect on our daddy. All I know is that Momma started loving me a bit less after Edelyn came into the world, the two of us little more to her eye than coins in a sleeve, the first one in, the first to get pushed out when a new Penny comes along.

As hard as it was to separate my feelings toward Edelyn from difficulties Momma and I would have had regardless, I couldn't understand why she all of a sudden appeared to dislike me. I still failed to see what sending me down here was meant to accomplish, but believed in my heart that sending my sisters to Picayune was the best thing Momma could have done for them, Edelyn especially. But as Gram was prone to repeat, the remark usually aimed in my direction, age and wisdom are requisite counterparts. Neither does a body any good until the other is fully installed.

These days, I possessed wisdom beyond my years, had known a love so strong it nearly broke my heart, could speak to loneliness desperate enough to let a man lay hands on you. That voice reminded me how much I love my middle sister, Edelyn, of the obligation I alone held to shed light on the futility of the path she's on with Massoud, how she must work to free herself.

"I don't need to set the path to predict the outcome. I've seen where you're headed from the bottom up. Been places I don't intend either of you to see," I insisted, holding steady on the pecan expanse of her skin, her complexion dotted with a light sprinkling of soft brown freckles.

"My way in life has taught me that you have worth, beyond any measure a man like Massoud can comprehend." I found myself again channelling Gram's words, only this time for my sister's benefit instead of my own. Felt a few of Gram's gray strands rooting themselves in among my unspoiled locks.

"I wish I didn't have to be the one to tell you, but that man doesn't respect you. What he does for you might on occasion look like love but, in the end, that man doesn't love you. A man can't love you until you're prepared to love yourself."

Regrettably, Edelyn lacked sufficient exposure to the wisdom Gram used to spout to sit back and let the healing soak in. She reacted no differently than I might have if confronted for the first time with a concept, the truth behind which was foreign to my ears.

"Your way in life can't do a thing to improve my self-worth," she said, her eyes refusing to meet mine. "To think I define my worth by how the man in my life is treating me, that I'm that small inside. How about you find some business of your own to tend and leave me to worry about where things are headed between me and my man?"

Edelyn searched the front room of Gram's house for some place to storm off to. But, with our new sleeping arrangements as yet undecided, she had to settle for making a beeline through the kitchen onto the back steps, a luxury their New York City apartment wouldn't have permitted. She could just as easily have stood her ground, the little bit of Gram's speech I had worked up inside my head unprepared for this much resistance from my middle sister. And folks consider Champayne stubborn.

I'll be the first to attest, the move to Mississippi can be traumatic in its own right. Being sent here against your every wish only adds insult on top of injury. The separation from Massoud eventually proved too great a shock for Edelyn's system to take, no matter how big she claimed to be on the inside. She was back on the train to New York before the month had run out, leaving me to accept that even if the man in her life was cancer, it was her cancer to kick, quit or let slowly kill her spirit.

Weed Gardening —

Gram's movement around the house was like the seasons changing. Take for instance the bird feeder she had hanging from a tree in the backyard. In its full spring glory, that tree bent down nearly low enough to touch the far end of the clothes line. I never once saw her fill that feeder. It never went empty either.

Each morning I'd watch the same flock of birds taking turns swooping in from the line of trees along the back fence to fill up on Gram's birdseed. Just when I thought the feeder might run out, it would appear the next day filled to the brim, the same birds bustling back and forth from feeder to tree like life was always going to be this way, just as they had always known it to be. And, just like that, another season would pass, the bright showings of spring again colouring each blade of grass, the petals on every flower, sprigs of cotton sprouting again from a long-forgotten field of brown twigs.

That's how my grandmother moved around Picayune: invisible in her endeavours yet highly effective with the results she produced. Yet, as much as the whole town was her responsibility, inherited but kept, the backyard was her sanctuary.

"God moves out here," she told me one evening, the two of us standing on her back porch to take in the peacefulness that had drifted in with the cool night air.

"What's God like?" I asked in response.

"God is infinite possibility," she replied. "Look at that sturdy oak," she added, pointing in the direction of the far corner of the yard. "You have never seen a more handsome tree. That tree has been here longer than both you and me put together. Roots run underneath this whole block. Only God could create something so majestic, a living thing for the whole world to see, to draw breath from, rest ourselves beneath its shade." Conversation came easily between the two of us at this point. She'd answer a question without my needing to ask. Would continue down a path for the sole purpose of arming me with the full benefit of her perspective.

"Took a lifetime of patience to raise that tree, that plus a goodly amount of sunshine and rain." She turned an eye toward the heavens to see whether God was listening, having appointed an angel to stand by and make certain she was telling it straight.

"What if I was to bring you a big 'ol tree, asked you to stand it upright in my backyard? You wouldn't know the first thing to do. Even if you did figure how to get it standing on its roots, it would take a whole corps of engineers to anchor that tree secure in its place. Still might not stand for all eternity unless the Almighty himself deems it so. God did that and more with the mere passage of time. Stood that tree tall for you and me to see. That's what God's like. More than I can ever be. That's all."

Eventually, even Gram's less subtle movements around the house became a distant memory to me. I could recall letting her hat and gloves and pruning shears sit for weeks on the front step, lying next to the row of shrubs she'd been tending, thinking she was gonna get back there the next day to finish the job. Moving those things would have meant I had accepted her passing. Yet, sitting there, all too still, they stood as constant reminders that my grandma was never again coming back this way. Eventually, the ache of one dread over-powered my reluctance to deal with the other and I returned her things to the potting shed she'd had some men in the neighbourhood build at the end of her driveway. In the end, I suspect putting away her things is what Gram would have wanted.

I woke up one morning, Gram having been gone for what seemed two eternities (time tending to run twice as slow underneath the burden of sad memories), and took stock of my surroundings: the bird feeder that Gram quietly tended had long gone empty, her flower garden lay in shambles. With Champayne's arrival in Picayune, I had taken up the task of tending both, picking up the reigns of unfinished business, flowerbeds and bird feeders getting equal attention again, sand-wiched in between duties around town raising korn.

The gardening wasn't so much gardening as it was keeping up with the weeds in the few beds Gram had going along the front porch. Then even the weeds weren't weeds as such. Daddy claimed Mississippi was the first place he'd known where a blade of grass refused to grow straight up and down. They have this long creeping grass down here that makes its way vine-like along the ground, creating a needle-point pattern of stitches, each grass vine digging itself in every few inches or so in search of fresh dirt.

With the slightest neglect, Gram's front yard gets overrun with tiny grass worms, burying their heads to shade themselves from the sun or duck the attention of a pesky bird. It was inevitable that some of that needle-point stitching would find its way to the flowerbeds where it was my job to undo the grass vines, each dug in worm letting go with one last satisfying little pull. Mr. Graves called it Bermuda grass. I wasn't sure how grass from Bermuda made it all the way to Picayune, but I could understand how it would take a grass from that part of the world to withstand this heat.

Champayne and I used the heat of the sun to split our day in two. We confined our morning activities to the back of the house, from bedroom to kitchen, with an occasional venture off the back steps to fetch clothes from the line. In the afternoon, we moved opposite the sun to the front room and the porch. I liked to get my weeding done early in the evening before the sun rolled down too far over the roof of the house. I put on a pair of gloves, a hat, and some floppy old shoes that

Gram used to wear most anyplace. I wore them exclusively for weed gardening. Startled the neighbours half to death at first how much I resembled Gram in that getup. Thought I might wear it as this year's Halloween costume. See if I couldn't scare up some ghosts around here for real.

I was out on the back steps the other day, waiting for Champayne to finish setting the table for dinner, when I noticed a few brightly coloured petals strewn across the lawn, fallen adornment from the climbing bougainvillea signalling that the wind must have blown through the backyard at some point, though you could hardly tell it from the still afternoon air.

The trees stood motionless, not the slightest ripple evident in the glass surface of the rain water collected at the bottom of Gram's wash bucket. On most days, a tragic little wind sputters fitfully through Picayune. One you must stand dead still to see, to feel, to hear rustling nearly imperceptibly amongst the leaves of only the tallest of trees, a stingy wind having found the effort too great under all this heat to blow with measurable strength.

I conjured the image of a high priestess having passed through the yard to distract myself from the heat. Imagined well-wishers borrowing flowers from the bougainvillea to throw at her feet. All the life drained from the yard now that the procession had moved on, only a windswept handful of fuchsia coloured petals left behind to suggest that life had ever before stirred back here. To bear witness to the place where my grandmother sought comfort, found solace beneath the shade of that sturdy oak. And in that vision, I saw another season without Gram slip past, fuchsia petals left to visit us again on the heels of the heavy springtime rains, falling from a sky painted twelve shades gray by days of endless cloud cover.

Broken Sky —

Champayne and I rattled around Gram's house for the better part of a week before venturing into town. I couldn't keep her locked inside forever, but still hadn't decided how much to tell her about the choke hold the circle had on Picayune, our family's history of shame at the centre of all that commotion. I was wrestling to form my own opinion. Still, I refused to let her stumble over the bones in Picayune's backyards on her own. Didn't want her to be that lost soul, left to wander the streets unsuspecting.

I woke her one Saturday announcing that we had errands to run. After helping me clear away the breakfast dishes, she took a seat at the kitchen table to lace up those skate-sneaker things of hers. I made a note to pick her up some regular tennis shoes. She was gonna stand out like a sore thumb flaunting her out of town ways in those gadgety things.

I sat working out an agenda for our excursion in my head. We'd start with the simplest of tasks: the post office, the drug store, plus a few quick items from the market. Something to get us out of the house, but nothing that would have us in town long enough to risk a run in with anyone whose affiliation I wasn't fully prepared to explain.

Truth be told, I needed my ends tightened up but I wasn't ready to venture back into the hair salon myself, much less with my little sister in tow. She'd learn all she needed to know about that bunch soon enough.

That's when she interrupted. "When are we gonna go across the street and say hello?"

I had promised Mr. Graves I would call over to Miss Spinnaker's as soon as I got back. She'd want to know how things turned out with my mother. "I'm sure we'll bump into her before too long."

She seemed less than satisfied with my response, but obliged by not pressing me like she ordinarily would, still a bit overwhelmed I imagined about the strange possibilities her new surroundings might hold.

Fortunately, the heavens smiled on me and we made it into town and back without major incident. Anybody I knew nodded from a distance to acknowledge how pleased they were to have me back in town, but kept their distance, respecting private time with my baby sister. Meanwhile, Champayne was a sponge by my side, dark stutter eyes soaking up everything in sight, undoubtedly gathering material to question me on later.

She started in again about Miss Spinnaker as we began our walk from the bus stop. Did she and I visit much? Had I seen inside her house? Was she nice to me?

"She's pleasant enough," I told her. "But I don't make a habit of going by to see her."

She latched onto my arm as we neared Gram's house, twisted herself around me like she'd spied someone she needed to duck. "That her?" she asked.

A thin brown hand was at its place in the window across the way, the curtains parted to allow a view onto the street.

"I wouldn't pay her any mind," I said, letting Miss Spinnaker get her fill from behind half-drawn curtains. "She's always at her post, patrolling the mean streets of Picayune." This I found especially amusing having just returned from New York, its streets crawling with wolves according to Momma's account. Having seen deep inside Picayune's belly, I couldn't begin to tell the foxes and wolves and hounds I'd observed lurking in broad daylight.

"Think of Miss Spinnaker as a one-person neighbourhood watch," I advised my sister. "Highly unnecessary, yet zealous in her duties nonetheless."

"That's what you call her, Miss?"

"What else would you have me call her?" I ask. "Girl, you've got to learn to pay proper respect if you're going to make it down here." She gave me that funny look again, wheeled away from me on her heels.

"You're just like your daddy," she said. "Never paying enough attention to question what's happening right underneath your nose. The whole sky is falling, but none of that matters so long as everything's okay in the world inside your head." I sensed some of what she was loathe to know about me swimming inside her head.

"You never think to ask what's going on outside

to make the sky fall to pieces. You keep on about your business, stepping over dented clouds, bits of shattered sky piling up around your feet. As long as no piece of broken sky lands on top of you, you figure you're all right." Now my look turned funny.

"You ever stop to wonder why she keeps so close at hand?" Champayne asked.

"Miss Spinnaker meddles in everybody's business," I answered. "I don't pay her any more attention than she deserves." She wheeled backwards down the walkway, placing herself a safe distance from the bits of shattered sky hanging loose above my head.

After supper, Champayne felt obliged to tell me, thought someone would have told me by now seeing how I had been down here all this time. She squared herself in front of me, sucked her breath in deep, then exhaled slowly to coax out the words. I listened, distracted by how much her face had come to look like my face, the elongated chin, those jewel shaped eyes, as my baby sister delivered the news: we were Miss Spinnaker's business, the woman across the street having given birth to our grandmother some many moons ago. A piece of broken sky hit me square in the head.

The family resemblance became immediately recognizable: Gram's mouth and nose, Momma's eyes, my thin brown fingers. I stood silent, as the impression I'd formed of Miss Spinnaker mutated inside my head, percolated against thin recollections of past encounters with her, returning in the form of the great-grandmother whose acquaintance I had yet to make—Edelyn's, Champayne's and mine.

A new kind of whistle blew inside my eardrum, anger twisting colours beneath the surface of my closed lids, glowing white hot from their own private sun. I no longer hated my sister, Edelyn. I couldn't fault Champayne either for having been left to deliver the news. That I needed somebody to tell me, to spell it out in the plainest terms punctuated the stagger walk I seemed intent on taking through life, one sharp curve after another sneaking up on me, realization not taking hold until I was already well into the ditch.

Even my mother was spared the brunt of my wrath. When I questioned her later by phone, the sound of disappointment buried as low inside my voice as I could muster, she claimed to have become so accustomed to silencing talk of Gram's mother outside of what she had been led to believe was true, the need to tell me anything different had slipped her mind.

I pitied Gram. The news must have hit her the same way it had done me, only more swift, like a sharp thumb to the windpipe.

I focused all my resentment on the spindly hand across the street. Despised the pink and green curtains that had succeeded all these years in concealing her shame, hiding the face of a woman who would give up her only child. She deserved every last insult Momma had hurled her way. I only wished for the opportunity to heap more of the same on her, sparing my mother what little energy she had left, her health quietly waning back in New York.

I never once took Champayne over to see Miss Spinnaker, neither did she venture to our side of the street again, like a rat suddenly exposed to bright light. She had to have known Momma wouldn't stoop so low as to send another child down here unarmed with the truth. With the need to respect any wishes Gram may have asked she honour out of the way, that's likely the first thing Momma shared with Champayne and Edelyn. Only she forgot to tell me, invisibility cream hiding me from view.

I turned my attention to the other truths Champayne might be inclined to unearth. Wondered what she might know about Gram's father, the legacy we had stumbled into unwittingly. Even if she knew, there was loads more I needed to tell her, scandal hanging over Picayune like an angry sky threatening at any moment to come bearing down on anyone even remotely connected to the circle.

Tuesday After Noon

Champayne caught me at the kitchen table in the middle of my grocery list. It had been ages since I needed a list, being in Gram's house alone. To this point, I had been content to manage day-to-day, taking in only what I alone could consume, letting tomorrow decide what my body would want next.

"Somebody's here looking for you," Champayne announced, poking her head inside the kitchen, her face lit with the prospect that some excitement might finally land in her new world. I didn't share her enthusiasm. People looked for me these days, sought my counsel on how to settle any number of easily mended disputes. I had no reason to expect anything out of the ordinary. Oh, the things that could occur on an ordinary Tuesday afternoon.

"Show them in," I said, barely looking up from my grocery list.

His blue eyes grabbed me up first, lifted me out of my chair until I thought I might rush across the room and leap into his arms. Fortunately, I found my voice before my feet set to moving, saving my ego an unnecessary bruising.

"What's brought you back this way?" I asked, directing him through the back door, out of earshot of my baby sister.

"I'm here on advice from my grandfather," August replied in a tone I might have found soothing had his sudden reappearance in Gram's kitchen not been so unsettling. "He told me to follow my heart."

"Evidently, your heart has led you astray."

"I suppose I deserve that," he replied, those blue eyes somehow managing to come off deflated.

"Let's not get into what either of us deserves," I answered, working to remain unmoved by his apparent show of sad emotion. "You don't want to tally that record."

A momentary close of his eyes erased some of their sadness. "I've had lots of time to contemplate what I want in life," he began again, his hands at work to mould his chin into a shape able to get all the way through whatever he'd come to say.

"I recognise the privilege I've been afforded. Let what I have fool me into believing my life was fulfilled, without having expended any real effort of my own. I never meant to squander that privilege. Wanted instead to find something worth reaching for, a direction to apply myself in that hadn't been laid out for me already." He adjusted his stance, steadied himself against the handrail leading away from Gram's front porch.

"My daddy and them, they're first generation made. Came up on the back of Granddad's good fortune to believe they're entitled in some way. From their first steps on the sunny side, they began to cultivate the notion that people who move in the same circles ought to be paired.

"The circumstance surrounding my introduction to my wife was marked by everyone pretending to be more rich, more refined, more deserving than any of us can rightfully claim to be. Only my grandfather remained true to any claims he made. Having achieved all he set out to accomplish in life and then some, he had no cause for pretence. Having patterned my approach almost exclusively on things I've seen him do, it's inevitable that I inherit some of his unsavoury ways too." He searched my face to make sure he still had my full attention, eyed the back door to see whether he might score an invitation back inside.

"Seldom do the things we have in mind for ourselves play out as we had envisioned. An opportunity presents itself before we're fully prepared to give chase. Even when the timing is right, we fail to recognise the value in pursuing an opportunity until the moment has already passed us by. Sometimes the need you have for something rises in you faster than you can get a grip on the urge behind the need. We find our hands full already when something we desperately want comes our way." His hands were at his chin again, easing out what he wanted to say next.

"To think I was destined to marry before ever tasting my first real kiss. Having no basis to navigate by, I agreed to leave fate in more experienced hands. All those hands knew to do is ensure the family name didn't take a backward step into the gutter—or the mud as was the case for a family of horse trainers.

"The courtship went by us like a breeze. With time, I found I could no longer move her. I'm not certain it was ever intended that I could. This past year, the two of us were out window shopping as the Thanksgiving weekend drew to a close. She clutched my arm as a first lick of winter's wicked wind hustled past, the holiday season seeming to have a regenerative effect on our connection to one another. A cognac diamond bracelet caught her eye as we turned the corner in front of a jewellery shop that, according to the stencilling above the glass door, has stood for nearly a hundred years. The bracelet was arranged in the window alongside a matching necklace and a tantalizingly long pair of dangling earrings.

"I knew she wanted it before the salesclerk motioned us in from the street. One look at the warm glow of shimmering brown stones against her skin, and I knew I needed to get it for her. I could have asked Granddad for the money. Could have borrowed my father's charge card, but that's been the story of my whole life, spent riding on one or the other of their coattails. The bracelet would have to wait if I was to make the purchase by way of my own hard work.

"I began stashing away the commissions from the little bit of luggage I managed to sell. I'd never have enough in time for Christmas. Valentine's was beginning to look like a viable possibility. My heart sank when I returned on Christmas Eve to find her parents had purchased the entire set for her, down to those dangling earrings. I believed her when she said she hadn't put them up to it. She hadn't put her parents off the idea either.

"That marked the beginning of the end between us. I struggled to comprehend what I wanted from her, tried to figure what, if anything, of consequence she ever wanted from me. I thought for awhile I knew—she wanted what her parents had, what my parents have worked diligently to upkeep, the two of us surrounded on both sides by people who subscribe to the simple notion that, in order to be happy, all you need do is look the part.

"In the end, we created the illusion of happiness, a bright paper wrapping to conceal a nearly empty existence together." He covered his mouth with both hands, drew his face together between anxious fingers, like the part of him that needed to get through all he had to say was about to come apart on him.

"But, one person can't be left to do all the figuring where two people are concerned. I tried to convince myself that real happiness didn't matter so long as we worked with equal strength to perfect the illusion. When you and I first met, I took the foolhardy approach. Neglected the responsibility on my hands and gave into the need I felt for you, placing my happiness above hers. But what happiness could I hope to find, disappointing her at one turn only to turn around and disappoint you at the next? No conscious man can live that life for long and still have any feelings left.

"It didn't hit me until that Easter weekend I didn't make it home to see her. I anticipated the upset being apart might bring, the two of us sharing the burden a lonesome holiday can lay on you. She, on the other hand, seemed more concerned what to tell her family, how to excuse my not showing up for Easter supper. Rehearsed into the phone how to answer to her friends having been left to attend Sunday service without me seated next to her in the pew.

"I tried with all my worth to stand by her in this position, recognising the need to get along as best we can settle itself in between us. That's when a trembling started deep inside my chest: a murmur, a passing thought. That tiny whisper of doubt finally birthed a panic that getting along is the best we'd ever manage to do for one another. It took that break between us for me to recognise my being in Picayune had more to do with sorting things out with her than any career anxiety. I realize now how selfish it was to insist on sticking it out alone, thinking the sacrifice would succeed in turning the tide on my misadventures in door-to-door sales."

He was beginning to go 'round about on me again, the dots between wherever it was he'd been and my grandmother's back step failing to connect. But I had grown wise in my years, stood tall above him on Gram's back porch, resisting the urge to again beg for him to choose—me or her, forever and ever more.

I'd had my fill of his long winded trail of events. Instead I offered him a bit of my truth. "My grandmother had a topaz pendant that she left stashed inside a velvet pouch well in the back of her top bureau drawer," I explained. "It's where she kept all her delicate things. Not hidden, mind you, but buried just the same. It was a keepsake from a long-standing connection, one that defies simple explanation, feelings she wasn't supposed to have felt in the first place. I wore that pendant last year on my birthday, lifted the pouch from the back of the drawer and wrapped myself all day in the history of buried feelings between my grandma and her person."

I straightened my spine an added measure, shaded my eyes against the afternoon sun, determined for a change to dictate the course between us. "You want love," I told him. "You go someplace where you can get that kind of feeling."

"I'd like nothing more than the chance to try, with you," he replied, too quickly for my tastes, the last bit tacked on like an afterthought.

"If you were here for me that would have been the first thing off your tongue. Instead you want to concern me with all the things you can't afford to give her." I waved a hand at him. "Man, you need to go on away from here."

His mouth bent in a way I had never before seen from him. "I don't need you to be angry with me. Not right now. Tomorrow, you can be as angry as you like, hate me even. But right now, I ask that you set aside your anger, hear me out. I have been apart from you, but not a day has gone by that I didn't think of you, didn't dwell long on the things you and I once shared. I know the hurt I've caused you. But you have to recognise that I've been hurting just as badly for you."

"It would take a lifetime of trying for me to hate you," I assured him. "I felt myself headed down that road at some point, but couldn't manage to get all the way there." I put my anger on a back shelf. Let him finish explaining how he's been hurting for me. 'Cause Lord knows how badly I'd been hurting for him.

He relaxed his shoulders, his eyes regaining some of their brightness. "When you're apart from someone, you inevitably seek small reminders to keep thoughts of that person close at hand," he offered. "Too much time apart and those reminders begin to take place of the actual person, the thoughts inside your head only vaguely recognizable as the person waiting on you back home. I got caught somewhere between too long and

369

not enough time in Picayune."

He disappeared inside himself, went to a place I couldn't help but imagine he and I had been to together. "Trust me when I say that I didn't set out looking for you. Didn't intend half of what took place between us. But we can't take any of that back, cram the feelings between us inside a jar, screw the lid on tight and get on with our separate lives apart from one another. Can't erase what we shared, though, getting over you is something I never aspired to do."

"Then you should never have kissed me," I said.

He rocked back on his heels, recollection of what he knew to be true clashing with my account of the circumstances surrounding our first kiss. "But you kissed me," he said, his face working to hide the first bend of a smile.

"Then you should never have kissed me back. You shouldn't have taken me home with you, kissed me on your granddaddy's porch steps. You shouldn't have come back to Picayune with me, kissed me again in my grandmother's bedroom. Most especially, you should never have left."

"I reached a point that I couldn't keep from kissing you," he admitted, that recollection jiving more with how I remembered it.

I caught myself reaching for his hand when he gestured in my direction, to wrap myself inside his arms before he could squeeze away again, when he let slip past his lips something that hit a wrong nerve.

"I'll admit. I left here thinking all I needed is time away to clear my head, to silence the thoughts rooting themselves inside me. I remember leaving for Picayune with a similar notion in mind, that all I needed was time alone to rediscover the benefits being with her would bring. The moments you and I spent have proven too numerous to dispel, and all the other good times rolled together still too few."

"So that's all I was to you, another good time?" I felt the insult as much for her as for me, the two of us lumped together in the most unfortunate pairing. "What do you expect me to do when the next good time comes rolling along? Let you run off for another eternity, hoping you might someday come back to me."

"I accept responsibility for everything I've done," he stammered. "Put you in the middle of a situation that was troubled long before you came into the picture. But you can't blame me for something I didn't do with my full heart."

"Simple as that?" I asked. "That you're not to blame for what your heart was feeling at the time."

"In a way, the explanation is just that simple if that's how you choose to look at things. At the same time, it's the most complicated thing you'll ever hear said." The thin smile left his lips, settling in behind pleading eyes, threatening to break what little hold I had left on my composure.

His hand reached for mine and this time I took it with less hesitation than I would have preferred. "You'll have to tell it for me someday," I replied, still unsure how far to let myself fall.

I thought for a moment I heard Champayne stirring inside the screen door. The last thing I needed was for my baby sister to see me go soft in front of a man. "Look, I don't have time for any idle chatter," I said, pulling my hand away from his.

"It's only idle if you don't want to hear what I have to say." His tone for the first time sounded insistent, this part of the conversation not as carefully rehearsed inside his head.

"It's not that I don't want to hear. It's a simple matter of not being able to hear you... Not right now."

"All right then," he said. His answer landed flat, indicating his intentions not to argue though his eyes, wide with emotion, showed how wholly unprepared he was to give up the fight. "If you won't hear me today, then I'll be back here tomorrow and the next day and the tomorrow after that, need be, 'til you'll hear me again."

I allowed the voice rattling inside my head to take command of my tongue. "I put all my tomorrows on a train and sent them back to New York." I leaned a hip against the porch railing to anchor myself. I grew drunk from the scent of August's skin, memories of his touch mixing with my thoughts, twisting my words. Had me telling things I hadn't intended to tell.

I gushed with pride upon learning that Edelyn had enrolled in City College, her mind set on becoming a social worker. I talked about seeing her perform at the spoken word cafe, how she wanted to be a poet, too. I motioned in the direction of my baby sister eavesdropping inside the kitchen on account of our momma laid up in New York, her black hair denied the opportunity to see gray. I thought about my daddy, trapped inside a glass cage, longed to see him stepping down from his perch to hug me again.

The tears were streaming down my face before I could catch them. I found myself trembling against August's chest before realizing I might crumple into his arms. I got that held safe feeling again—the strength of my daddy's arms around my neck, his grip on my shoulders, a reassuring kiss against my forehead. I might have missed all that had Champayne not seen fit to intervene, recognising how badly Daddy and I would miss not seeing one another.

August cradled my head against the firm knot of his shoulder, my tears staining his shirt sleeve. This was the only time I could remember him showing up in anything less than a button-down shirt—just jeans and a cotton T-shirt. He looked rustic, cowboy cute minus the ten-gallon hat.

I straightened my arms into August's chest, pushed myself away in a pitiful attempt at pulling myself back together. When I looked into his face again, I saw the tenderness in my grandmother's eyes that I had far too often mistaken for disappointment before learning the details behind the circumstances that made her so tough. I felt the warmth of my mother's arms in his embrace, saw in her thin smile the desperate need for me to love her back, to forgive her for any time her love for me might not have been so evident.

I wiped my eyes with the back of my hand then I asked that he forgive my outburst. I assured him that my tears hadn't meant a thing, that I would be fine. He didn't seem to believe my promises, but apologised just the same for the intrusion then left through the side yard to avoid having to pass my baby sister again, as broke down a look on his face as any grown man had the right to muster.

I hate that I didn't have the strength to call him back. Hate even more that letting him go again might rob me of what little strength I had left.

"Who was that?" Champayne asked on my way in from the back porch.

"Nobody," I muttered, raising a trembling hand to conceal my red Rudolph nose, the puffiness in my lips.

"Worked you up like he was somebody," she said, wrinkling her brow at me.

"He used to be somebody," I replied, shading my eyes from her view. "Now he's nobody." I searched the kitchen for some chore I might assign her to preempt any further questions about my used to be somebody.

"Looks like somebody to me."

Looks like somebody to me, too.

Untold Tomorrows

My mind was a jumble of unkept thoughts. I attempted one thing after another, but couldn't manage to hold a single task through to completion. I had trained myself over the years to keep my desires at bay, to quiet the yearning. Then August showed up, promising to focus untold tomorrows on me and I couldn't see clear to stand by and let him do it.

With all the added responsibility I'd taken on in recent years, the ways I'd extended myself on behalf of people around me, I needed time alone to consider the irrational, impractical possibility of having August in my life again. I offered Champayne some made-up excuse about needing to clear my head then set out in search of the tallest hilltop at the farthest end of town. With a dead baby buried at the top of one hill, the shame of having raised korn buried atop another, my choice of hilltop retreats in Picayune was growing scarce.

I showed up too late to catch the sun setting, but was rewarded by the wonder of her spectacle nonetheless. Layers of colour stacked on top of one another like a rainbow pulled taut along the horizon. The red skirt of the sun, long ago disappeared from view, lay nestled between the hard earth and the lingering glow of the daytime blue sky. The hem of her skirt ran upward from blood orange to the peel of a tangerine, turned ripe with age. A rust coloured sash appeared, marking the line beyond which night time would eventually fall, layers of red disappearing beyond the horizon.

The whole affair dissolved in a shade so dark even the grimiest night crawler might lament the sun's passing. I was left to navigate the way down the hillside by light of an anxious moon, still flickering to reach its full potency against a charcoal sky. I arrived at the edge of town wanting to see August again, needing to see him. If a rainbow could lie on its side stretched end-to-end along the horizon, then I could accept that eyes that blue could show up after all this time, welled over with sadness.

I sent word for Mr. Graves. He had a way of knowing things, and I figured he would know something of August's whereabouts around town. He showed up the next morning carrying an accordion style folder, the kind used to safeguard invoices, bound together by a self-attached elastic band. He placed the parcel on the kitchen table as he sat, never bothering to explain its contents to me.

His eyes looked sad too, but then they always did. Though, on this particular occasion, his eyes seemed to betray the characteristic detachment required of his position as undertaker. Today his eyes looked like they had witnessed the first ceremonial handfuls of dirt thrown on the casket of his closest kin.

"Tell me you're not here to confess that you're my grandfather?" I asked as I poured a stream of freshly brewed coffee into a cup for him.

"I wouldn't want to disappoint you in that way. Your mother was already eleven, twelve years old when I finally met your grandma good. I wish at times I had known her forever, that we had been high school sweethearts or something. But our high school years didn't overlap in a way to have made our meeting that early in life possible." The sadness in his eyes deepened as the morning light grew to fill the space inside Gram's kitchen.

"Somebody once told me that a man who wants to do right needs a righteous man inside his shirt pocket to remind him of the path he ought to be traveling. I've come to accept that a man who needs constant reminding of how to do right is gonna slip after too long, despite a righteous man ridin' along with him," he said, slurping coffee from his mug. "The only time I've truly done right was on your grandmother's behalf. That it's her I was doing for is the most wrong I'll do in my lifetime." His expression went blank just like I'd seen Gram's do, seated at this very table, staring into her palms, hoping to find the face of somebody who loved her beyond measure staring back.

"This is no life for anybody to lead, loving someone

from afar—when the two of you can manage to keep your distance, your heart beating away across town. No other heartache is more persistent, until your heart breaks for good." He set his mug down on the pine tabletop.

"I met your grandma at her daddy's funeral. She was tough as nails even way back then. Still, you could see the fright percolating behind silent eyes, left alone with a little girl to raise, no sort of momma around to pave the way," he began to explain. "Whereas the whole rest of the world expected her to be stronger, wiser, braver than most days she knew how to be, I permitted her to be her true, unadulterated self. Alone with her, I could be my true, unadulterated self, too." He suddenly became conscious of his rambling, seemed to recognise by way of my vacant stare the gap in knowledge I possessed of past history with Gram. Realized that gap was bigger than he'd be able to fill in a single conversation over morning coffee.

"With your grandmother's passing, I lost whatever good might come between us. Though her departure has cleared the path for me to do right again, I have little time left to make good on all my broken promises. recognise that with the right shift in circumstance, what I have at home might never have been." I imagined August sitting there, working to resolve the same conflict inside his head. With the right shift in time, I might never have known him. A shift in the opposite direction and he may never have left my side.

The need to explain himself continued to pour from Mr. Graves, like he understood the surrogate role he'd been left to play, in part on August's behalf, the rest for my grandmother. "As for Missus Graves, I know she doesn't set well on most people. But I always pictured myself growing old with her, getting to see that satin head of hair of hers go salt and pepper before turning all together gray. I see us chasing after grandkids, taking turns spoiling 'em rotten. I'm just not certain how to knit the time together between now and then to make us growing old with one another a viable possibility."

He slid the parcel to my side of the table as he gathered his hat to leave. I had nearly forgotten about the folder he'd come to deliver. I was lost in the realization of what he and Gram must have meant to one another, their silent need for one another receding largely unseen to the far reaches of the circle. For the first time, I missed Gram's presence by my side for somebody other than my own sorry self.

I sat alone at the kitchen table for the longest while before mustering the nerve to unfasten the elastic band. I reached inside the folder to find a bundle of unopened letters nestled in amongst its accordion style folds. Mr. Graves had organized the letters by postmark, from oldest to newest, the face of each envelope addressed in August's hand to me.

The thought of August having been close by all this time, some little part of him resting within easy reach inside one of Mr. Graves' office drawers, sent a small panic through me. I spread the letters out across the knotty pine table, taking care to preserve their order, and began piecing together the lost time between August and me.

The first few letters read like correspondence from one pen pal to another: he wanted to know how I was getting along, asked about the weather. The weather was fine from wherever he was writing. Lots of words, but still nothing said between us. His next few letters conveyed a sour mix of anger and sadness. Anger that I hadn't returned any of his previous letters, sadness that I likely never would reply.

Through waves of shifting emotion, a sombre realization started to stick inside my head—August had been just as sick without me as I had been without him, even though our being apart seemed to be of his choosing. It started with the simplest statement of regret, the closest thing to remorse I would hear in any of his letters:

I would rather you stand on my toes, scream in my ear, cry a river of tears down my neck, than remain silent, that you never speak to me again. That you will forever more know me solely from an outside vantage point, that you will never know the true feelings of my

heart. I've come to realize I'm going to lose
you simply because of how desperately I want
not to. I struggle with the notion that things
will end this way, without another word said
between us. That nothing we shared will have
mattered if I'm never able to speak with you
again...

His next letter seemed to presume I was angry with
him, having discovered that least little bit of himself that
he'd held back from me. He figured part-way into the
letter that she was angry with him too, for the little bit
of himself he'd allowed me to steal away from the two
of them. My insides went fuzzy again. I condemned him
for having shared with me that least little bit of himself,
for leading me to believe he had more of himself to give.

I stayed glued to the kitchen table for the better part of
the day, sifting through the details of August's letters.
I'd read one passage that would send me looking for
something he'd said in a previous letter about how
much he missed me, how he'd been unable to silence
memories of our time together, to see whether his feelings had changed.

Lunchtime came and went with little more than
a cold cup of coffee by my side. I missed my daytime
TV programs, skipped my afternoon nap, postponed
my customary stroll down the walkway to check the

mailbox. In true Miss Spinnaker garb, I had hemmed and hawed my way, stammered through what I needed to do, wasting the better part of a day. Still, I was unable to get all the way through the folder filled with August's letters.

Fortunately, some internal clock ticked silent inside my head in time to gather the folder and put it away before Champayne came busting in to tell me about her day, her eyes filled with excitement that she had finally made a friend or two, that she was beginning to make her way at school. I tried to fix my attention, but found as we sat through an early supper that I was only half listening.

Champayne went to bed early that night, concerned no doubt that she'd done something to quiet my mood. Regret swept through me as I studied the silhouette of my sister's lonesome backside. I crept out to the front room and slid into the sofa-bed next to her. August's letters would have to wait another day.

The next morning, I retook my post at the kitchen table armed with a fresh cup of coffee, a pot simmering nearby in case the task ran long again. I waded through another handful of pen pal letters before eventually coming across one that, though the briefest in the stack, took the greatest effort to get all the way through. Anytime I thought I understood the sentiment behind August's words, I had to start over again. Read something different in his tone each time I attempted a second read:

> *Had I chosen a single path in life to follow, I might have become something separate from the person you see today. Given the chance, I'd have been something different for you, something to bring you fulfilment without asking a single thing of you in return. I'd be the blue streak in a rainbow leading the march across the springtime sky, or a twinkling star sent at twilight to remind you that you're not alone in the world. I'd be a forgiving wind, blowing just strong enough to move the air around you, but not so brisk as to disturb anything you didn't want moved. I'd be the gleaming skin of a silent river waiting for you to push through her honeysuckle defence to remind you of our connection to some distant land. If I could choose, I'd be whatever you wanted me to be.*

Each letter ended the same—*Yours, August.* But how can that be, given that I'm here alone while he's God knows where? That's when I noticed all the envelopes appeared the same, Birmingham PO stamped round at the top of each envelope just above my name and street address. The postmarks ticked off the days in regular succession, August averaging nearly a letter a week interspersed by several long pauses where I imagine either he had gone home to Maryland or she had travelled to be with him in Alabama. I didn't believe I should hate him for it, but wished for more than a second that I could.

At one point in his letters, it was over between us:

You are sure to believe by now that I am through with this, have gotten over all that we shared, the bond we formed. Then you must not have felt the dream I had of you last night. You were here with me, in a place you could not possibly have been, close like the moon, peeking in beneath my window shade. I touched you. And you touched me. Splendid, forever kind of touching, like this was meant to be. I'd like to think you felt that dream, that you felt forever with me. But I fear that you didn't, that forever between us is something that cannot be.

Momma tells me that even a man who's grovelling at your feet will hold a bit of his humility in reserve. That way if he succeeds in winning you over, he'll have some dignity left in front of you, can hold his shoulders back when he cocks his head to proclaim that he's your man, his most determined peacock strut on full display.

Once you've gotten to know a man up close, you only need see his eyes to know the depths of his humility, a shallow breath rattling inside his chest providing sufficient evidence of genuine remorse resting in place of any affectations toward grovelling.

August let go of all his humility inside his letters, bared his soul for me to see.

If things between us are to end this way, I want you to know the profound impact knowing you has had on my outlook. My grandfather tells me that I most want what is least easily attained. When I had you, if ever I had you, I still wanted more.

No matter where life takes us, a single fact remains: I saw you and I know the way that you saw me, in my truest form. Prior obligation took me someplace else. The need for propriety, to get on with life, took you someplace too. It's no longer my place to know where you've gone or what you've gotten up to. But know that at some point we were both right there, together.

I don't say this to diminish the time we shared. In some ways, time and distant memories are all we have. In other ways, the time we spent brought more than either of us deserved to know about one another. When it's all said

and done, there will be other fulfilment in life,
time spent with someone different, for you
and me both. And undoubtedly, other regrets.

The last letter I read was postmarked nearly a year to the day prior to him showing up again in Picayune. His tone had turned notably resolute, his voice more desperate than it had seemed anywhere else along the way. It's like he was seeing into the future without me. Only the wheels as conjured inside his head had already started turning. He hadn't been here to witness the events unfolding firsthand, but his heart had informed him all that was about to transpire:

I feel you on the verge of meeting somebody
new if you haven't found someone already.
I imagine he's a decent sort. I can't see you
accepting anything less in your life. He'll treat
you like you want to be treated. Will care for
you in ways I only wish I could. Will be there
for you at times my present circumstance
won't permit.

I see you in time falling in love with this
man. But your connection to him will never
match what might have been between you
and me. The bond you share with him more
conscious than felt against the memory of
private moments together with me directed

along the most haphazard trail of emotions.
From a distance, it will appear that his love
for you has no rival. But close in tight, where
only you and I can see, you'll know how
much I love you, how much I have always
loved you. I will forever hold a special place
for you in my heart. Even if it means losing
you, I'll want to see you happy again.

I found his jealousy pathetic. I was especially put off by his assertion that no man could ever love me the way he had. That he chose to imagine me paired with someone else as a way of torturing himself seemed all too hypocritical when that's precisely the pain he left me to endure. How can August accuse me of being untrue when I'd stopped looking for love the moment I found it in him? When I knew all the ways that I had loved him, that we had loved each other, like no one else could love. Not in this lifetime.

I decided not to read anymore letters, entertaining a one-sided conversation. Still, I couldn't quiet my curiosity over Mr. Graves. Why he had taken such meticulous care of August's letters, with no apparent intention of ever sharing them with me? The pecking order on this side of town again sprung to mind—the ministers followed by the undertaker. Sitting well down the line, the postmaster was obligated to fulfil whatever wishes Mr. Graves had imposed on him to intercept any letters

Mr. Graves would see fit to keep from me.

He claimed to have kept the letters on my grand-mother's account, hoping to spare me the burden the two of them had carried for one another. Then he shows up the other morning with a folder full of August's letters to read, like it's okay all of a sudden for me to bear the pain of loving this man, of wanting somebody I might never truly possess. Perhaps he'd been standing silent the whole while, waiting for me to ask to see August's letters, for me to realize I'd eventually find myself wanting to hear from this man again.

My Shadow and Me

August failed to come looking for me the way he had promised. Or maybe he had come looking, stood long at the edge of Gram's walkway then turned back, fearing I might refuse him again.

I set out looking for him instead. But how do you look for someone whose intentions you no longer comprehend, whose whereabouts for what seems an eternity are still a mystery? I had only managed to see him on occasion he'd come to see me. Now the task was on my hands to find him.

I headed in the direction of Richardson. Everything was coming up new of late over there. Maybe August and I would have a chance at a new beginning over that way, too.

I hadn't anticipated the commotion that met me on my way out of Picayune. People were milling about as though caught on the eve of a hurricane, unsure from which direction the wind might blow. Except no two people I passed seemed headed the same way, toward some safe haven away from the storm's direct path.

I found myself swimming in a sea of anxious expressions. The eyes said all I needed to understand their predicament, the urgency of their stares focused in a way that left the rest of the face frighteningly expressionless. The closer I looked, the more I came to realize that nobody appeared to be fleeing. Each person I passed seemed on the path of something, someone they desperately needed to see, bodies spilling in every direction at once, anxious to say their last, clinging good-byes.

Eventually I gathered from bits and pieces of hurried conversation that word had gotten around: the circle was under attack, the credulous faces around town in their final twist of denial before giving way to the truth. Bulging eyes peered past me to bid their final farewell to that lone someone before the lights Miss Thula had spoken about switched on.

Having assumed responsibility as ceremonial chair at the centre of the circle, the task of coordinating the door-swinging around town on my hands, it came as no surprise that I would be kept in the dark about any sort of uprising. The attack, at least in principle, aimed squarely at me.

Miss Spinnaker's words bit at the base of my skull as I stood in the wake of the crowd moving past me: 'This place ain't bigger than nothing. How are we not gonna know?' Believe me when I say, nothing rocks a whole community like the one thing even the simplest mind can't help but see coming. It's the thing that had always been waiting to happen, the possibility it might never come to pass more frightening than the thought that eventually it would. That it let you slide another day, resting on false comfort that a time of reckoning wasn't looming on the horizon, a call to judgment close upon you for all that you've done.

I touched each shoulder that passed, looking for someone to spare a moment to explain where everybody was headed, where I needed to be. Eventually a body eased close by me, leaned into me and said, "Miss Thula will be needin' you at the hair salon. You should get right over there."

Missus Graves' chalk white station wagon was parked directly behind one of the cars from the used car lot, *McCullough Auto Sales* hanging where the license plate should have been. It looked from the way she had squeezed in on his bumper that the two of them had raced there, to see who would get the coveted space beneath the royal empress shade tree adjacent to the shop's front door.

From the urgency of how they had parked, the bumpers of their two cars nearly touching one another, it was more likely still that Missus Graves and her circle of hens had chased Mr. McCullough here, her car blocking his exit like she was law. All she needed was a blue light and siren to cement her authority. I found myself wishing it might rain again and turn both their cars to dust, sparing me whatever commotion lay wait inside.

I walked onto a scene straight out of a nightmare. I was relieved to find that Missus Graves had but one of her cronies in tow until I recognised Missus McCullough by her side, a heavy covering of mint-green eyeshadow plastered in place, the two of them having trailed her husband here from the used car lot. Missus Graves stood posted in the middle of the shop floor casting aspersions on anybody in earshot, looking for the first time like she needed her hair done, though the wild look in her eyes lent the impression that she wasn't the least concerned about the state of her hairdo.

According to her account, Miss Thula was the lowliest person to ever walk the earth. Stealing scraps of time from a broken-down fool like Mr. McCullough who sat trapped in the back of the room like a deer caught in the roadway, his hooves stuck to the pavement. I'm not sure what her commentary had to say about Missus McCullough, left standing in the way of Missus Graves' tirade, hoping to steal that same time back with her broken-down fool of a husband.

Cecile and Sharaine were more of the same, junior home-wreckers in training. Only their actions couldn't be helped, their way in life an inevitable consequence of the company they had chosen to keep. The two of them stood uncharacteristically dumbstruck on either side of their aunt, caught in the path of Missus Graves' glare.

Lamar stood silent toward the back of the shop with the patience of a fire, waiting to burn, his full

attention trained on the gyrations of Missus Graves'
wild hair. Having made her rounds in the room, Missus
Graves eventually turned to heave a series of insults in
the direction of his station. His crime in her estimation
was being too common—to see her, to know her, to
even dare speak her name.

In the end, it became clear that he had been keeping
close company with Mr. and Missus Graves' daughter,
Lula Mae. Lamar was too far below their daughter's
station despite the extent to which Lula Mae had
dogged herself down over the years. Truth be told, Lula
Mae had needed Lamar's help to regain her self-worth,
not unlike me. And, in return, she helped him find a
sense of belonging in Picayune, something I still sorely
missed.

I only doubted momentarily that Lamar hadn't been
seeing Lula Mae alone. It would appear from the way he
kept their relationship so secretive that he wasspending
his affections elsewhere, Lula Mae the woman he kept
on the side, their secret connection marking his price
of admission into the circle. I should have known
better than to question the integrity of the one man I
had grown to count on above anyone else, whose face
I turned to whenever I found myself in need of a bit of
comfort, resting in the warmth of my daddy's eyes.

Slowly, Lamar's conversation started to burn, in
deliberate spurts as was his tendency to do. "I don't owe
you any explanation. But I have done no wrong where

Lula Mae is concerned. I brought her back here all the way from Baton Rouge knowing she'd need family by her side to fully get herself back on the path toward right. I don't know what it says about you-all that she needed to carry herself across state lines to begin to try. Recognizing I alone can't provide the support she needs, I brung her back here to be with you. Now it's your choice to make whether or not to help your daughter."

"How are you gonna tell me what I need to do for my child? Tell me, who are you? You're not even a real man, standin' up here all day, your hands full with other women's hair, your head lost in the details of their tired conversation. How you gonna even turn your head my way to say a solitary thing?"

"Seeing how little understanding you have left of what a real man should be—caring on top of compassionate, flawed at times in his approach yet committed to you nonetheless, I take it as a compliment that you don't see me as one."

I always knew a battle of some sort would unfold in Picayune, a war between righteousness lost and righteousness long forgotten. Have everyone choose sides, each person taking a stand. Let the chips in the circle fall where they may.

I envied Mr. McCullough, tucked away from the commotion like a spectator, acting as though he'd never played any part in the circle. Wished I could crawl over silent and take a place next to him, the two of us sharing a hiding spot toward the back of the room. But, from the way the hairs were standing up straight on the back of my neck, working to get a better view of the commotion, it was evident that I wouldn't be so fortunate on this day to avoid the direct line of conversation.

Stumped by Lamar's open defiance, Missus Graves turned her attention toward me. "And don't think for a minute, Miss Penny, I can't see you standin' over there. Always tryin' to keep your head below the radar. Now that your luggage salesman is back in town, I don't reckon that's going to be so easy to do." Missus Graves had seen August and me once, holding hands, coming back from a stroll along the riverside. We vowed that day to break it off, to start over as friends. It was like falling in love all over again, only faster, deeper in love than we'd fallen the first time around.

I took charge of the situation, sensing Miss Thula was in no position to do so. Even Lamar was unable to come to my rescue, his private circumstance as much under attack as that of anyone else's in the hair salon.

I motioned in the direction of Cecile and Sharaine. "You-all go on home. There's nothing more either of you can do here today." Mr. McCullough was cowering next to Lamar's station, arguably where I should have been. Missus McCullough had reached the point of feeling sorry for her husband, one hand clutching her chest, the other covering her mouth for fear she might let out a cry.

Missus Graves appeared to have momentarily lost command of her anger though her eyes spit fire whenever she looked in the direction of Miss Thula's chair. I positioned myself between the two of them, Miss Thula's head lowered, unable to meet Missus Graves' full stare.

"What is it you want here?" She seemed to take offense at the very thought of my having addressed her directly.

"I'm here to call you and everybody like you to account."

"So, you're here acting on God's will. Is that what you would have us believe?"

"I'm here to see justice done, to put an end to everything you represent. God being on my side is a mere consequence of how I've chosen to live my life, walking in the way of what's right."

"No one is questioning how you've lived your life. All I'm asking is what you're looking to accomplish, getting everyone riled up this way?"

"And there she is," Missus Graves observed, clucking to herself. "Your grandma in the flesh, all of her slick talk passing through you like a sieve."

"What's so slick about wanting to restore order, to get folks to act civil toward one another?"

"Order!" A loose strand of hair flopped positions on the top Missus Graves' head as though acting in direct response to the elevated agitation in her tone.

"You can't restore order from chaos you yourself have stirred. It simply cannot be done."

I sat wondering what chaos had I stirred. I had come to view personal accountability as extending no further than the ends of my fingertips, to the top of my baby sister's head, to the sound of Edelyn's voice by phone to let me know she had arrived safely back in New York. Missus Graves could only have meant August. But August had gone off to Baltimore or Birmingham or wherever he was supposed to have been. If he had come back to me as he claimed, then he had done so of his own free will. Lord knows I would have brought him back here far sooner had I possessed that kind of command over his whereabouts. "I'm afraid that I don't get your meaning."

"There you go, working to keep a foot on both sides of the fence," she responded. "You condone certain behaviours around town, set up elaborate schemes to let untold indiscretions pass unchecked. Then you show up like an innocent bystander, wanting to know what all the fuss is about. You are content to let bedlam rule as long as the perpetrators pay their dues. Those dues intended to soothe any sore feelings, leaving the rest of us to accept these false shows of goodwill as part and parcel of this makeshift belief system you seem to have bought into, where one kind deed can make up for any amount of turmoil wreaked on another person's existence, good karma leading the way to do your bidding.

"Ruth Ann, how many times would you say your husband traipsed over this way to mend a screen door, or to help install a new garbage disposal?" She didn't leave but a half-second for Missus McCullough to attempt to answer. "Countless times," Missus Graves spouted.

"Countless times," Missus McCullough nodded, her hand still clutching her chest.

Missus Graves trained her words on me again. "I should wish to see this whole thing come tumbling down around you, everybody's dirty laundry piling up in the streets. But this is our home. Picayune not a playground for you to do with as you please." She spoke as though she had her entire circle of hens at her side. "There are people who still care about maintaining a level of decorum around here. I am no longer willing to stand by and let you tear the fabric of this community to shreds."

She buckled under the weight of her anger, paused to make sure her animosity was at full strength before continuing. "You put a couple curls on top of a couple of heads, sew a hem into a dress or two and you're supposed to be absolved of any wrongdoing? Let me assure you of one thing, Miss Penny. Karma doesn't owe you diddly. Karma failed to bring Mr. Graves home to me faithfully at the end of each day. Karma can't hope to return your luggage salesman to wherever it is that he belongs."

I began to recognise the source of her animosity, her aim not fully set on anybody in the room, not on me, not on Lamar, not even on Miss Thula. "So that's what you want, for Gram to turn up here and face you once and for all." I waved my arms in front of her. "Send an apparition to fly around the room in her place, the fright straightening everybody's hair permanently?"

"You must take me for somebody's fool," Missus Graves answered in response to my feeble attempt to lighten the mood. "Let's hear what kind of joke you have to tell once your baby sister catches wind, one way or another, of all that has gone on around here. How is she bound to react the next time someone takes a shotgun to his wife's head and it's the woman's blood on your hands.

"What I want is to see your Gram stand up and take responsibility for all the harm she has done, to bear her share of the blame for the crumbling mess this side of town has become. Lift a hand and try to make right the destruction that took place under her care."

I set humour aside, met her face on, the same as I imagine Gram would have done had fate placed her here in the room with us, Missus Graves' one wish at last coming true. "My Gram is dead and gone." It was the first time I can recall having let those words past my lips, affirmation of Gram's demise fully uttered. "Whatever pain she caused you should well have died with her. Yet here you are, arguing on behalf of all the love lost in the world, when you're the only one among us who truly has a man at home."

"I wish I can say he has always been there, standing beside me. But that has hardly been the case."

"Be that as it may, today he's right there waiting on you. Yet you're standing up here, spending precious time working to convince us of what's right in the world. What interest can you possibly have in how any of us have lived our lives?"

"To see you get what you deserve."

"Now tell me, how will that bring you any closer to setting things right between you and your man?"

I'd like to say that I succeeded in turning Missus Graves on her heels, that in the end I'd gotten her to see my point of view, to appreciate the things in life she still had to hold onto: a husband who loved her despite his one indiscretion, who stayed with her in spite of strong feelings he developed for somebody else, a daughter who had struggled her entire lifetime to live up to impossible expectations, who was struggling still to earn her mother's approval despite how far she'd come. I'd like to say all that but realize at best I managed to wear her down, to exhaust her patience.

Eventually, Missus Graves gathered Missus McCullough into her chalk white station wagon and drove off. Mr. McCullough drug himself out of the corner once the sound of Missus Graves' car was a safe distance down the roadway. He started in the direction of Miss Thula's chair but I stopped him in his tracks, feeling neither of them deserved to offer the other any explanation for what had just transpired. I sent him on his way, telling him he needed to get right what he had at home. I hoped Miss Thula had the good sense to heed the same advice.

The chaos outside the shop had only intensified since I'd gone inside the hair salon, the bodies in the streets seeming to have multiplied, feet zigzagging up and down the block the same way a hen crisscrosses her steps in search of sustenance. The same fleeting glances met my stare, holding my gaze just long enough to make a positive ID before flitting off in search of their one special someone who was undoubtedly wandering glassy-eyed and lost somewhere across town, as desperate a look on his or her face.

Suddenly the urge to see August struck me again, to look into his face and see whether his eyes were bulging, the same as those gaping in my direction on the overcrowded walkway, desperate to see me again. Part of me was still a bit burnt, stumped by his jealous assertions that no one would ever love me again. Still, the need to see him was stronger inside my chest than any anger I felt toward him.

By the time a light drizzle had begun to fall, Missus Graves and her chalk white station wagon had long disappeared to the other side of town, had turned to dust as far as I was concerned. I wanted to put my hands on somebody. Grab them up and shake 'em, shape them into what I needed them to be. For so long in life, I'd taken what people had given me and not taken it well. That night I wished to tell someone what I needed from them and have them do it.

Go home to your husband. Go home to your wife. That's what I'd told Missus Graves, Mr. McCullough, Miss Thula by direct implication. Go to them, even if they don't want you anymore, even if you no longer want them. Lock yourselves in the house together and make it seem so. That's where I need for you to be.

I wanted to shake Miss Spinnaker into the past, shape her into a momma for my grandmother, a grandma for my mother. Draw a solid line of mothering for me to pull cues from. I wanted to squeeze the life back into my baby's tiny body, push her back inside my belly. Let her stay there until she's ready to come out on her own. I wished to let Curtis be a boy again, his shirttail tucked neatly inside the waist of his trousers, his sights set on nothing more than obeying his momma's every word. August, I'd leave alone. Let him find his way back to me if this is truly where he wants to be.

Anger cut loose again inside me. Whatever weight I'd been left to carry, compounded by the wrongs I had committed on my own, should have been repaid by now, ten times over. I leaned my head back and let go my loudest scream on a violent gusting of wind, hoping to find someone in earshot to feel my rage. I searched the heavens, wished to find a silver moon looking back at me, my gram reaching down to instruct me on which way to turn. Instead, my cries were met by an empty sky, black inside an even darker blackness, defying me to return its cold-hearted stare.

That's when I remembered something Mr. Graves had advised as he laid the folder filled with August's letters next to me on the kitchen table: *'A man will tell you all you need to know if you listen carefully enough. He may not say it in the way you want to hear, but, given sufficient space and time, he'll bare all his soul for you. Just keep in mind that a one-sided conversation seldom comes out right. Go to him directly if you find you still lack some understanding.'*

I set out again in the direction of Richardson, working to keep my eyes from bulging as I searched the faces that passed. The crowd began to dwindle the further I got from town. Pretty soon I found myself alone on a street. This stretch of road, though familiar to me, stood eerily still. I thought I heard footsteps shuffling in the dirt behind mine, a shadow creeping up to take my soul.

I began to think that things couldn't possibly end this way, finding myself more alone in this world than I'd ever been despite my luggage salesman having made his way back to town. My heart pounded halfway up my throat, looking to make its own escape even as fright held me paralyzed. Just when I thought to run, August's voice rose out of the darkness. "Have you had enough?" he asked, his calm baritone filling the air between us. "Enough chasing your own shadow, enough working to right a wrong that was never yours to carry?"

All I wanted to say, my chest full with the words, was *yes*. I had had enough bearing the weight of the world on my shoulders, righting a wrong that was never truly mine to keep. That I had had enough of being alone. That I still loved him.

That's all I wanted to say, but the words rebounded inside my head, dancing with the fate of every woman I'd ever had the chance to meet. I forgave my sister, Edelyn, for the innate ability she seemed to possess for picking the absolutely worst man for her. I willed her to find the insight to consider in our father a template from which to build rather than accept as unavoidable the layers of pain inflicted on her by the likes of Massoud and the careless disregard he had shown for her wellbeing. To find a gentle soul on which the full strength of a man, caring on top of compassion, might grow in time, committed to her until the bitter end with the aid of her steady hand to nurture its development.

I wished Gram peace, solace to recognise the comfort she and Mr. Graves found in one another despite the hurt their negligence inevitably caused. Forgiveness for the havoc she brought to another person's happiness, for the burden she added to someone else's distress.

I wished my mother peace and solace and forgiveness as well. May she ultimately find the perspective to forgive herself, to find in herself something worthy of the love she believes she's missed out on.

To Miss Spinnaker, I offered time. Time to contemplate her shame, to consider a lifetime of regret that she worked tirelessly to conceal. Time to let go of all she has, to forget all she knows, to leave the past in the past and allow the future to take charge of care for its own wellbeing.

To Missus Graves, Miss Thula (Sharaine and Cecile by association), I offered one another's pride, one another's guilt, one another's pain. I don't mean to suggest they deserve one another, but, through some awful twist of fate, neither of them would be complete in her regret without the other close by to stir her emotions. In the end, having each other to contend with is all either of them has in life to truly count on.

I saw both sides of the river, began to understand Bunk's wife with her failed attempt at removing herself from the circle, ridding herself of the only life she'd ever known. I bemoaned her last, struggling effort to escape that slow train rumbling down on her, to reconcile the guilt for her open defiance against all that is seen as right in the world, leaving her husband decidedly on the outside, oblivious only to the reason things had to wind up this way between them.

To August's wife, Nora, I offered my heartfelt apology. I have done to you what I would least want done to me. Took from you something I myself found impossible to live without. I will not burden you with well-wishes, will not belittle your suffering by claiming to understand your pain. I can only begin to comprehend the hurt I've caused you. Will live till my dying day wishing I could take back what I've done, can send him home to you pretending no one like me ever did exist.

When I asked August whether he'd been out looking for me, he admitted to having been there the whole while, outside the hair salon to make certain I was in no real danger. Suddenly, I felt the strength of my daddy's arms, the warmth of my mother's eyes, Gram's soothing tone, even Miss Spinnaker's spindly brown fingers looking over me on the mean streets of Picayune. He promised at a time that he would never abandon me. I trust that he never will. Have always known that close in tight, where only he and I can see, no one could ever love me the way he does.

He escorted me to the end of Gram's block, his jacket pulled across my shoulders to shield me from the rain, still working to find its rhythm. He told me to get some rest. There's something he wants to show me in the morning.

In Deference to Your Mother's Daughter

August picked me up the next day in a loud, brooding pickup, the kind that has two sets of wheels sandwiched beneath each of the truck's rear fenders—even his little man car had grown up. He drove with the deliberation of an ungainly old man as we made our way out of Picayune, allowing the truck to slip forward before easing off the gas to silence the engine's thunder at work under full charge.

Runyon Farms was painted in faint lettering on either truck door. I recognised the same moniker on a wooden placard hanging loose at one end as we turned up a dirt drive at the far end of Richardson. We stood staring at a sagging barn door, the field overgrown with patches of long weeds, their flowering heads trembling against a wind still deciding whether it intended to blow with measurable force. In the shadow of the barn stood a dilapidated farmhouse that might once have been the source of great pride. Not as grand as the one that anchored the landscape on Mr. Gossett's estate, nothing to turn your nose up at either.

August seemed to sense my puzzlement. "There are two kinds of people to engage in the business of breeding racehorses: those who earn their fortune at the task and those who lose all they own. You're looking at the seedy underbelly of the horse racing business that granddad never wished to speak about. It spells the end of the road for some hapless soul where land and money, his animals, his prize possessions, even command over his staff, are lost by the mere stretch of a nose across the finish line.

"This farm is the business I was sent down here to tend to in the first place. I'd proven how miserable a job I could do running an already thriving stable. Granddad was interested to see what I might do with a business in need of a turnaround. Nearly had her back on her feet before I was called away again. I should say Mr. Runyon's head groom and I nearly got her back on her feet, Mr. Ramsey being the only stableman willing to stay on or unable to let go for reasons he alone comprehends."

The mention of August having been *called away* stung more than I wished to admit. I didn't recall it that way. Instead recollected opening the door to find his wife standing on Gram's front porch, the burden of shame landing on me double its weight, having been left to answer for August's behaviour on top of my own, the incessant flowing of tears that nearly succeeded in washing away everything pure inside me: hope, faith, belief. The pain of him being pulled away from me, the emptiness echoed back any time I look for some sign that he had fought to stay, an ache that still nags me to this day.

But, if a rainbow can lie sideways along the horizon, then I could bear to indulge August a bit longer. "What brought you back?" I asked.

"I went home to Maryland for a spell. My parents were in the midst of selecting new doorknobs for their home's interior, despite their old knobs having dutifully opened all those doors over the years. Just the latest upgrade in a long list of change in their perpetual state of rearranging, the two of them always on the lookout for some way to freshen their surroundings.

"Having replaced every movable furnishing, they've gotten to swapping out permanent fixtures. Picked out these heavy pewter levers rounded off at the ends. I couldn't help but remark how the weight of those curves pleased my eye, how their shape fit my hand as it glided gently over their supple contours. Each handle I touched reminded me of some small pleasure, taken a bit at a time with you." His eyes went shy, the little bit of distance that remained between us leaving him embarrassed at having shared something so intimate out loud.

"Mostly I came back here looking for you." He continued, his eyes studying his hands before shyness could take hold again. "I don't ordinarily dream in colour, can only recall the vaguest details of my dreams. Then one night while sleeping in my parents' study, one of the rooms my brother and I had grown up in only now it's filled with couches and leather armchairs and wall upon wall of towering bookshelves, I dreamed you up whole. Put my mouth on yours, tasted you with my tongue and realized that I still need you."

"What need of yours can I possibly fulfil after all this time away?"

"At the end of last year, my father called a special meeting, appealed to the board to set aside a portion of the livery proceeds to benefit victims of Hurricane Katrina. My mother's folks are scattered across the Gulf Coast region. Thankfully, my grandmother made out all right, but a good number of her friends and relations lost all they had.

"When my father handed my mother the first check to send along, she reminded him that her mother had never been especially fond of him. He replied that her mother liking him had no bearing on him loving her daughter. I didn't know he could still make her cry, not in a good way. I decided then, if I was to ever have a chance at loving you, at making you cry in a good way, I'd have to get myself back down here and try. Simple as that."

"What led you to believe I'd sit here content, waiting on you?" I wanted to put my hands on *him* at this point, shake him from the past and bring him back to me for good.

"I didn't expect you to wait, necessarily. Had

411

hoped the part of you that managed to connect with me wouldn't rest easy just like some part of me hasn't rested, an erratic beating inside my chest, since I last held you."

I sensed the remaining distance between us begin to slip away, but time had taught me that you couldn't truly know a man until you'd crawled inside his head and seen how broken down he is with your own hand. Measured with your eyes where he needs your help to build himself up again.

I needed to know one thing: "There is a point where we could have exercised better judgement, left one another well enough alone." His eyes locked on mine, registering every word. "Why didn't you leave this alone?" I asked, pointing a finger from his chest to mine.

"I wouldn't have known you otherwise."

"And you just had to know me?"

"In that moment, there's nothing I wouldn't have done to know you."

"Then why'd you choose her over me?"

"Because she asked me to, presented an ultimatum I didn't feel at the time I could refuse. When I'm being completely honest with myself, I recognise it as a choice I should have made on my own. I believe deep down you would have wanted the same thing, for me to get clear inside my head where I wanted to be and choose. Only she put it into words."

"Tell me then that you want to be here, that you're not here simply because coming here was the easier of the two paths to take."

"Getting back here, the right way this time, is the hardest thing I've ever had in my life to do." His hand again went in search of the end of his chin.

"I have never been much at ease standing still. That is my particular defect. I don't shun contentment. I simply believe things between two people ought to continually evolve, continue to improve even if they're good already. The difficulties between me and her began with an aversion for discord pitted against an expectation that the quest for change between two people paired together in this world should be never ending." His eyes twinkled with renewed brightness, only different than when we first met. Time had wound down his intensity a good little bit, but his sincerity seemed more rooted in the person he was aiming to be rather than working to be whoever the rest of the world had in mind for him.

"She and I had known of one another forever. What I found missing is the wondering, that desire to discover new things about one another. When you've already seen all there is to know about a person, you're left with what you thought you had, reflected against a shaky rendering of your own desires.

"I sat down one morning to write a letter, to clear the air between us. Things are always clearer in the morning. It wasn't long before I realized I wasn't writing that letter to her. I was writing it to you. Of all people, I most wanted you to understand the full weight of my regrets." I began to see with my own eyes how broken down he was.

"A couple days at home and the truth began to unfold. I'd lie awake at night weighing the choices I'd made, fearing a wrong turn somewhere along the way had caused me to miss out on something truly remarkable. It was even more frightening to consider the very thing I want might still exist, perhaps not in easy reach. But, if I can only get myself back down here, the thing I want may still be attainable." The tenderness in his eyes continued to melt, threatening any second to gush over on me.

"Some of us know what we want without needing to see it first," I offered, having seen him in my dreams before he showed up on Gram's doorstep. "Far too often the thing we want vanishes before we ever have the chance to hold it good." I needed to choke back the tears, this a conversation I intended to finish without going soft in his arms.

"Sometimes you don't realize what you want until you've seen it already, had the chance to hold it close," he replied, his dreams not working the same as mine.

"Then what took you so long to get back here?" I asked.

"I had things to attend to. Needed to spend time with my grandfather."

"How is your grandpa?" I pictured his granddad rocking the day away on his front porch, his white T-shirt pulled tight across his thin chest, the quiet sadness in his pistol gray eyes staring off into the spring-time sky.

"We buried him last winter..." Somehow sorry didn't seem enough. Couldn't hope to fill the void, just like words alone had never succeeded in helping me overcome the sadness of having lost my grandmother.

"I wish I had known."

"You can't possibly have known," he replied, then broke off suddenly. Tried to move the conversation someplace else. "I've been trying to reach you."

"I've been away."

"That's what I hear," he said. "Not that I've been checking up on you. I just needed to see you."

"Tell me. Why?"

"I sat alone with Estelle the night before my grandfather's funeral. Half the county had been by the house throughout the course of the day, a steady procession of sorrow having lain wait through years of his declining health to pay their final respects. We sat alone in the house, held our own private wake.

"Granddad was a wonderful story teller, but he never offered much in the way of a sound, easy to follow recipe on what a person should do next. He feared I'd fail to see his point without the benefit of his white hair, without a lifetime of his wisdom to pull from. Worried he couldn't relate to my dilemma having left behind the years of foolish optimism I still possessed. He offered the only advice he felt qualified to give: *'don't grow old without living your life first.'* Miss Estelle on the other hand told me that I needed to get beyond the wrong I'd done at some point and try to do right for a change. *'Get straight to it whatever you're planning to do then don't let up on the follow through.'* It's what she'd urged him to tell me, what she would have appreciated seeing him do for her." The wind rattled through once more, pretending it had the stamina to stick around for a spell.

"If I can split myself in two, I'll spend the rest of my days making up for the hurt I've caused you both. But that's an impossible task to fill. What I know today is that loving another person is one of the most complicated things you'll endeavour in your lifetime to do."

"More of your granddad's advice?"

"Sadly, it's a lesson I've been left to learn on my own. Even the simplest gesture, holding a hand or failing to, can land you further than you ever imagined from your original intent. I've reached the point that I no longer recognise the chicken or the egg. Did I lose her when I left for Picayune? Or, did I flee here on the realization that things were already lost between me and her?" His eyes went off to check on things in the other side of the split in his world.

"I wanted to tell her a thousand times, but the truth

wouldn't find my tongue, not the full truth. When I finally came clean, she seemed to know already. Even her darkest suspicions had long been confirmed by the things we no longer looked to one another to do. She just hadn't reached the point of believing this had to spell the end of the line for us. But I wouldn't have said anything had I believed there was still some hope between us. Would have been content to choke on the truth for the rest of my days had I felt there was some way to piece things back together.

"Ultimately, I determined that doing right required that I alter my circumstance. Give this a proper chance." I was touched by his humility. I hate that he took so long to find the need to explain himself, but simply love that in the end he did. But again, once a man gets to talking, especially about his feelings toward you, I've learned to let him keep on talking to make sure he doesn't leave anything out on you.

"We always used the words *I love you*. But, until my grandfather's passing, I didn't recognise how deeply she cared for me. That she loved someone who had loved me, appreciated how much time with him had meant to me. That's the first time she stayed with me in Birmingham. Even our wedding night was a compromise in duelling interests.

"Granddad's house had always been the focal point for family gatherings. The centre of her universe was rooted back in Maryland's Eastern Shore. We held the ceremony early in the afternoon then boarded a plane in time for a twilight reception on the Inner Harbour. We spent the next two nights in Ocean City with a good number of her close friends in tow.

"But, on the ride back from Granddad's funeral, she announced her intentions to spend the night. One night became two. Two nights became three until we'd been there, the two of us together, for the better part of a week. We stayed in one of the upstairs bedrooms. Slept in a bed that at this stage in life is barely big enough to hold me let alone a second full grown person. I was moved, to inconvenience herself like that solely for the benefit of my comfort, convinced me how short sighted I'd been in judging the depth of our bond.

"We talked most nights into the wee hours. Held our voices low like we didn't want anyone in the house to know we ever talked. I asked if she regretted marrying me. She said there was always something about me that she liked. I liked something about her too. But seldom do like and love stick around together, waiting to see which will win out in the end.

"On our last night there, she confided in me that she wanted to have a baby, but, given the uncertainty between us, no longer believed that a good idea to pursue. After all, the last thing she wanted was to bring a baby into the world without the full commitment of the child's father by her side. She'd lived that reality firsthand, her parents like mine being distant lovers at best. That a part of her legacy she didn't intend to carry forward." He drew small circles in the dirt with the heel of his boot.

"I don't know what kind of father I would make, but I know I want someday to be a grandpa. Having witnessed the love Granddad had for me and my brother, different in his approach yet equal in intensity, I know I'll make a better father than I would have without the benefit of his example.

"That night, she and I decided it would be best if we not think about kids until things between us were on more stable ground. In the end, we realized that holding onto something that might never be would do more damage than simply letting go.

"I won't stand here and proclaim for anybody's sake that I don't love her, because I do. Even to this day. But the two of us could only stand around for so long waiting on that moment to arrive when things between us might click. After meeting you, I knew that moment would never come." His eyes went shy again, this part of the tale something he didn't especially wish to tell.

"Once she moves on, and I trust that she will, it won't change how badly I've hurt her, how badly I failed her in my duties as a husband, as a partner in this world. But letting her go, allowing this last gigantic hurt between us, is small compared to the pain either of us would have to endure struggling to maintain a one-sided affair. It's an awful thing to realize the best you can do for a person is to leave her to get on with the rest of her life. But, I reached the conclusion that letting her alone is precisely what I needed to do."

"How long will you stay?" For once I seemed to have caught him off guard, sent him clutching to regain his balance with the simplest of questions. "If I take you at your word this time, how long will you stay?"

"As long as you'll have me. As long as there's something between us to cause you to wonder where either of us would be without the other."

On the way back to Gram's house, he winked one of those smiles at me that started sideways in his mouth and I found the way to let him back in. That night, he made love to me like the earth moving beneath my feet. Not violent or trembling. No volcanoes erupting. Just terra rock-firma swaying in rhythm to the movement of my oceans, my river, my current.

I tried for a time to keep him quiet, to keep myself quiet, fearing Champayne might be lying awake in the next room, eavesdropping on our reunion. After a while, I didn't care that my sister might overhear. Prayed she was asleep already 'cause I couldn't help her overhearing otherwise.

Momma speculated on how the woman has all the power before she makes love to a man, then afterwards he gains all her strength (especially if the love making is any good). Making love to August again for the first time had sparked a new life force between us—a living thing, part him, part me, sent to bind us irreversibly to one another.

Mr. Graves warned that I'd never be able to tear myself away if I let August in again. It's like he knew ahead of me that I'd eventually let him back, that I couldn't help myself. But I swear, August lying there next to me, if I were to force my arms to let go, he couldn't tear himself away either.

Outside Forces

I formed the opinion that a body doesn't age from the inside out. None of us is destined to rise and fall based on sheer will alone. It's the outside forces acting on us that ultimately determine our fate.

My mother succumbed to the outside forces acting on her in the 32nd year of my life. She would have been fifty-three. Daddy laid her to rest in the most dignified way he could muster, on a gentle hillside in Picayune next to her mother's headstone, all her daughters by her side, despite someone else having taken charge of his family in the end.

The night following the funeral, I asked how he and my mother had grown so distant, how their lives became separate seeing how close they seem to have started out.

"We stopped dreaming the same dream together." He waved his hand past his brow to dismiss the notion inside his head, the way a horse uses its tail to swat a fly, sending a quiver to its ears, followed by a shoulder, its hind quarters, to keep the annoyance of the fly's pestering from landing too steadily against its skin.

I understood my father's meaning, having heard my

mother's side of the tale. With care for my sisters and me on her hands, our three mouths to feed, she had to force herself to let go of the dream percolating inside his head where success comes easily, where love between two people lingers well beyond the energy either has left to tend to its upkeep, where pain is a condition you pity someone else for having suffered. My sisters and I bound our mother by duty to live her life outside the dream. Even if the man she hitched her wagon to was destined to float for the rest of eternity beyond the grasp reality had thrust on their existence together, she certainly couldn't afford to do the same. I am eternally grateful to her for all her sacrifice.

My daddy, on the other hand, most people judge by what he hasn't done, by the things he's failed in his lifetime to accomplish. He too had never officially abandoned our mother. He just became so adept over time at slipping away that his presence in our household became obsolete. He knocked wood at having never been formally fired from a job. Still, he kept many a job he would never have taken had he given the slightest consideration to his own desires, ambitions he undoubtedly held down somewhere deep inside his subconscious.

I recognise my inability to see him with anything other than a child's eyes. Have seen him invent rhythm, create music with the mere strum of his fingers on an otherwise silent tabletop, discover song in the sound of the wind whispering past. He can win both sides of an argument without raising an eyebrow. Like he doesn't care which side wins so long as he has his say. He is most accomplished at any occupation that requires little more of him than the passage of time: guarding an empty bus depot or waiting for the grass to grow on one side of a park that is full on the other side with grass he's just finished cutting. Still, I don't fault him none. After all, he's my daddy.

Champayne and I set up post on the evening of our first full night's stay at Runyon Farms. I drew her attention to the thin line taking shape along the horizon as the sun started to set.

"Those clouds are about to capture the sun," I told her. "Which clouds?" She asked. "Wait," I answered. "You'll see soon enough."

And there it came to pass, a tiny nugget of wisdom passed from big sister to little. At first, the sun fought through, surfaced momentarily, its face turned orange with exhaustion from the day's work before giving way to the assault. We stood in silence as the sun surrendered itself inch by struggling inch, a sea of blue clouds quietly celebrating the sun's untimely demise.

I watched Champayne's jaw go slack, the look of bewilderment clouding her eyes. I slipped an arm around her shoulders. I assured her that things don't always wind up this way, different than she had imagined. Eventually, I gave into the truth that things do on occasion end this way, defying everything we believe to be true.

I tried to get Daddy to stay on with us in Mississippi, with August, Champayne and me. He begged off the invitation. "I'm leaving you in good hands, baby girl," he assured me, any hint of disbelief buried so low in his voice that I couldn't detect it. "You're gonna do just fine. Besides, your sister Edie is determined to get herself back to New York. I can't stand to see any of my babies left out in the world alone."

Having seen my father through a child's eyes, I trust that he never will leave any of us to stand alone. Not my daddy. He will do all he can to protect his baby girls. This, above all else, I know is true.

Long Last

There is a line between two people, sometimes straight, sometimes not so straight that connects them to one another regardless of how far either has travelled from the other. The connection that August and I share has persisted throughout the years, teetering on the verge of disintegrating, either that or spilling over, dousing me with a lifetime of my greatest hopes and desires wrapped in fond memories with him.

August felt obliged to explain on our first official night back together that whatever existed between us, that heat, needed to be stripped bare. We'd see what grew in its place.

I still have difficulty sleeping. Only these days, on nights I can't sleep, I sense August somewhere nearby, unable to sleep either, and I take comfort in knowing that I'm not alone staring off into the darkness, that I'm not so strange after all.

I accompany him to the occasional gala affair, courting investors, suitors, clientele needed to propel his fledgling business, sputtering to bring itself back to life. He's close at hand whenever I need someone to wash my back. Sometimes he joins me in the tub. Other times, we sit and talk. Though I've never married, I suspect this is what marriage is like. Once you survive the bleary-eyed possibility of a person, you begin to appreciate the deeper folds of his personality. Once you've seen past the things that make you smile, you begin to understand how certain things would bury your insides if ever they were taken from you again, would fill your lungs with sand, stop your heart from beating.

I still sense that slow train bearing down on me, rumbling up my back. Today I know that train isn't meant to carry me anyplace. Sometimes the fate that awaits us is lying on the opposite side of the track, eyeing the same stream of cars wondering which move to make. It's only after the train has passed that either of you recognises the other, standing in a cloud of dust working to make sense of the hazy image staring back at you. That slow train sent to trick the fate of someone still foolish enough to believe what she wants in life is forever on the verge of passing her by.

Champayne and I joined August out in Richardson shortly after work got underway to transform Runyon Farms into a welcome stopover for a horseman and his traveling stable. He planned to keep a few horses on hand for anyone seeking a weekend getaway, a sort of bed and breakfast with horse riding privileges thrown into the deal. As renovations drew to completion, August approached me with a simple proposal: "I want you to marry me."

"I'm not saying I will. But, if I do agree to marry you, it's only right that I tell you I intend to keep my father's name. That way my sisters won't have to endure a single moment's time wondering where they belong." August consented with a wink of his eye, having himself spent a lifetime in limbo, his granddad's would-be first son living beneath his parents' roof.

We will build a life here together. And, with that, a name for the establishment was born *Gossett-Hill: A Horseman's Hitch and Post*. We adopted as our standard greeting a single question, meant to remind us of the connection we all share, the commitments we must work to maintain: *'How long will you stay?'* Privately, I suspect each of us hopes for the reciprocal question in return: *'How long will you have me?'*

Epilogue

Last Generation

Goodnight World

The clock ticks, and another day goes by. Night falls and I witness another year slip past. The years pass and another part of me moves on, another piece of my soul departed from this earth to face a new kind of rain, a new kind of moonlight, a different sun.

I've seen more than my share of people come and go in this world. Have known them in many strained and peculiar ways. I've seen 'em at their worst. I've witnessed them from a distance, struggling to do their very best. I've known a girl who wanted to throw her baby out the window. Watched that baby grow into a woman, raise a baby of her own, grandbabies even.

I've been that woman. I've been that girl. Wanted to throw my baby away then struggled ever since to protect her, a ghost of a hand intent on setting them on the gentlest, most forgiving path.

I've grown to accept that my only daughter left this world ahead of me. Today, her only daughter went to join her. It pains me to no end. Though, I'm not the least surprised to see things end this way, with nary a kind word said between us, the whole lot of them cut off from my reach. Can't say I deserve any better. Will wish 'til my dying day that I had found some way to do right by them.

Penny has just begun to set herself up in a way that might lead to another round of babies coming into this world. A new generation of hope that doesn't need my meddling hand to find their way in life.

Seeing how miserably I failed my daughter over the years, her only child even, I've resolved in my head to leave this earth. Not with a bang or a flash. I didn't enter the world with such fanfare. There's no reason I should leave here that way. Instead, I'll slip quietly into the shadows, let one finger go and then the next. Eventually the last finger will undo itself. And finally, I can let go.

I leave behind a world filled with turmoil for the next generation to sort out, the last traces of my existence on this earth. I bid you-all farewell. Goodnight world. Goodnight my sweet babies. I pray the Lord your souls to keep.

About the Author

Jedah Mayberry was raised in southeastern CT, the backdrop for his fiction debut, *The Unheralded King of Preston Plains Middle*. The book was named 1st in Multi-Cultural Fiction for 2014 by the Texas Association of Authors. It went on to win Grand Prize in Red City Review's 2015 Book Awards. In 2018, Jedah completed the Hurston-Wright Foundation Workshop in fiction during which early refinements were made to the present work, *Sun Is Sky*. His work has appeared at *Loose Leaf Press*, *Linden Avenue*, *A Gathering Together*, and *Black Elephant*. Jedah resides with his wife and two daughters in Austin, TX.

photo by Kristal Winston